I0630786

ALSO BY ROBERT GAGE EVANS

FICTION

OTHER BOOKS OF THE SOJOURNER SERIES

Book Two
SUTTER'S FORT
ALTA CALIFORNIA
1838

Book Three
OMROD SMYTH
A COD FISHERMAN FROM BRISTOL TOWN
1579-1634

Book Four
JAMES CATHCART
SLAVE TO THE DEY OF ALGIERS
1785

NONFICTION

PINE FLAT: A QUICKSILVER BOOMTOWN (2005)
PINE FLAT: FAMILIES OF THE MODINI PRESERVE (2016)

YOKUTS WARRIOR

Spring 1792

ROBERT GAGE EVANS

THE SOJOURNER SERIES
BOOK ONE

YOKUTS WARRIOR - SPRING 1792 by Robert Gage Evans
Book One of the Sojourner Series

Copyright 2017 by Robert Gage Evans

All rights reserved.
This is a work of fiction. The literary perceptions and insights are based upon extensive research, but all names, characters, places, and incidents are products of the author's imagination.

Editor, revised edition: Jocelyne Thomas, Branwen Books Editing Services

Interior graphic: Satellite photo of California in 1851 by geographer Mark Clark

Cover design and interior layout by Ellie Searl, Publishista®

ISBN-10: 0998342521
ISBN-13: 9780998342528
LCCN: 2017949799

Previously titled TIPNE MAN

PINE FLAT EDITIONS
Sebastopol, CA

Dream Mountain

Chauchila Village

Tachi Village

Tulare Lake

Tulumi Village

CHAPTER 1

Spring 1792
Tule Lake, San Joaquin Valley, Alta California

ULATI WALKED INTO THE LAKE WITH the serene gait of a Sandhill Crane. After a dozen paces she turned to look over her shoulder and beckoned to me with one hand. "Come along," she said, "join me for a pleasant swim."

It was her idea of a joke, of course, but I couldn't force a smile. "It will take another twenty days of hot weather before I put a toe in that lake, maybe longer."

She turned to face me. "Now, now, a Tachi warrior does not shirk the test of a little cool water. Come along, and we'll swim together out to the first little island."

I refused her taunt. "Go ahead; enjoy yourself. Swim out to the island. Check the heron nests for eggs if you wish."

My mother. A clever woman: smart, beautiful, and in past days, a constant tormentor of her fifteen-year-old son. I waved my hand at her as if she were a stubborn puppy. "Go. Go. Don't wait for me." In this particular matter, Ulati could not trick me into a foolish venture.

I knew the lake was filled with frigid water. I saw the skin of her breasts puckered from the cold and the smile she offered did not mask her intention. I felt no glee at her discomfort. "Go—what are you waiting for?"

In the next instant Ulati came crashing through the water as if fleeing ten large water moccasins. Tule Lake reeds barely rippled as she passed them; a low moan escaped her lips as she raced the last ten paces to the beach. "Insolent child!" she yelled.

Now a hint of laughter slipped from me as I handed over a rabbit-skin towel to my mother. She kicked sand at me and returned my frail smile with only a little sadness showing. Two months now, two cycles of the moon from phantom sliver to brim-full. Two months since my father was killed.

We sat on the warm beach until the goose bumps disappeared from her body and a true smile returned to her lips. "Well done, Coyote Boy," she finally said. "You didn't fall for my foolish bait. Not too bad for a young warrior of fifteen years."

It felt good to hear her tease me, and better to see her smile. The tears were gone, and our hair was beginning to show a hint of growth. The tears shed from the moment of his death and through his cremation were finished. The *berdaches*, those men of two-spirits who served our Tachi village in so many ways, had taken the ashes of my father to some remote spot where they could bury him. They had admonished the spirit of my father to remain in Tipiknits Pahn and to enjoy the company of other spirits in that heavenly place. The berdaches had also admonished the spirit of my father to not bother those in our Tachi village who might retain malicious thoughts against him.

Those who killed my father with stones, for instance. Those of our village who had yelled foul words at my father as he died.

I sat up and looked at Ulati. "What will we do now, Mother? They burned our lodge and all of our food and tools. What's next for us?"

She remained prostrate on the sand with hands under her head and knees slightly elevated. A raven complained from a nearby willow tree, and ducks without number dabbled about in every open spot of the lake.

"Is Uncle Podnow our only option?"

"Please! Let a little more heat seep into my bones before we discuss our future."

"Uncle Podnow is the elder brother of my father and shaman to all the Tachi people. How can we deny his invitation to live in his lodge?"

"I was hoping for a suggestion from my only son. What do you say, mighty warrior? How can I avoid the courtesy offered by a fat lecher and his dreadful wife?"

I drew myself up. Yes, I had given thought to help my mother. "What about this option?" I offered.

Ulati remained silent.

"Your husband was the best antu doctor, physical healer, of the Tachi. He set broken bones and cured the illnesses in our village, and he also performed the same services for those who lived in other Yokuts villages. You were his assistant in many, many cases. Why not continue with the work?"

Ulati raised her knees a notch but remained silent.

"There are a few empty lodges we could occupy. Together we could survive through the next few seasons with my hunting and your income as a healer."

Ulati sat up in slow discrete movements and looked directly into my eyes. "They killed your father because he failed to cure the sickness suffered by the chief of our village." She drew a deep breath. "My husband promised the chief and his family that they would live, but the chief and his wife and three children all died, so the relatives of the chief killed my husband, as was their right and privilege."

I remained quiet. All of this I knew in both head and gut, but surely we had friends enough to carry us through difficult times. There were the boys and older girls that I played soccer with and the many women of the village who held Ulati in high esteem. Surely the harsh memories of one extended family would eventually dissipate.

"Therefore, Kiyu, as you certainly must realize, it seems unlikely that my services as healer would receive a positive response in Podnow's village."

"There is no choice but Podnow?"

"None."

⸺

My mother, Ulati, and my father, whose name I may not use because he is dead, had frequently smiled at me, often without cause or pause in their activities. We three had led lives of great importance, and each evening was spent in a review of our accomplishments. I regaled them with my heroic deeds on the playing field. Ulati told of clover patches found or the completion of a tiny feather basket. My father was held as the most important antu doctor in our Tachi village and in fact was frequently called to other Yokuts villages in the southern part of the Great San Joaquin Valley. My father was also a resolute listener, and his telling of the tales of gossip, imparted to him from one family about another, often brought gales of laughter from my mother. As I grew older, I also came to understand the foibles of men and women and joined with their mirth.

Now I lived with Uncle Podnow.

The evening had been the best time of day with my father, beginning with the moment that the sun set and before many stars could be seen in the sky. "Come," my father would say, "down to our secret spot to conduct our secret sport."

Ulati and I always followed closely. Our secret spot changed with the weather and seasons, and Father was capable of making the first part of our evening into a game of hide-and-seek. On our last evening before his death, he had us on our backs, staring in random directions and listening for the call of owls.

I heard a raspy, hissing screech. "White face!" I whispered.

"Answer our friend," my father said, and I did.

"Describe your friend," my father said.

"Flat white face, white belly and underwings, both with brown spots."

"Listen," my father said.

A mellow whistle of sweet intensity came from a dense clump of alder and willow trees. I answered in perfect repetition, and the owl answered with immediate concern. "The little owl with the big heart," I said.

There were eight owls, altogether, for us to count on that last night, but my favorite was the little owl with the big heart.

Now my father is dead, and I may not say his name. None in our village can utter the name of anyone who has died. If anyone speaks the name of a dead person, it is likely that the offended spirit would leave the beautiful red mountains and green wetlands of Tipiknits Pahn to haunt the dreams of that skeptic of our village traditions.

———◆———

Of the two paternal uncles who survived my father, it was Shup who was favored by me and Ulati. In fact, Shup was friend of all the People, while his eldest brother Podnow was the Tipne Man—that is, the chief 'spirit doctor' or shaman of our village. Podnow was deferred to by all of the Tachi villagers, but he was not loved. Our chief spirit doctor had great power over all of the people, while the Rattlesnake Doctor—the healer for wounds of the flesh, or medicine man—had little power but great favor with all of the people, at least in Shup's case.

Shup could, by virtue of his rank and wealth, maintain a lodge of his own, but in fact he slept and ate with the bachelors of our village. Don't mistake my observations: Shup did not live in a lodge with those men holding two spirits—the berdaches—but with the older men who had never married or were divorced, or men merely looking for a good night's sleep away from annoying wives. Those warriors and the village rattlesnake doctor enjoyed their own lodge and servants, constant rounds of gambling, and many raucous jokes.

Also, Shup was a singular exception in our extended family. He was not very smart or very tall. He had a big head, a big voice, and a few very stale jokes. He often trailed after Hineh and me to watch us and applaud our every action. Uncle Shup was like a big brother who never said a mean word—a big brother with a big smile and an occasional question.

"Do you boys remember the days before you received your names?"

"Sure," I said. "I remember one morning in my father's lodge when Hineh grabbed a piece of dried salmon from me and popped it into his mouth."

Hineh, my cousin, gave me his small twisted smile. "Oh, come on, Baby No-No, where is your sense of humor?"

"Listen, Cousin," I said. "I want you to know that it makes me angry when you call me Baby No-No. In fact, I want you to scrub that insult from your memory and stick with my true name: Kiyu, the Coyote."

"Ah, yes, Kiyu, the cunning trickster," said Hineh. "Trickster or No-No, either name will suit you, my little cousin."

"Now, now, the two of you. I named Kiyu after our quick-witted Coyote spirit," our Uncle Shup said.

"Well, I thank you for the delicious joke, Uncle Shup. I have no doubt that either Trickster or Baby No-No will serve my little cousin through his tiresome little life."

"Not a joke." Shup gave us both a serious look and repeated: "Not a joke."

Hineh gave a quick bob of his head to our uncle and then turned to me. "Just keep your facts straight, little cousin; you now live in my father's lodge, and your father is dead. It is my father who gives orders to you and your mother, and he has every expectation that those orders will be obeyed."

Anger rose in me at that tiresome taunt. "Listen, Hineh, you must understand that my mother still mourns for my father, and it is not fair for your father to make demands upon her."

"Ha! Baby No-No wants his mommy."

"Ulati does not want Podnow, and that is the truth! You must honor my mother and the memory of my father."

"Pay attention, No-No. Ulati lives in my father's lodge, and she must obey my father's every command."

Shup put his fingers in his ears. "Stop, stop, you boys. No arguing. Please be friends. My ears hurt with your insults."

———◆———

The evening meal was complete. Traushnah, wife of Podnow and mother of Hineh, was silent. Hineh looked at his toes. Three cousins and two aunts became mice, hunkering in shadows to avoid capture by a large hawk. The days of early summer were pleasantly warm; the unending onslaught of torrid heat was still pending. Geese were still tending their goslings; fawn and mother were never more than a few paces apart.

Podnow stared at the fire for an eternity and then began speaking in a loud voice. "Tonight," he said, "tonight Ulati must begin her tenure as my second wife."

He looked briefly at Ulati, then back to the fire. "She must become the second wife to the greatest spirit doctor in the Great Valley. All in this village understand that when a man dies, his wife becomes the wife of his surviving eldest brother. The family must remain together. The children of the deceased brother must remain with the father's family."

He waved his right hand to admonish the fire pit. "The spirits will tolerate no more of this unseemly behavior from Ulati. The spirits of our ancestors have whispered to me that they are angry at this clear violation of their laws, and they are angry with Ulati's disrespect of me."

Ulati said nothing, but sat with her back straight and stared boldly at Podnow.

Podnow bugged his eyes at Ulati and waved his arms as if conjuring a troop of helpful but dangerous spirits. He tried to yell one final word of censure to the wife of his dead brother, but no sound pushed past his lips.

Ulati continued her piercing gaze.

Podnow diminished his gyrations until both arms hung as limp cords. He looked briefly at Hineh, turned, and walked from the lodge.

No one moved until Ulati said to me, "Kiyu, would you care to walk along the lakeshore with me this evening? We may by chance hear the tiny black bird with the huge voice."

"You don't have much time," said Traushnah. "The ceremony will begin with the first stars."

"Certainly, wife of Podnow. We will return when the village elders make their appearance in this lodge."

CHAPTER 2

Summer 1792

THE FIRST WOOLY FINGERS OF fog drifted up from the lake, and the Tachi villagers began to wander toward Podnow's lodge. The old men and old women came through the open door and took their places near the fire, and Podnow's family followed. Next to arrive were the singers and dancers, who found space to sit around the outer edge while the important younger men scattered wherever they could find room. All sat quietly. Some ate bits of tobacco with pensive rabbit-like nibbles, and others thought their important thoughts. Old men scratched at legs and underarms; old women sat very still with eyes wide open. Many lesser citizens of our Tachi village sat near the lodge, quiet and well-mannered, all within the sound of their tipne doctor's voice.

Podnow sucked smoke deep into his lungs. "This is good jimsonweed," he said.

All were quiet.

"It is from the desert people, the Kawaiisu Utes." Podnow waved his pipe at the eldest of the elders. "The thieves, they require an equal weight of shells for their magic weed."

The eldest of the elders nodded his head but said nothing.

Podnow smiled toward one friend after another and drank tobacco tea from a small basket. In a repeating sequence he took a deep pull on the pipe, then a sip of tea, then bestowed his benign smile on the entire crowd.

When Podnow was nearly finished with his second pipe, his deep courteous voice suddenly boomed into all quadrants of the lodge: "Listen, chosen People of the many spirits. I am ascending into my dreams, so follow me into the sky. Follow me beyond the stars."

"Yes, yes, we will follow," the elders murmured.

"See! There!" Uncle Podnow stood and pointed to the roof of his lodge. "I'm traveling the ghost trail of the Tachi. I see the insurmountable red mountains. I see the happy spirits of Tipiknits Pahn." His voice lowered to a soothing whisper. "All is peaceful in Tipiknits Pahn."

"Ahhh," the elders said.

Podnow gripped the tiny wooden pipe between his thumb and first finger. A red spark glowed from the bottom of the charred bowl. He looked beyond the roof of tule thatch, past the red clouds. "Welcome, Middle Brother," he said. "I see you riding your sorrel horse among the gliding eagles. I see the huge birds as they give you food and baskets of clear water."

"Ahhh," the elders said.

My father.

Podnow held both arms toward the ceiling. "Look, my friends, the eagles provide my middle brother with pipe and tobacco."

"Ahhh," said the elders and important men of our Tachi village.

"Pay attention, friends and neighbors. Look at the sweet life of Tipiknits Pahn." Podnow stood on his tiptoes for the second time that day. "Every need is fulfilled. Every desire is satisfied, and all antagonisms are forgiven in Tipiknits Pahn."

"Ahhh," murmured those who were crowded into Podnow's lodge.

"Ahhh," chorused those who were seated outside the lodge.

The oldest woman of the village smiled and began to clap.

Podnow turned full circle, arms outstretched. "My brother understands the necessity of death. Look, see how he smiles and how gracefully he accepts his death. Notice that he blames no one for his departure from our village."

The elders joined with Oldest Woman in her steady, insistent cadence. The important younger men made agreeable sounds in their throats.

Podnow turned his head upward and pointed at the roof. "There! See the lovely tule marshes of Tipiknits Pahn. Do you see the red mountains and sky-dancing eagles?"

More of the villagers joined in with the quiet clapping of hands.

Podnow positioned himself to speak to the spirit of my father. "Brother, listen to me. Tonight you must listen to me with the diligent care required of your position in our family."

"How may I serve you, Eldest Brother?" The voice of my dead father rumbled through Podnow's lodge, and his image became larger and larger until two gloriously red eyes encompassed the entire roof over our heads and glowed down upon us.

"Good, you are here," Podnow said. "Listen, spirit of my middle brother, for I need a small favor from you. Tell Ulati that she must share her blanket with me, as is the tradition of the People." Podnow drew deeply on his pipe, held the smoke in his lungs, and then slowly let the tanai fumes drift from his open mouth back into his nose. It was a very good trick.

The spirit of my father retreated to the far horizon and settled his horse in a stiff-legged stance.

The village elders shook cocoon rattle-sticks at an increased tempo, and the singers joined with a chant of prayer. The middle son of Podnow's father studied the red sky and, far below, the mountains and eagles. Then my dead father sang.

> *Thou, the one!*
> *Come to me, to this place.*
> *Eagle!*
> *You and me, circle.*
> *Circle around me again and again.*
> *Circle around me again and again.*
> *Eagle!*
> *Come to me, to this place.*
> *Eagle.*

The song drifted into my ears and wandered through my eyes and mouth; over and over and over, the song vibrated in a tortuous route from ears to toes. A fierce wind blew feathers in twirling eddies about my dead father. The golden eagle of my father screamed; the sorrel horse moved his wings with the slow majesty of a white vulture. My dead father smiled from beneath the golden feather shroud that covered his shoulders, and finally he spoke to Podnow.

"The white invaders have strong magic. It was they who sent the sickness, not I."

Podnow dropped his arms and shrugged his shoulders. "What could the People do, my brother? You failed to cure those who were dying. You were the medicine doctor and failed in your duties."

Podnow raised his right hand toward the red eyes. "What about Ulati?"

The drums and rattles filled the silence until my dead father spoke again. "There is no fault upon the People. I was the antu doctor and could not stop the burning fevers or the honeycombed blisters. I did not stop the thick black water oozing from eyes and mouth. No, honored brother, the Tachi were correct in killing me." The red eyes blinked three times, then three again. My dead father sang his eagle song over and over and over again.

I felt immersed in a warm blanket held on one side by my dead father and on the other by Ulati. The hot ember from my stomach disappeared, and I joined in singing.

> *Eagle!*
> *Come to me, to this place.*
> *Eagle . . .*

Then, in that moment of warm intimacy, during the mutual embrace between my mother and father—at that very moment!—Podnow yelled, "Stop the singing! Middle Brother, you *must* listen to me." Podnow stomped his foot as if he were killing a fat scorpion. "The laws of our ancestors demand that Ulati assume her role as my second wife, yet she refuses my sleeping mat. Refuses! Your son replaced his birth name ten seasons past. He is nearly a warrior, yet Ulati stays near him."

Podnow put his hands on his hips. "The behavior of your wife is unseemly. Know these facts and tell Ulati to honor my dignity—tonight, my brother, tonight!"

The rattles trilled. Smoke billowed. A golden eagle plunged through the mist with bent wings and issued loud, piercing screams. The bird spread its golden wings and golden tail feathers at the last instant to settle lightly on a roof beam of Podnow's lodge. The spirit of my dead father sat next to Golden Eagle. His voice was louder now and sharper at the edges.

"The White Others, honored eldest brother, have powerful medicine, but the medicine of the Tachi is powerful also."

"Certainly." Podnow pawed at the black-and-white paint that covered his face. "Every child can confirm such a simpleminded assertion."

My dead father ignored the insult and continued with his even-tempered speech. "The spirits honor us above all others. We are the People. Our ancestors guide the People. All the spirits protect the People."

Oldest Woman again started with her delicate clapping beat.

"Listen, my friends," whispered my dead father. "Listen, all of you in this village who threw stones to kill my earthly body."

The entire village, young and old, joined to clap while the singers hummed like a hive of bees. The dancers stood and jumped and bowed and threw their arms up into the air. The singers chanted my dead father's eagle song. The elders clapped with sticks and hands.

Fog oozed up from the marsh in cool wisps. Those who sat outside Podnow's lodge wrapped rabbit-skin cloaks over youngsters and moved shoulder to shoulder with their neighbors. My dead father sank deeper into the gray smoke that swirled through the rafters.

"Listen, People of our village. You must send messengers to all of the Yokuts villages. You must send gifts to those of the People who hold old grudges of one village against the other. We Tachi must send gifts to the Miwok, who are our cousins. You must say to all of the Yokuts and Miwok: "The feuds are over. All of the People and their cousins, the Miwok, must recognize only one enemy, for if each village stands alone, we will all die. If we stand together, we can continue to serve all the spirits in the same manner as the parents of our parents."

Podnow turned from his spirit brother. His face seemed made of soft clay. At first, with slow, tentative steps, Podnow began dancing in a small circle around the fire. Then he moved faster and faster until the eagle feathers stuck through his ear lobes jiggled to the same rhythm as the clap-sticks. The white stripes painted across his face, arms, and fat belly gave the impression of a flop-jointed skeleton. Podnow danced and danced until sweat erased the white stripes, and his lips puckered like a fish in a late-summer stream. He stumbled and stopped. All became quiet. Podnow looked cautiously at the distant red eyes. "Must we send gifts to all the villages?"

"Yes."

"Expensive gifts, even to the Miwok?"

"Gifts are important, Elder Brother. Gifts will encourage those of each village to forget past indignities. Gifts will open their ears to the tactics you propose. Send many gifts and tell the People and the Miwok that the spirits favor them over all others."

Podnow rubbed his sweaty stomach. "Yes. I will send gifts, Younger Brother, just as you say."

The spirit of my dead father straddled the back of Golden Eagle. "Good. That is your part of our bargain, honored brother, and this is what I will do." His voice thundered like boulders down a mountain. "I will speak with Burrowing Owl—Pokook—and send him flying about the Great Valley and into the hills and high up into the mountains. I will have Pokook announce the annual mourning-of-the-dead celebration to all of the People and to the Miwok. I will have Pokook lead all of the Yokuts villages and the Miwok villages to this Tachi village for the *Lonewis*."

"The Lonewis," Podnow asked, "here, at our Tachi village?"

"Yes, Eldest Brother. It will be the greatest mourning ceremony in the memory of the eldest elder."

Podnow sucked in his gut. "We will invite all Yokuts and the Miwok to our village, here, among the Tachi?"

"Yes, Brother, bring them here, to the village best-loved by all the spirits."

Podnow's shoulders squared from a straight back and now nearly-flat stomach. "I hear you, Middle Brother."

My dead father's voice was now a raspy whisper: "When the People and the Miwok are assembled, the plans to destroy the white invaders will germinate and grow."

Podnow whispered to all present in and around his lodge. "I will send the gifts. I will send time strings to announce the Lonewis. All of our People and all of the Miwok will follow Pokook to our village."

"Together!" shouted those gathered in his lodge. "Together, Yokuts and Miwok will stop the white invaders!"

Podnow took a slow, deep breath into his massive chest. "Now, my younger brother, is there anything more from the spirit world?"

"No," my dead father said in a faint, distant whisper.

"Good." Podnow squinted with his left eye. "There is one small remaining detail that we must discuss: what about Ulati?"

Thick smoke suddenly filled the lodge. The elders coughed and coughed and crawled toward the exit. The young men emerged after the elders, and all quickly departed down the well-ordered streets. In a few moments they were settled in their own lodges. Even the babies and dogs were quiet.

Podnow stared at the empty rafters. The smoke became thicker and the silence heavier. He stretched his arms toward the ceiling. "What about Ulati?"

There remained only the silence—a smoky, tired silence.

Ulati pulled the blanket over her head, and I drifted down under my own soft rabbit skins. Even from across the lodge, I could perceive the smile on her lips. I smiled in return.

She whispered, "That was a good show the old man gave us tonight."

"Very impressive," I answered. "The red eyes and loud voices were especially good."

"He's the best of all Yokuts tipne men, my son. Never underestimate your uncle Podnow."

"My father is dead, and the Tachi still die in large numbers."

"Stay close to me, Kiyu. Listen only to me, and no one else."

"Certainly."

I dozed for a moment, then felt the soft touch of my father. "My son," he whispered, "were you able to understand how Podnow created the red eyes and booming voices?"

"I'm not sure, Father. Something about his voice in combination with the songs and dancing. Whatever his bag of tricks, it was a very impressive spectacle."

"Was there another element of the evening that extended beyond your normal expectations?"

"The smoke was excessive for such a small fire pit."

"Good, my son. You must study under the tutelage of your uncle Podnow and learn how to manage all of his tricks. He is a very smart tipne doctor."

"I hear you, Father."

"However, my son, you must beware of your uncle Podnow," said the spirit of my father.

"Certainly," I said.

"Beware of your uncle Podnow," my father whispered. "Listen only to me or to Ulati."

"Certainly," I said.

CHAPTER 3

Fall 1792

FROM DAWN TO SLEEP, THERE was nothing but preparing for the Lonewis. In the entire Tachi village, infants and elders, poor servants and rich doctors, all held no thoughts but of getting ready for the Lonewis.

Ulati looked up from pounding acorns into flour. She scolded me as though I were a small boy and not a warrior of fifteen years. "No! Do not ask again."

"Please, Mother, the big boys from the Wowol village have challenged us to a soccer match."

"After the Lonewis you can play soccer until you collapse, and not before."

"The older girls call us women-men if we don't face our opponents on the soccer field! Please!"

"Why do you use that unpleasant name for our two-spirit men, my son?"

"Never mind," I said.

Twice Ulati sent me to retrieve a pestle left along the riverbank by some woman or another, and both times that I completed her assigned task, she ignored the opportunity to give me a brief smile. "If you finish one job, I want you to start another without complaint," she said.

Aunt Traushnah squawked at me to gather baskets of acorns from the large storage bins, and in a most demeaning manner, two women of no rank in the village ordered me to carry firewood to the Lonewis celebration site.

Hineh, on the other hand, followed his father from lodge to lodge to listen while the elders organized the Lonewis. Whenever Hineh passed me on a lane or in a field, he called out in his magpie voice, "Fine work, my boy." The tenth time he called the insult, the juices in my head boiled. I dropped my armload of wood to pick up a solid stick, and threw it at Hineh. The missile missed his ear by a finger width and came to rest at the foot of a small tree.

My cousin giggled like a little girl thrown high into the air by her father and ran toward me with the speed of a cougar. He kept yelling, "Servant, servant!" with each blow from his hands and feet. Traushnah stood nearby as Hineh made blood gush from my nose and mouth.

Hineh was also bleeding about his face, but in the end, he was the victor. I did not move for a long time after the beating. A whispery wind dried the sweat on my back. Red finches chattered on and on, oblivious to the pulsing pain of my ribs. The big girls screamed with the joy of scoring a goal against the big boys. There were never tears on my face, so Hineh saw no tears before he left me in a heap.

Later, in our lodge, Ulati saw no tears as she washed blood away with a damp wad of moss. She spoke to me in her calm, reasonable voice. "Listen carefully, Kiyu. If you cannot learn how to remain calm while under verbal attack, you will suffer in a most grievous manner for the rest of your very short life. Your impulsive behavior mimics that of a badger, and not that of a warrior of the Tachi people."

———◆———

Our village chief sent messengers—*winatum*, they were called—in every direction. These winatum carried gifts of shell money and tiny feather baskets and a string made from deer tendon with twenty-one knots tied from top to bottom. The messengers said to each of the Yokuts and the Miwok villages, "At each sunrise, remove one knot from this string. The Lonewis will begin at our Tachi village with the last knot. Come and share your grief for those who have died this past year. Come to the greatest Lonewis in all memory."

———◆———

My dead father kept his promise and sent the messenger owl, Pokook, up and down the Great Valley. I heard the little burrowing owl speak with the dead spirits throughout the day, and even when I woke in the night he maintained his persistent c*o-hoo, co-hoo*. I heard the Tachi women say that the Miwok people were reticent to leave their villages but that Pokook continued with his constant *co-hoo, co-hoo* even as the Miwok talked and argued. *Co-hoo, co-hoo,* Pokook sang, and eventually the Miwok began moving toward our Tachi village.

Pokook led the Miwok from their hills down to the Yokuts' beautiful marshlands and lakes. He demonstrated how they could travel from one tiny island to the next, and also how to navigate around the interminable morass of reeds and bottomless sinkholes of our swamps. *Co-hoo, co-hoo,* he called.

———◆———

Ulati peeled and twisted milkweed fiber into a strong string while I tried to follow her example. My left hand held the completed string between thumb and forefinger, and the right twisted the supple fiber toward my stomach. It was a simple matter: twist the new cord over the old and repeat until finished. I'd practiced the same twist and turn since the days before my name was given to me.

"Tighter! We will snare ducks with this string, not grizzly bear." Ulati leaned forward to examine my effort. "No, no, no. Undo everything and begin again. How many times must I show you? Just move the fiber over and toward your stomach, and maintain the tight weave with your left hand. Twist with your right wrist over and toward your stomach. It is all very simple, my warrior. Keep your mind on your task of the moment."

"Woman's work," I said.

She ignored my displeasure, and I slowly unraveled my cord.

Ulati stopped her fingers. "If you cannot restore some semblance of friendship, then you must ignore Hineh," she said.

"His insults have increased in number and malicious intent." I started again with the string and held each firm twist with my left hand. "What can I do?"

"Not much, for we depend upon Podnow for our protection."

"Why don't you agree to his constant request? If you become his wife in fact, then we can both sit by his side at all times."

"Do you think I should become the second wife to Podnow and a slave to his first wife?"

"You already serve Traushnah. Is the other part so distasteful that we both must live in constant distress?"

"There are many people in this Tachi village, and also in both Yokuts and Miwok villages, who hold us in esteem. Let us keep our present situation intact for a while longer. Our situation in Podnow's lodge is more annoying than distressful."

"For you, perhaps, but I have a constant storm in my stomach with the worry about Hineh." I worked at my snare for a stretch of time and then leaned toward my mother. "Do you have another man in mind to replace my father?"

Ulati waved me away, an annoying fly. "Certainly not. Can you think of a possible replacement for such a man as your father?"

"No," I said.

"Then let us make the best of our condition, my son. If you allow Hineh his little insults, your stomach will never settle. You are both marvelous soccer players, and you are both admired by everyone in the village. Ignore his insults."

"I will try my best, but I make no promises."

Ulati tapped my shoulder with her soft hand. "Look at my string and notice how it mimics the spider webs scattered throughout the tule marsh."

"I said I will try, but—"

"I will tie this string into a filmy snare and place it across the trail of a green-headed duck."

"Hineh is so persistent—"

"First, my son, I must twist the string in the proper manner, and then I must discover the trail to a nest, and finally I must set the snare. Every step is conceived with thoughtful regard to possible problems, but my ultimate success depends upon the strength of my snare."

"But—"

"You can snare Hineh with words. He will kill you in a contest with rocks or fists, but you will eventually triumph over your cousin by using words as your weapon."

"Hineh is much heavier and stronger than I am. If I call names at him, then he will beat me."

"What happens to Traushnah when she calls me odious names?"

"Traushnah is a witch."

"Traushnah is not a witch. She is the mean-spirited mother of an arrogant son."

"She's a witch."

"Traushnah frequently calls me a witch." Ulati touched lightly under my chin. "Occasionally Traushnah calls you a witch."

A small bird with an orange beak stared at us from a clump of reeds. It sputtered *kid-ick, kid-ick* and disappeared from sight.

"Am I a witch?"

"If another believes you are a witch, then you are indeed a witch in their eyes."

"Can I make Hineh believe I'm a witch?"

Ulati stood when I asked my last question, and much later that day she smiled when I brought six green-headed drakes into the lodge. I threw the snare-caught ducks on the floor for Ulati to gut and clean, and then I gave Hineh my best witchy smile.

"Are you ready for another beating, my servant boy?" Hineh yelled.

Over the next days, Ulati and I added our few ducks to the hundreds of ducks and quail and geese and deer captured by the Tachi for the great Lonewis. Many of the men and boys disappeared for five days on a long-distance surround of the giant elk. I stayed with the old men and women to dip nets for small fish and to pole tule rafts out onto the wide lake. We speared trout that were as long as I was tall, and sturgeon that were larger than Podnow.

When the first strangers arrived for the Lonewis, I stayed in the background. Many of the young men and women I knew from village soccer matches over the past few years, and they were no threat to me in any fashion. Many of our Tachi children, however, saw these strangers as ugly and ferocious creatures, with strange clothes and misplaced tattoos. Even the village dogs ran whimpering into the tule reeds when the strangers appeared. All was quiet for a time, and then the big boys began playing their rough games with the strangers, and Hineh and I brought our gang into a contest with strangers of our age. Very quickly the gambling sessions among both men and women grew into celebrations. Wild hoots and laughter echoed in and about our Tachi village.

Some strangers were fat and stupid; others skinny and stupid. Most were like the Tachi, however: fat and skinny, stupid and smart, and every conceivable mixture in between, for they were the People. All of the strangers were either of the Yokuts or our cousins, the Miwok, and together we were invincible.

Our Tachi chief sat under the shade of a willow lean-to and smiled a welcome to each visitor. He was the first stop in our village for every guest. He gave them fresh water from large baskets and listened to the small details of their journey. He placed each group in camps up and down the river and nearly to the lakeshore. The chief welcomed the Nutunutu and the Wowol, our nearest neighbors, and also those who came from the far hills to the east and those who followed Pokook from the dry western slope of the Great Valley. All these strangers he treated with great courtesy.

When the last knot of the string was untied, our old chief called the headmen from all of the villages together into his lodge. They sat and talked about the days before the white man, and they drank their tobacco tea and waited. When the moon and stars were bright, our old chief stood, and all the talk stopped. In his old, soft voice, our chief said, "Tomorrow the Lonewis will begin."

CHAPTER 4

Fall 1792

T HE LONEWIS BEGAN. WORDS STUMBLED among tears, but the Yokuts and the Miwok listened carefully to each expression of grief. An old Wowol woman told us of her dead brother. She described a young man who tackled a woman from another village during a soccer match. This exuberant young colt lifted that woman from the opposing team over his shoulder, and despite the riotous efforts by both teams to impede his progress, he carried both the ball and the beautiful woman across the goal line. We all cheered this exemplary deed and laughed with the discovery that the young hero eventually married the woman he had tackled.

The old woman went on to describe the progression of her brother's death from the invaders' disease. She told us of the first headaches and final tortured convulsions. The ground of our village was soaked with tears.

When the Miwok spoke, Yokuts listened with heartfelt compassion. Even the ferocious Chauchila listened and cried and laughed and dropped their cougar smiles during that first day of the Lonewis.

As evening came, the sun framed the western hills in poppy gold, then through a short transition in vermillion, and finally, as the last mourner stood to leave, we were bathed in resplendent deep purple.

My legs tingled for the first twenty steps as Ulati led me toward her favorite part of our tule marsh. She whispered again the story of my father's first snare-caught bush rabbit. The night heron croaked as Ulati told me how my dead father developed a special powder of willow bark and soap root to cure the aches and miseries of our elders. She grew animated in describing how her husband had learned to set broken bones and cure the normal fevers of young children.

She held me close as she talked. "The Tachi named your father the best antu doctor of their village," she said.

"But they killed my father," I said.

"Yes."

"Tell me again why they killed my father."

Ulati looked through my eyes, and each word plopped into my stomach. "Our village lost many to the white invaders' curse; so the relatives of dead people came to our lodge and killed your father."

"How?"

"With stones and knives."

"Did he resist the attack?"

"No. He welcomed their gift of death."

Ulati released my eyes, and we both stared into the twilight. "You know perfectly well, Kiyu, that your father could not cure the fevers or remove the black pus. You saw the People kill your father, and you know that they were correct in killing him."

I sat still in Ulati's soft warmth. A thrush joined his rolling, flutelike song with the crickets and frogs. The creatures of our tule marsh sang about the greatest antu doctor of our Tachi village. I finally interrupted the lovely chorus, a hard edge to my voice as I spoke. "Today I saw those who killed my father sing and dance. Did they forget his blood-soaked body?" My nose was full of snot. My eyes on Ulati's eyes. "How can it be that his ignorance of the white invaders' disease allowed his murder? How could those fools kill my father at one moment and now celebrate him as the greatest antu doctor of our Tachi village?"

"The spirits speak of proper behavior through our spirit doctors, my son. The Tachi are the best loved of all creatures on this earth, so it is that the spirits direct us along a path that will guarantee our survival."

"It was Podnow who directed the murder of my father."

"He is our Tipne Man. Only Podnow can clearly her the voices of the dead spirits." Ulati held her hand for my silence. "It happens occasionally that the spirits give what seems to be mistaken advice; even wicked, in fact. You must remember, my son, that the spirits gather experiences from uncounted number of generations of the Tachi people. It is from this massive collection of options that the spirits whisper the single correct action into the ear of our Tipne Man."

"Podnow killed my father."

"You are young, my son. Listen and learn before condemning your Uncle. He loved his brother, and loves him still."

"He killed your husband. Now he says the spirits require that you become his second wife."

"Shush! No more of such talk."

"Big fires!" a thunderous voice called.

Ulati sighed. "Ahhh, your Uncle Shup. When he shouts, leaves fall from the trees."

"Leaves?" I shook my head. "Ears fall from your head when Uncle Shup yells."

"Get ready for singing and dancing," the voice roared.

Ulati stood, and I quickly followed. "We'd better hurry along. Shup gets louder and louder if people dawdle."

"**Hurry! Hurry!**" Shup admonished.

The first tentative flicks of blue flame groped among the twigs in the ceremonial fire pit. Babies in their cradles stared in silent admiration as the fire reached in greedy bites for small branches, then began swallowing large tree trunks. The first evening star emerged from behind the bright snow-covered mountains to the east.

Nearly every village had their own fire, all scattered erratically around the huge central flame. Everyone shushed. "We are ready," our old chief said.

Ulati whispered, "Listen to the singers standing near our chief, for they are paid to lead us in our grief." She pointed toward six men painted all black, with white face spots and white stomach stripes.

Ah-hah-now`uh. Ah-hah-now`uh Wuk`ele`o. Ah-hah-now`uh.

We are crying. We are crying. We cry again. We are crying.

I felt my father's spirit between us, and we three were immersed, one with the other, and enshrouded by the People. I smiled. There were no tears in my eyes, yet I joined my mother in singing, "We are crying. . ." I followed Ulati around our small fire. I matched her steps with mine, and Ulati's tears fell onto my strong arms, and soon the spirits joined us. They cried with us until I felt the first tear burst and trickle off my nose.

We are crying. We are crying.
We cry again. We are crying.

When the stars were bright and the mist began easing up from the tule reeds, the crying song ended. We sat, all quiet for a time, then the professional singers began clapping, and the Yokuts and Miwok around the many fires joined with them. The singers brought us together in the same cadence, and on each fourth beat they had us point to a friend or neighbor. We laughed and clapped and pointed, and the singing and dancing and crying began again.

On and on this celebration of joyous grief continued until I floated into the dream world and told my Brother Coyote of the sights and sounds. In my dream, Brother Coyote began to cry for my dead father and I saw his tears. I felt his sad-happiness. I joined with my spirit brother, and together we cried for my dead father.

———

On the third night of the Lonewis, I watched Uncle Shup as he slipped the smooth skin and feathers from the great blue heron over a neighbor's head. I saw Shup tie the two feather horns and watched as he mounted abalone-shell eyes above the two peek-holes. Before my eyes, the man disappeared. An apparition stood in place of the man who lived in the lodge next to Podnow. The spirit raised its arms. "*Rooarr*!" it said, and all the young children scooted back to their mothers.

"His name is Huyupah," Ulati whispered.

"Yes, I remember from the last Lonewis at the Wowol village." Ulati was a bothersome mother at times.

Huyupah's long blue feathers swung free, and the short pieces of willow fastened across his shoulders held ghostly rattles that floated in and about the fire.

"His feet never touch the ground," a nearby child said.

"So it seems," I said to the youngster.

The People made a game of hiding things from Huyupah, and he always found them. They put beads in tree branches or under logs, and he found them. Huyupah danced and whistled and looked at people to call *ho-hoo`no,* and then he found the items that were hidden. Even the Miwok joined in playing with Huyupah on that third night of the Lonewis.

———

The next night, the fourth night of the Lonewis was the best of all nights.

War!

Antu doctors against tipne doctors.

The winatum made seven fires—three in a row on each side and one especially large fire in the middle. Uncle Shup stood in front of our chief and shouted, "The fires are ready!" His echo settled among the distant stars. Our old chief answered, "*He`ahn than`hin*" in a quiet voice, as if he were speaking to his first wife or eldest son.

Uncle Podnow went to the central fire. He wore his feather skirt and headpiece and moved with the grace of a well-fed eagle. All the other doctors found spots near the other six fires and began singing their special songs. Soon they began to shake clapper sticks and swing basket trays, first over one shoulder, then the other. Podnow was the first to move away from his station, and soon all the doctors were dancing in a ragged line past a tall tree trunk buried upright in the ground and covered with valuable gifts. Podnow beat the ground with his basket, and all followed his lead.

"Look!" I pointed to the gift tree. "A string of shell money fell for Uncle Podnow but not for the next doctor."

"The second is an antu doctor," Ulati said. "Don't tell me that you have forgotten the certain pecking order of our people?"

"But why the difference here at the Lonewis? All the doctors dance and sing in the same manner."

"Watch, and remember that it was the same the last time you attended a Lonewis, and the previous ten times also. When will you understand that the power of tipne doctors is vastly superior to the antu doctors? When?"

There is one mother that I know in a very intimate fashion who can be as persistently annoying as any mosquito on a hot, calm night.

I leaned forward, like a hawk on a tree branch over a gopher mound, and watched each detail of the dance unfold. The doctors danced with the same motions and all sang the same song:

> *Ha-lahl`mo hah`ha*
> *Ha-lahl`mo hah`ha*

But only the tipne doctors received the beads and money and feather baskets from the gift tree.

"Listen, Mother mine, there must be a simple answer, but I still can't understand why the tipne doctors are favored over the antu doctors. Could you please help your stupid son understand this mystery?"

She smiled but not with her eyes. "It is simply a fact of nature from time before knowing. It has been the tipne doctors who have the power to speak directly to the spirits. Antu doctors fuss with herbs and splints. Other folks lead the hunt for grasshoppers or make baskets that retain water or construct bows and arrows with great facility. But it is only the tipne doctors who can gain the trust of the spirits." Ulati leaned forward to better make her point of information clear to the mind of an extraordinarily stupid son. "It was but a few nights past when we had this same discussion. If we have any hope that the entire business of the village is successful, then we must place our trust in the spirits as expressed by our tipne doctors. In exchange for this trust, the People are held in great favor by all the spirits. It is really a very simple matter."

I tried to study Ulati's eyes for deception, but she looked away from me and toward the central fire. "So you say, mysterious mother, but it remains my contention that neither the spirits nor their spirit doctors here at this Lonewis are serving the People in an honest manner. Beyond that, I still contend that Podnow had his brother killed so that he could have you as his second wife."

"Enough of your twaddle, Kiyu. I suggest that you listen and watch for a change. You may even learn something new, my son."

I shrugged my shoulders and turned away from my mother.

The doctors moved with the precision of flying geese. They smashed basket trays on the ground, and small arrows appeared in the trays with each thump. They spun slowly in place until, with no apparent signal, they stood still. Shup threw logs on the fire, and each length of cottonwood tree snapped at the other like a rabid dog. My stomach grew hollow, then nearly exploded with vomit as the doctors started to hurl magic weapons at each other. I saw a doctor from the Miwok stumble and fall down. A skinny doctor from the western hills turned a somersault and crashed full-length in front of Podnow. Shup sent his winatum into the circle to pull one body, then another, out of the action and back to the smiles and tears of friends and neighbors.

The doctors stalked one another like bobtailed cats after quail. They hid in smoky shadows and jumped into combat with ferocious howls. A few antu doctors from the largest villages held their own against the tipne doctors, but most of the antu perished at the first attack.

Ulati thumped me in the ribs and pointed her jaw toward our chief.

I tried to make sense of an apparition that stood before our village chief. It was dressed in a hodgepodge of beaks and antlers and feathers and wiggled about like an impatient child.

"*Cuksa!*" Ulati said.

"Yes!" I said. "The clown."

The apparition leaned toward our chief as if accepting detailed instructions for an important mission. The chief nodded, and Cuksa turned to jump and scream and smash his ragged tule basket on the ground. The doctors all stopped fighting. Podnow spoke to an important Miwok tipne doctor, and Cuksa threw bits of harmless acorn shell at them. Cuksa danced on pointed toes, waved his arms in a dizzy, uncoordinated frenzy, and stuck out his tongue at Podnow.

"Ooooo!" the crowd moaned.

"*Rrrroarr!*" the remaining doctors roared at Cuksa.

Cuksa turned his back to my uncle, bent his head nearly to the ground, and raised his red-painted bottom toward the most powerful tipne doctor in the entire world.

"Ooooo!" the crowd yelled.

Cuksa wiggled his bottom as would a docile she-elk to a lustful bull.

The People howled with laughter, rolled on the ground, and churned their feet in the air. Neighbors slumped against one another, weak with pleasure.

"What is Cuksa doing?" I yelled to my mother.

"He gives Podnow a sweet insult to a known adulterer."

"Who would dare to insult Podnow?" I was being only slightly facetious.

"Watch!"

The doctors turned on Cuksa like an avenging army. He fell among the feet and fists, mortally wounded.

"**Boooo!**" the Yokuts and the Miwok thundered. Women shook their fists. Children screamed, "No! No! Don't hurt Cuksa!"

A squad of Chauchila warriors stood and moved from the shadows into the bright firelight. "**Hold!**" they yelled.

The doctors drew close, and Podnow nodded toward Cuksa. They knelt to pull arrowheads and small rocks from the clown. They massaged Cuksa's limbs and cooed soft words into his ears.

The People stopped yelling, and the Chauchila retreated. Shup and his winatum threw logs on the churning fire.

Cuksa sat upright, studied the doctors, smiled, and jumped high into the air. Higher still! Higher! Until, in an astonishing display, Cuksa flew through the air over our heads. He waved and giggled and shouted the names of boys who trailed after him in his orbit round and round the central fire.

Cuksa fluttered slowly to the ground, dashed through the audience, and vanished. The Yokuts and the Miwok said, "**Ohhhh**" and beat their hands on the hard-packed dirt.

"See," I said, "there is some justice in our world."

"The best part is over, my son. Now we must watch Podnow collect his due for a temporary indignity."

I made a face. "Uncle Podnow, best loved by the spirits."

Ulati pulled my ear. "Stop teasing, my son. Just watch your uncle display his power, and no more words."

Uncle Podnow threw magic missiles at those doctors who remained standing, and one after the other they fell. A final few combined their attack, but Podnow spewed eagle feathers into the air, and they succumbed to his power. After the last opponent was vanquished, Podnow roamed around the fires, from village to village, to receive gifts that recognized his great victory. Miwok villages gave him baskets of soap root and rabbit-skin blankets. A few of the southern villages gave him baskets of corn and gourds, while those of the tule marshes gave weapons and honey and strings of money. All gave what they felt was due the most powerful tipne of the Yokuts and the Miwok.

But I saw a few frowns when his back was turned and little of the exuberant pleasure that normally complements the giving of gifts.

It took six of Shup's winatums to carry the treasure from the fires to Podnow's lodge. Ulati followed my eyes with hers and made little ticking noises with her tongue. *Tic, tic, tic,* like the wren warning her children of a dangerous intruder.

Ulati put her arm around my waist to pull me to her side, but I held back. She pulled even harder. "Stop," I said. "I don't want to hurt you."

She gave another sharp tug, released me, and walked away into the darkness.

On the last night of the Lonewis I sat next to Ulati but we didn't talk. I was tired of the restrictions required by a Lonewis celebration. I felt itchy because no bathing was allowed, and I missed the flavor and texture of meat. Ulati had kind words for our neighbors but none for me. There was no Cuksa or dancing or beating on the foot drum, just the many mourners who carried tule-reed mannequins toward the central fire.

I fussed and squirmed and immersed myself in a great warm pool of self-pity until I noticed a family of mourners with a warrior mannequin. The dead man's finest clothes and his favorite weapons covered the well-crafted tule reeds. The family stopped at the inferno's edge, hands all together, and threw their father or son or husband into the flames. I sat up straight with my shoulders back. A tall Miwok walked to the edge and threw a mannequin covered with an antelope shawl and beads into the fire. Family after family carried tiny tule-reed children, all swaddled in rabbit-skin blankets, and pitched them into the fire.

Small bumps emerged along my arm. Spiders scurried about my neck. I leaned to my left. "Did you burn my father?" I asked.

"We burned his spirit, not his body. Your father's mannequin was dressed in his finest clothes. All of his tools and weapons and secret medicines went with him to Tipiknits Pahn."

I felt a lump grow large in my throat. "His body. What of my father's body?"

"He was buried in the ground." Ulati watched two mannequins disappear in the flames. "He was buried by the two-spirit men. They buried him deep in the ground, and they admonished your father to go away and never to return."

"Do you mean the women-men?"

"Listen, Kiyu, I mean the men who manifest the spirits of both men and women." She paused briefly to stare into my eyes. "I speak of the worthy men of the People who honor us with their necessary skills. We name those of our village, those very men whom you and Hineh so much admire, as two-spirit men."

I shook my head a little. "You smile as if my feelings have no merit, Mother mine. Let me tell you that it is no joke when one is called a two-spirit in front of friends."

Ulati stood and then pulled me to my feet. "Come, Kiyu. It is time for us to join the celebration."

I followed my mother into the crush of sweating bodies to circle the huge fire.

> *Ah-hah'nah*
> *Yoo'e uh'la*
> *We-ah'la hah*

We sing. You are going to burn. We are crying.

Fog settled over higher ground and turned the sentinel oaks into ghostly guardians. The People sang and threw mannequins into the fire and cried. My mother spoke with my dead father through eight turns around the fire, and I felt honored that most of her stories and anecdotes were about me. I again felt the joyous emptiness of shedding tears for my father. I felt the warm blanket of his protection settle upon my shoulders.

The celebration continued through the night and until the sun made a silver disc through the morning fog. Then, although a few continued to walk slowly, silently about the tired fire, most of the Yokuts and Miwok drifted away into the gray mist. There remained three young women kneeling shoulder to shoulder in the ashes, crying and singing praise to three dead spirits. It was a peaceful moment, an instant frozen by the tinkling echoes of meadowlarks. Our chief stood and dismissed us. *"He'ahm than'hin,"* he said.

There were scattered cheers, and most of us moved toward the river. The dancing and crying were finished. We could wash the dirt and tears from our bodies and prepare for a great feast. The mourners could eat meat again and let their hair grow. The Lonewis was over.

"Ahhh," Ulati said. "Please. Wash my hair again." The servant woman, likely someone born of an anonymous father, stood behind Ulati and kneaded crushed lily bulbs into the long black strands. Tiny rainbow bubbles skimmed along the river. "Ahhh," Ulati said. "Now soap my shoulders and back. Ahhh. The water and soap feel so good on my body. Thank you."

Ulati closed her eyes and sloshed water over her breasts. "Now," she said, "please do the same for Kiyu, except I want you to shampoo his hair twice."

We returned to the river shore, and the servant woman dried us with an old rabbit-skin blanket. Then she helped us step into new clothes, and we returned to our lodge. I fell immediately into a deep sleep to dream of endless rows of food stretched along the horizon. Brother Coyote raced with me toward platters of baked fish, toward the mounds of dried grasshoppers and steamed elk. We ran until our tongues lolled. "Faster," Coyote said. "Hineh is stealing our food. Faster!"

I stumbled to the ground. My shoulder hurt. My head wobbled back and forth. I opened my eyes to see Uncle Podnow over me, with his hand on my shoulder.

"Follow me," he said.

CHAPTER 5

Fall 1792

S HADE HUNG LIKE A THICK spider web under the cottonwood trees. A small bird warbled incessantly along the upper branches, alternately ending his song with rising, then falling, inflections. The river moved at our right hand with the quiet *shuss* of wind through pine trees.

Uncle Podnow looked briefly around the clearing, then waved Hineh and me to a spot near the stacked firewood. We sat away from the dignitaries, but close enough to see and hear the proceedings. I ignored Hineh, made myself small, and listened.

The village headmen and tipne doctors sat in a large circle. A few talked quietly to neighbors; the rest were mute, with unfocused eyes. The bird suddenly stopped his busy warble, and our old chief whispered, "Let us begin." He swallowed his tobacco, smiled, and started speaking.

"As a young man I traveled from one village to the next and learned to speak the words of others." His smile moved every wrinkle upward, and he nodded in friendly recollection toward an ancient

Miwok tipne. "I traveled to the west and traded with the Ohlone and Chumash. They had many villages—although none as large and numerous as ours. They were rich—although not as rich as the Yokuts."

His smile disappeared. "I stopped going to those villages when the white invaders arrived."

Another old man said, "Yes, it was the same with me."

Our chief continued. "Now the Ohlone and Chumash are beggars and slaves. The white invaders serve as their masters." He shut his eyes and looked into his memory. "Once, long ago, I traveled to the north beyond the White Mountain that sends smoke to Tipiknits Pahn, past the Modoc people who trade the beautiful black glass. I went even farther north to a place where ferocious Cayuse and Nez Perce meet to trade for horses and women and shells. Here, at this place so far away, I saw a white man."

A chorus of men said, "Tell us. Tell us of the white man."

"He was hairy and smelled like a dead goose. He had an exploding stick that could destroy a small basket at a distance of one hundred paces."

No one spoke.

"This white man tried to intimidate the Cayuse and the Mandan and the Walla Walla. The red men laughed at the single white man. They said, 'You are one and we are many. Can you kill us all before we kill you?' The warriors laughed like girls washing their hair in a warm stream as they took the magic stick and broke it against a rock."

Everyone around the circle smiled. Even Hineh and I smiled from our distant outpost.

"These warriors tied the White Other to wooden pegs nailed into the ground. They peeled small strips of skin from his arms and chest and stomach. After four days the White Other stopped screaming and died."

Our chief sipped from a small clay cup of tobacco tea. He drained the brown liquid and chewed the limp leaves. He belched, and the other headmen and tipne doctors waited, as silent as stones. "On another occasion," our chief said, "when I was older, the Mohave Others showed me the bones of White Other warriors and offered white children in exchange for my goods."

"Those Mohave folks are tougher than a grizzly bear," a Chauchila chief said. "They are very, very tough."

Our old chief nodded. "There are many lessons for us to learn. Our rich and friendly neighbors to the west no longer exist as they did in the days of their ancestors. They listened to the white invaders. They shared land and women with the white men, and now they are dust."

He let the silence spread beyond the circle, then asked, "Tell me brothers, what are we to do about the white invaders who now threaten our villages of the Great Valley?"

A squat boulder of a man from a Tulamni village leaned forward and began to speak. "Now listen to me, Yokuts and Miwok sitting here together. The magic sticks of the white invaders spit fire only once. They can kill at a distance farther than our best arrow, but only once. Brave men can draw the evil magic into themselves and leave the remaining warriors to attack the white men at close range."

The Tulamni chief looked around the circle for a response to his observation, but all remained silent. A crow flew overhead and called a small insult. The warm autumn sun filtered through giant cottonwood trees, and the Tulamni chief sat back into his former position.

Far away, I heard cries of triumph and outrage from the playing fields. The sweet smell of baking meat drifted through my nose. A woman's gambling song filtered in among the trees and made me think of Ulati's quick hands and relentless victories. The same crow passed silently overhead, and a Miwok chief spoke.

"You Yokuts of the low hills and plains are vulnerable to attack from the White Others. They will ride swift horses over the western hills and descend upon your villages in a flash of lightning. You have seen the White Others destroy the coastal people and thus have great cause for concern." He held his right hand toward Podnow. "Listen, cousins: the Yokuts are more numerous than the Ohlone and Chumash." He stood and extended both arms to the circle. "And all the Miwok stand as your ally!"

All the men stood in fierce jubilation. They shouted in raucous cacophony, "We are all united—together, the Yokuts, Miwok, and the spirits!"

The Miwok chief raised his hand for silence. "Not too quickly, my friends. The white coyote is cunning and deadly. Remember how the white invaders taunted each Ohlone and Chumash village with reminders of old grudges and feuds. They took the side of one village to destroy another, and soon all were destroyed." The tall, handsome chief dropped his voice to a whisper. "They will play the same tricks with us."

"No!" the young leaders yelled. "We will stop the white invaders!"

The old men moved as if red ants were marching over their toes. They huddled together, all those with stiff fingers and long memories, and made soft, cackling noises like white geese on a cold winter morning.

The Miwok chief sat down and waited until all were seated and quiet. "Podnow, of this Tachi village, has warned us, and I admonish you in the same manner. We must listen to our ancestors. We must join together as one village. Only by thinking and acting together can we keep the white invaders from your Great Valley and our sacred mountains."

Two jays squawked overhead. All the men nodded, heads bobbing like lupine stems in a breeze.

After it was clear that the Miwok chief was finished speaking, Podnow stood. "I recently spoke to my dead father, and he told me of the days when there were no horses in the Great Valley. There were many elk and deer and antelope, but no horses. Now our warriors hunt from the backs of horses, and the Yokuts have grown accustomed to the sweet flavor of horsemeat." He waved an arm toward the south. "From the swampy lake country to the high plains, stallions lead ever-increasing herds, and the elk and deer fall to the joining of horse and warrior."

Podnow stretched and rubbed his belly. "My father studied the horse when it first appeared in our territory. He welcomed the horse. He honored the spirit of the horse, and soon the horse became part of our life. We must study the white invaders, and perhaps we can reach an accommodation with them. If we can establish a system of trade that benefits both, and if our spirit ancestors mingle as well, it seems possible that both white and red can honor the other."

"Never!" interrupted a Chauchila chief. "They have already destroyed the coastal villages in a blink of time, and it seems likely that we will suffer the same result. If we must all die or become slaves, what is the purpose in even considering our surrender to the white invaders?"

Podnow nodded his head a few times and then continued his oration. "We must certainly avoid closing our eyes like the Chumash wren. We must also mimic Brother Coyote and flash our sharp teeth at the invaders. But consider this, my friend: the invaders also have sharp teeth. Yes, indeed, and even at this moment all of our villages suffer grievously from their mysterious diseases."

The shadows began moving at a faster rate toward the east. The aroma of baking meat and acorn bread settled as a thick cloud under the trees.

"This is what we must do," Podnow said. "The Yokuts and Miwok in every village must develop a warning system. The winatum of the Yokuts will move to the western hills and watch for the white invaders. Those villages that are threatened with attack from the white warriors will send all women and children to safety." He sucked in his gut. "Listen to me! We will let no one pass who would harm us. We will kill those who would kill us."

The older men thumped the dirt. The younger men waited.

"We must behave as one village. All must deal with the White Others as if it were *your* lodge under attack, as if *your* women and children were threatened."

Podnow held out one finger. "We must develop a system of signals from the highest hills and a cadre of fast runners who will report to the war chief of each village."

He held two fingers to the crowd. "We must stockpile emergency food and weapons. Every village must prepare caves and gullies—those places that are thick with vines and hidden from sight—for our families."

Now he held three fingers aloft. "Of greatest importance, we must learn everything possible about the white people. It appears that they are here to stay, and they certainly will not disappear with the winter rain."

Podnow dropped his hand and shrugged his shoulders. "Maybe we can make profitable trade with the White Others, and maybe not. Maybe we must live with the constant threat of war. Whatever happens, we must learn how to survive in this new world."

The Chauchila chief again shouted. "Maybe we should kill them all!" He stood and shook his arm at Podnow. "Kill the White Others. Attack them before they become any stronger! Kill them now!"

A few of the younger men also stood and gave tentative support to the Chauchila. The rest sat and waited for Podnow to continue.

"My brother, the second son of my father, followed the tanai smoke into my nose and gave me some good advice. 'Send our sons to the White Others so that we may learn the secrets of their magic.'" Podnow shrugged his shoulders again and held his arms outstretched. "So be it. We will send Hineh and Kiyu to the White Others. They are both smart and powerful young men: Hineh with the proper white-tailed eagle spirit, and Kiyu's name speaks for itself. They will learn the White Others' words and style of thinking. They will discover their tricks. In two summers or so, these two young men will be ready to serve the People. Until that day when they are fully trained to encounter the White Other magic, we must build a fence of bodies to protect our land. We must always remain alert and ready to die. We must act as one against the White Others."

His shoulders drooped like a small plant in the hot sun. "That is all. I am finished."

Podnow sat amid the silent tapping of stubby little pipes. Soon a wreath of smoke and the demanding odors of food covered the conclave of headmen and tipne.

Our old chief tapped the burnt tobacco crumbs from his pipe. He stood. "Now we shall eat. We must have food and sleep, and after a moon or so, perhaps we will make war with the White Others or perhaps we will trade with them. This old man cannot see more than one meal into the future, so let us adjourn and eat our fill."

The men clapped and laughed and joined together to walk along the path through the trees and up a small hill toward the village. They behaved as if they were all cousins and uncles of the same village. I heard them proclaim Podnow and the Miwok chief as two who shared the same vision. I heard them proclaim me as a spy of the white invaders.

A spy! I wanted to ask questions of Podnow and to discover the plans that he and the Miwok chief had for me, but Hineh scooted past me at a trot, and I hurried after him.

CHAPTER 6

Fall 1792

ULATI WAS WORSE THAN A badger with bad teeth after the Lonewis. When Uncle Podnow waved for me to follow him, she snagged my belt and kept me at her side. Later, on the same day, when Hineh suggested a soccer game, Ulati hissed at him like a wounded bobcat. Then, when Hineh in turn called me a woman-man, I ran at him in blind rage to strike a blow. He dodged, tripped me with a stick, and kicked me three times in the ribs. Ulati chased Hineh down and smashed him three times on the head with an oak branch. Traushnah flew into the fray with nails and teeth and feet, and Ulati hit her with the same branch and then kicked the first wife of Podnow three times in the ribs.

The villagers stepped from their lodges to laugh as Hineh and Traushnah ran like whipped dogs, but Ulati didn't crack a smile. She narrowed her eyes and stared the entire village into silence.

I didn't know whether I should laugh or cry, but I managed a small and bloody smile at my mother. In return she threw her weapon at me and then walked away toward the lake with a rapid but sturdy gait. There was no essence of a beautiful crane in her flight—more of some larger bird born of nightmares.

During the evening meal, Podnow yelled at Ulati, "Stop raising dust in my lodge!" He looked at his son and wife dabbing bruises. "Why don't you teach Kiyu to fight? He's allegedly a warrior, yet I see him flopping in the dust after any encounter with my son."

"My son is not a bully. Why don't you teach your son to withhold his insults?"

"Now, now, I'm merely observing a tested fact. You're better with a hefty stick than any Chauchila warrior with a lance, so just go ahead and teach your son the same skills."

Ulati kicked dust on Podnow's bare feet. "You can just leave Kiyu alone until I say he is ready for this silly sojourn you have invented." She put both hands to her hips. "And also, Big Belly, you must leave me alone!"

During the night, Traushnah whispered lies to her husband that everyone in our lodge heard, and in the days that followed, Traushnah told the same lies about Ulati and me to all the women of the village. She claimed that I was a woman-man and that Ulati was a witch to the White Others. That Ulati and her dead husband were both witches and spies who would assist the invaders to destroy the Tachi. Hineh repeated the stupid lies to the boys and young men and practiced his evil looks upon me.

Ulati laughed at the lies and sneered at Hineh's ugly face. She took me into the tule reeds to gather roots and high into the chaparral country for chinquapin nuts. Everywhere we traveled, she taught me the secrets of animals and plants. Best of all, better than toasted grasshoppers or watching Hineh cry big tears, she taught me how to gamble in the same fashion as my father.

"Watch the eyes, my son. Watch the eyes and the wrinkles above the eyes, never the hands. Let your opponent watch your hands. Divert him from the prize with your hands."

"Your hands move too quickly!"

"Your eyes move too slowly," she said. "Look for concealed patterns. Anticipate surprise. Think like the spirits, not like our brave warriors. Spirits seek life. Warriors seek death."

When I showed the least reluctance to follow her instructions, Ulati smiled and poked my chest. "Listen to me, my only son. I'm smarter than Podnow and smarter than your spirit brother. Only your father could best me in gambling."

I held both hands open and spoke in slow cadence. "Listen to me, my only mother. I am more than your son. I am a man, and you must treat me with greater respect."

Ulati tilted her head to stare into my eyes. "I am sorry, Kiyu. Tell me exactly what you want from me."

"Go slower with your teaching, and explain with intimate detail why I must do one thing or another." I paused for a moment. "Let us drop our mother-child bond in exchange for that of an honored elder and young warrior."

Ulati smiled. "My goodness, do I hear the voice of your father in my ear?"

I hid my smile. "Certainly not, Ulati. You hear the voice of Kiyu, a Tachi warrior."

Ulati permitted Shup to tag along after us on the condition that he keep his silence. And he did. Shup never used his great voice in the presence of Ulati, nor did he intervene during Ulati's lessons.

"Watch for thin, wispy clouds trailing from the south. If lower clouds follow from the southwest—lumpy, curdled mare's-milk clouds—then, Kiyu, we shall have two days of heavy rain."

Shup sat on his haunches and listened. He never added information of his own or contradicted Ulati. He just smiled. When Ulati showed me a noxious root or a poisonous mushroom, he smiled. When she told me how to prepare a paste for the tip of arrows or how to drop a special poison into the food of an enemy, Shup merely peered over our shoulders, nodded his huge head, and maintained his tilted-moon smile.

Only in the sweathouse was I apart from Ulati, my honored teacher. Most of the men and boys were already in the sweathouse when Shup and I arrived each morning, so Shup led me through the deerskin door, between Podnow and the elders, to the only available seats against the far wall.

A few days after Ulati's attack on Traushnah, all present in the sweathouse listened quietly as the village elders talked and talked and finally levied a fine on a family for taking acorns from an oak grove without permission. Shup and I continued our silence as the old chief gave a ponderous report from two of his winatum who had traveled up the valley and north of the great saltwater bay to visit the Pomo and the Wappo. He finished his oration by suggesting that the Tachi might wish to send a large group of villagers during the next summer season to visit and trade in that benign and productive area.

On the very next day Podnow called through the hot mist, "Shup! You must serve as Kiyu's guide."

"No!" Shup shouted.

"You must." Podnow leaned toward us, a shadow through the steam. "I have discussed this matter over and over again with the village elders, and we have decided that *you* are the one to serve as

Kiyu's mentor. *You* are the one to accompany him on his sojourn to the northern boundaries of our great valley."

"No. I refuse."

I spoke into the mist. "I understand the need for my sojourn, Uncle Podnow, but I am unclear about why my uncle Shup was chosen as my mentor for this task."

"We have considered all the options and decided that Shup is the best qualified for the job at hand, and further, that you and Shup both must accept our decision in this matter." He paused before another admonition. "You two must show respect for your elders."

"I am not satisfied with your answer, Uncle Podnow, and respectfully request that you explain in detail why I must go on this sojourn and why Uncle Shup must serve as my mentor on this journey."

Podnow only squinted his eyes. "There will be no further discussion of the matter, young man."

———◆———

When Ulati learned what Podnow had said to me, she was furious. "No!" she said. "You must ignore their pitiful plans for a sojourn just as we have ignored their pitiful lies." She marched head down through the ankle-deep water of the marsh shouting, "No, no, no! You may be a big soccer hero and think that you are ready to lead a young woman into the tall grass, but you will not leave on any sojourn until I say that you are ready! Do you hear me?"

———◆———

I heard the whispers in our lodge during the night, and I heard the Tachi villagers yell at Shup, "Go! Take Kiyu on his sojourn!" And during every sweat-lodge discussion the men applauded Podnow's plan and counseled haste over patience.

"The White Others grow stronger with every moon," the elders said.

"The People grow weaker with every moon; both Hineh and Kiyu must begin their separate missions," the old chief said.

Uncle Podnow stepped around the jumbled, sweaty bodies, clamped my arm in his hand, and pulled me to a seat next to his. "Your time with Ulati is over," he hissed.

The old chief spoke into the steamy fog. "Kiyu, your training must begin. My winatums have traveled up and down the Great Valley. They have also whispered to the Gabrielño and Chumash along the coast, and all give me the same information: the villages of the invaders grow, and the villages of our ancient neighbors die."

Uncle Podnow motioned for a young man to spill water from a basket onto the hot rocks. "Kiyu! Stand before me."

I stood to face the greatest tipne doctor of all the People; a foot drum throbbed in my head. My eyes blurred beyond what the steamy mist could cause.

"Kiyu! You must learn how to conquer the White Others. You must steal their magic. You must teach the White Others to dance with their eyes tightly closed." Podnow's red eyes burned through the churning clouds. "Your wren days are over. Now you must be Kiyu!"

Podnow put me back on my seat with a quick nod and spoke in a respectful cadence to the assembled men. "Shup is the proper teacher for Kiyu, for my brother travels with equal facility in this world and the spirit world. Kiyu must learn the wisdom of small creatures before he can meet the white invaders, and since Shup is the smallest of all men, he will serve as Kiyu's best teacher."

The elders coughed up phlegm and spit yellow gobs onto the hot rocks. They sipped tobacco tea and murmured agreement to Podnow's remarks.

Podnow turned toward Shup. "You must leave at the next full moon."

"No!" said Shup. "I refuse!"

Podnow made his nostrils flare and spoke in a louder voice. "You and Kiyu must travel to distant and lonely places. The training will likely take two years. Certainly that is sufficient time for Kiyu to learn how to cure his many flaws."

He pulled his shoulders back. "The spirits *demand* this sojourn." Podnow waved a magic white-tailed eagle feather toward Shup. "There is no other option."

Shup began to tremble.

"What is the matter with you?" Podnow said.

Shup remained mute, but his trembling grew more intense.

The elders stared, embarrassed, as Shup shook like a newly captured slave girl. Our old chief coughed, untangled his legs, and shuffled through the deerskin door. The others quickly followed.

I sat alone beside my uncle Shup. The fire went black, the steam lodge cold. Ulati yelled from outside the door. "Kiyu! Shup! We need to harvest some seeds. Come out and help me."

Shup continued with his shaking, but he didn't move. Ulati threw two sticks at the sweathouse and then yelled, "I'll wait for you on the riverside by our oak grove. Take your time." Her steps faded to nothing.

I rubbed Shup's arms and legs until he was nearly calm, and after a very long time he managed to whimper. "Tell Ulati . . . I can't . . . sojourn with you."

"Why?"

"I'm scared, Kiyu. Very scared."

"You? Scared? A rattlesnake doctor, scared?" A nettle picked at my stomach. "Only little girls are scared."

Tears dropped from Shup's eyes and slid over his fat lips. Snot dripped from his nose. "I'm scared," he said.

I bit hard on my tongue to prevent equally childish behavior. "Why are you scared? I don't understand, Uncle Shup."

Shup blubbered. "I don't know nothing; I've never killed anything. I don't want to go far away from here to where I've never been."

I hung my head. "I don't want to go either." We cuddled like two puppies left in the woods. When a crow cawed three times, and three times again, Shup stopped hiccupping and dripping snot on my shoulder.

"Let's go find Ulati," I said.

"Yes, find Ulati near the oak grove. Ulati will tell us what to do."

We returned to the lodge in time for our evening chores and a meal that was silent of words but loud with grunts of annoyance. After dinner, Ulati waited until the last basket was stored on shelves and the fire was replenished with small, dry logs, then she crab-walked around the fire and sat knee to knee with Podnow. "You are wrong," she said. "All the elders are wrong."

"Ahhck!" Podnow raised both hands. "Stop! No more!"

"You will kill Shup's pride and his smile." Ulati leaned forward. "Shup is our village winatum. He can do nothing else."

"This is your last warning," Podnow said. "The matter of Kiyu's training is a man's decision, not a woman's. I have been generous in sustaining you as part of my family, but you must shut your lips or leave my lodge."

"Shup has never lived among strangers," Ulati said. "He has yet to kill his first animal. Shup has a loud voice, a big smile, and some jokes. His large head is empty of all else."

Neighbors from adjoining lodges heard the loud voices and came through our front entrance to gather in rows around the fire. They listened in shocked silence.

Podnow sipped his tobacco tea. Two dogs outside the lodge argued over a bone. When he finally spoke, it was with the tone he used toward slaves or the children of poor relatives. "Listen to me, wife of my dead brother: you are not to bother men with your foolish thoughts. Shup will get over his sulk and serve effectively as Kiyu's mentor."

Ulati stood and screamed into Podnow's face. "Listen to me, Big Gut. It is *my* son whose life is in jeopardy, not yours."

"Seize the witch!" Podnow yelled. "Cast her into the river!"

All remained silent. No one moved. I had to pee.

Podnow spit phlegm into the fire and hunched his shoulders forward. He coughed a few times and then began to speak in a quiet voice. "My dead brother warned us of the impending danger from the invaders. Now my son and the son of my dead brother must learn how to live among the invaders. Each young man will remain in character with their spirit brothers, yet both will discover the invaders' secrets in a separate manner."

Ulati raised both hands. "Ahhh, a fine plan indeed, but only if the two live to become warriors, and only if they are smart enough to infiltrate a powerful enemy, and only if our villages survive another two years."

"Yes! It is a weak and foolish plan," said Podnow. "I admit to all Tachi here gathered that we tipne doctors and village chiefs from the entire Tachi and Miwok territory seem unable to devise a better plan. It does in fact seem as if we are throwing two clever young leaders of our village into a river at spring flood. My son and yours."

Ulati stared at Podnow for a moment. "My husband always held you in high esteem," she said. "He admired your humor and wisdom."

"Thank you for remembering the integrity of my dead brother," said Podnow.

"My husband once mentioned that at one moment in time you considered the happiness of slaves and women as a valid part of your office." Ulati managed the smallest of smiles. "I, of course, never argued that particular point with my husband."

A hint of smiles rippled through the crowd; a rash of coughing consumed the eldest cadre of women.

"No one has ever argued your wit, Ulati, or the devotion you held for your husband." Podnow let the crowd settle into silence again. "I have spent the past days speaking with my dead brother about our sons. For what it is worth to our wives, we brothers agree on a sojourn for Kiyu and an apprenticeship with the Chauchila war chief for Hineh." He held both hands up for silence. "I plead with you, Ulati— let the cousins move forward with our fragile plan."

Ulati spoke in a detached manner. "Kiyu still has much to learn. If you truly want him to gain the magic held by the White Others, leave him with me for another summer or so. Then, after he's learned what I need to teach him, you can send him on a sojourn for an additional summer."

Ulati moved backward a step. "There are ten or twelve men in the village that could do a good job teaching Kiyu how to control other men."

Podnow maintained his quiet voice, as if he were sharing an important secret. "Listen, wife of my brother. To become a powerful hunter-warrior is not what I want for Kiyu. He must learn how to rely on the spirit of his father for survival. We want Kiyu to learn how to watch and listen and remember. It is our conclusion that Shup can best teach him these skills."

"Not Shup!" Ulati cried. "He is not a warrior. He is not a teacher. You must not send my son on a sojourn with Shup!"

Podnow nodded his head for a long time before responding to Ulati. "Please consider that I speak for your husband and for all the spirits. I need your help in this matter, so I ask for a treaty of peace from you at this time. Help us, Ulati, and let us join in sending Kiyu on his sojourn."

Ulati stayed still for a long moment. A single tear slipped from her eye and coursed slowly down her cheek. She brushed it away, as if it were a fly or bit of dust. She stood, and then in a quiet, slow motion, walked from the lodge.

The nettle poked at my stomach with vicious persistence. Uncle Podnow was the greatest tipne of all the People. Shup was my friend and protector. Together we would make the sojourn: Shup and me, together.

CHAPTER 7

Late Fall 1792

I T WAS LATE FALL, THE season to harvest acorns, and Podnow's instructions were brief: "Follow the large north-flowing river until it meets a large south-flowing river. Always stay on the east side of the Great River, and always stop at each Yokuts village to introduce yourselves. Find your way through the numerous swamps and lakes until you can follow the huge south-flowing river to its source." After a long pause he nodded to Shup. "Let Kiyu decide where to locate his lodge. I expect Kiyu to return after eight seasons, and I also expect Kiyu ready to confront the white invaders."

Shup made no effort to answer his brother, and I was equally silent. To my mind the task was simple: just walk north to the twin volcanos, say hello at each village, and get permission to travel across their land. Eight seasons later, return using the same protocol. Even Shup understood the assignment.

We had just finished passage through the land of our immediate neighbors, the Wowol, when a heavy two-day storm turned the Great Valley into an endless journey of swamps and rivers. Each stream, each river, was a challenge to ford. Often it was best to find a way up the eastern hills until a smaller portage could be found. On two occasions Shup and I were forced to hike into the remote mountains before finding an acceptable spot to cross a tributary. More often, since the days remained hot and the water tolerable, we went upstream for half a day, found two logs, and with vigorous kicking managed to float diagonally across the tributary until we gained the opposite shore.

Twice Shup needed my assistance in surviving the river crossings, yet even in the process of drowning, he maintained his silence. During the first few days of the sojourn, my patience was exhausted by his petulant refusal to talk with me. After the second near-disaster, I joined with his grunts and hand signals as our only form of conversation.

At the end of the north-flowing river was the last Yokuts village, and then we moved through land owned by people who were little known to me. On one occasion we found a few days' shelter with a small Wintu village, and further north, one night with an even smaller Yani village. Antu doctors in both villages made an attempt to revive Shup's volubility but were quickly defeated.

"Was this creature always silent?" the Wintu doctor asked.

"No sir. He was the village rattlesnake doctor and always verbose in his manner."

"Strange business," the Wintu doctor said.

"When did he stop his tongue?" the Yani doctor asked.

"On the very first day of my sojourn," I said.

"He is very sad," said the Yani doctor.

"Have you a medicine to mitigate his malady?"

The Yani doctor was bone-skinny with enormous eyes. "No," he said. "There is nothing I can do to make him talk. When next he smiles, then his tongue will behave."

I maintained my role as the awkward navigator, with Shup as my morose follower, and at last a series of lumpy hills marked the northern end of the Great Valley. We wandered about for a few days, moving through dark little valleys filled with whitewater streams, until I stumbled onto the remnants of an ancient family lodge.

"Uncle Shup," I said. "This place is where we will spend my sojourn."

Shup dropped his carry-basket to the ground, pulled two blankets from the top, and made his nest against a moss-covered log.

I could barely move. The last decent berries were two days past, my fingers seemed useless claws, and nothing made sense in the fog of my mind. A small creek mumbled over green rocks; all else was silent. Sleep was my only option, and we both slumbered, heedless of any threat from man, beast, or spirit.

The first sunrise in my new home was well established before I stood to pee and look around. Shup sat in the shade of a yellow-scaled pine, eyes open and silent. There was no wind. Nothing seemed to move.

After a dilatory amble up and down the stream, I returned to the collapsed remnants of the ancient lodge. It had been big enough to hold a large family when first occupied. Now it was a crumpled pile of debris. As a first step, I pulled brush and tiny trees from the mud within and around the foundation. Then I made an effort to separate the solid-core beams from the useless rotten beams. When it came time to place the first heavy solid-core beam on the central support platform, and then to lift the other end onto the surrounding earth wall, I was stymied by the impossible task.

"Honored Uncle, help me," I called.

Shup turned his back to me and pulled a blanket over his head.

Toward evening of the second day at our new home, Shup shuffled past me and down to the creek. I heard him sucking water into his mouth like a deer, but I continued in my struggle to move and lift the roof beams. When the sun and moon were equidistant above the horizon, he stood, walked a few paces, and made water against an alder tree. With the last shadows he climbed up onto the dirt foundation of the old lodge, and after studying the dilapidated remnants scattered about, he moved a few steps to lift one end of the old center beam. He remained in that position until I was able to hoist the other end. In slow increments I extended my quivering arms and placed the beam atop the existing earth frame.

Shup dropped his end onto the appropriate place and returned to his blanket. We stared at each other until it was too dark to see, and only a thrush made any comments about our successful effort.

Over the next two days I ate some berries and grubs and made a thatch of willow whips and fir boughs to finish the roof of our lodge. Shup sat and watched me.

Blackberries were abundant, but the frosty nights of early winter seemed to produce few that were not spotted with sour red bumps. Rotten logs produced sweet white grubs, however, and I shared them with Uncle Shup. He refused my offer of astringent brown beetles, and after one foul-tasting attempt, we both ignored the brittle black beetles.

My hunger and the erratic jolts of changing weather patterns increased the necessity to store some food for the inevitable blizzards of this country. Grub-filled acorns I stored in our carry-basket, and I managed to spear one late salmon and snare a few white-tailed rabbits. Cold fog oozed up from the distant river bottom and over our creek until it covered the land and trees with a blanket of drenching misery. Morning shards of ice made our ritual of a daily bath in the creek more pain than pleasure.

I managed to keep the fire going, even when the southwest wind brought rain streaming through the roof. The gathering drips and drops formed a miniature river that tumbled past my small basket of acorns and out through the only door. Shup carved a small cave for himself under the western perimeter of our lodge, and he apparently slept through the foul weather.

Each morning after the storm, I followed a trail that passed between two huge boulders and checked my snares. I found three tiny bush rabbits on consecutive mornings. Together with some lily bulbs and withered bitter green leaves, each rabbit provided a tasty stew that fed us for two days.

A few days past the last rabbit, I found a raccoon enmeshed in the cords of my new milkweed snare. I killed the large snarling animal with an oak branch. "Die, raccoon!" I yelled. "Leave this world!" My blows bounced from the beast's eyes and snout and ears. "Die, die!" I cried.

The raccoon's rich, fat soup inspired Uncle Shup to a series of magnificent farts, and I was driven from our lodge into the cold, clean air. Our most prominent star glowed in passive tandem with a smaller star until both disappeared into the abrupt bank of black clouds. The first spitting drops of cold rain drove me back into the fragrant company of my uncle, and the rain continued with a steady throb for two days.

At first light on the third day of this second major storm, I opened my eyes to a strange silence. There were no dead leaves brushing one against the other. No water drizzled through my willow thatch. I peered through the door of my lodge and saw only a white expanse obscuring every familiar sight. I walked about the perimeter of our small clearing, sprayed a large yellow circle in the snow, and returned to snuggle under my blankets.

The quiet whisper of falling snow continued for one more day, and then the storm transformed itself into a howling, roaring beast for three more days. I could not move. The outside edge of my blanket was anchored in a frozen puddle. The fire pit was black ice.

Snow turned to rain, frozen puddles melted, and eventually moonlight trickled through the shredded willow roof. I pulled my blanket free from the mud, draped it over my shoulders, and stepped through the pine-branch door. Twenty or so paces from our ragged lodge sat Brother Coyote. He looked up from a fresh mound of dirt spattered upon the snow and smiled at me. After a moment, he returned his gaze to a shuddering eruption of earth.

I sat on my haunches to watch as Brother Coyote assumed a crouching stance. Every hair on his body quivered in focused attention. Gopher popped from his hole like a submerged stick from water. Coyote clubbed at the rodent with his forepaw and knocked him away from his sanctuary. Gopher stood on hind legs, puffed his fur, clicked his teeth in a rapid beat, and prepared to meet his antagonist.

Brother Coyote smiled through squinted yellow eyes and jumped into the fray with joyous abandon. He clubbed Gopher to the ground and with a whirling flash of sharp, white teeth threw him high into the air. Coyote resumed his ready-attack posture, on guard to prevent any opportunity for Gopher's escape. The pair danced and danced until Gopher departed for the spirit world. Coyote studied the inert form until he was confident the game was over. He looked first at Gopher, then at me, stood, shook himself with satisfied vigor, and disappeared into the first tentative shadows of dawn.

I stared at the dead gopher until the sun drew the last puddle of fog into its warmth. When I placed Gopher before Shup, my uncle sat up and began hunting through the fur to snag fleas and lice and ticks and pop them into his mouth. He took his sharp flint knife and skinned the animal. Shup looked at the fire pit, noticed the cold, wet clutter, and then he shook himself before slowly disjointing the gopher and eating each tiny appendage with silent intensity. My uncle finally finished the meat and offal, licked the bloody pelt, licked his fingers, and rolled back onto his bed.

I stepped from the lodge into the bright sun and the taunting laughter of Acorn Woodpecker. The bird giggled a few times and flew in his undulating swoops to a long-dead fir tree. He disappeared into a hole and quickly emerged with a hazelnut in his beak. Woodpecker held tight to the rough bark with his talons, turned his head, and dropped the nut. In quick, silent succession, the bird repeated his ritual five more times, then cackled his hysterical laugh and flew away.

I walked to the base of the tree, picked up the nuts, and cracked them in my hands. The first two were sweet; the third was filled with a delicious white grub. It was rich with fatty meat—crunchy and substantial in my mouth. The last three hazelnuts were all filled with grubs.

"Thank you. Thank you," I called to Woodpecker. After a moment I gave a feeble bark to Brother Coyote, but there was no answer. The forest was quiet again. The dead fir tree stood over me like a comforting old woman. I put my arms around her rough skirt and looked up the scaly, blotched trunk to the wispy thin clouds easing over the Dream Mountain. Both hands fell to my side. I turned and slid down to the snow-covered ground.

A jay called from far down the stream, and I felt a whisper niggling at both ears. "What? Speak louder. Is that you, Brother Coyote?"

Soft, crumbly bark cushioned me from the melting snow. I sat for a long time and listened to the whisper. The sun grew warmer. The wind hissed through yellow pine boughs, and finally I stood.

"Tell me, Brother Coyote, what is the meaning of this spoor?" I pointed to ancient beetle trails etched onto the tree trunk. Snow flopped from overloaded tree branches. Explosions sounded as the glutted stream slammed boulders around, one into the other. Near my foot lay a sharp rock, somewhat larger than my hand. The wind and water keened in hypnotic harmony. I saw Brother Coyote peer from behind a jagged stump and then disappear. I took the stone and began chopping at Mother Fir Tree. Tiny chips of rotten wood were followed by slabs of fibrous, grub-filled treasure. Twice, small clumps of yellow termites slowed my progress. I grabbed entire handfuls and threw them into my mouth to swallow without chewing and ignored the fluttering movement as they descended toward my stomach.

With the warm afternoon sun, Shup emerged from the lodge to sit and watch my efforts. At dusk I pushed Mother Tree to the ground, and Uncle Shup stood beside me as we studied the large cavities filled with hazelnuts and acorns. Near the base of the tree, directly under the shattered splinters my axe could not cut, squirmed countless termite grubs.

Uncle Shup grunted and we both started to eat—slowly, one nut and one grub at a time. It was the time for thrush and the small owls before we stopped.

In the morning I found a fat hare in my best snare and knew that we would survive. I would survive another season, and Uncle Shup would continue as my esteemed mentor. We would survive season after season until the end of my sojourn.

"Brother Coyote," I hissed. "Am I ready to defeat the white invaders now? Grubs and tiny rabbits fall to my hand—how are the white invaders any different?"

Shup farted.

A little owl laughed.

Brother Coyote was silent.

CHAPTER 8

Winter 1793

WET WINTER SLIPPED INTO A blur of seasons.
I added willow branches to the roof of our pathetic lodge. I maintained snares in various places, and my moments of triumph improved over time. On an indifferent morning, Uncle Shup spilled dirt on his arm, added a glob of spit, and rubbed the mud up and down until I said, "Clean." Shup nodded his head, and I smiled.

The tiny sweathouse was made with a simple willow-branch frame and covered with a double thickness of fir boughs. There was a small opening with a large piece of pine-tree bark as an adequate door. After each mindless interlude of silence, smoke, and sweat, we swam in the cold water of our stream. Mindless. Silent smoke and silent Shup as companions. Mindless of thought except for the brief visions required for surviving another day and night.

Shup's private sign language remained plain and simple. His desire to eat was a hand-to-mouth motion; eyes shut with head askew was his intention to sleep. For his daily walk to study the great Dream Mountain, he moved the fingers of one hand across the other.

My mentor ate the morning mush that I prepared, took his hot steam bath in a structure of my invention, and snored through long afternoon naps. Shup ate whatever grubs or mice or small fish or snare-caught songbirds I could capture for our evening meal and slept from dusk to dawn.

Shup, my mentor.

During my first effort to stalk and kill the huge redheaded woodpecker, I lost six round rocks of perfect weight from my sling. I screamed my frustration into the woods and heard only an echo. It was only toward the end of that first summer of my sojourn that I was able to kill a sufficient number of the lazuli buntings and pileated woodpeckers to fill a small basket with their feathers. I met my neighbors, the Wintu, Yana, and Yuki, and offered first my respect and then my feathers in exchange for their dried salmon, toasted grasshoppers, and dried roots. It was in this fashion that Shup and I survived our second winter with fewer ribs exposed than after the first miserable season.

I eventually found that one rock was sufficient to kill one bird, and my stock of feathers increased in a dramatic fashion. Since I posed no threat to my neighbors, they welcomed my trade. The Wintu heard from the Miwok of my sojourn, but the rest saw me simply as a strange young man who sold beautiful feathers and was a gambler of unwholesome skill. They called me "the young peddler of blue and red feathers" to my face, and "the young gambler who always wins" in loud whispers behind my back.

"He is spirit-guided," an old Yana tipne doctor said.

"An *evil* spirit guides his hands," mumbled a Yuki man who had lost a favorite bow and six perfect arrows to me.

From the beginning of the second summer of my sojourn, stones and arrows flew with uncanny accuracy to their target. The storage baskets were always full of acorns. Shup's gut spilled over his belt in three directions.

Early in the second fall season of my sojourn, I looked up from the mink pelt I was scraping clean. "Uncle Shup," I whispered.

He nodded his head without looking at me.

"Uncle Shup. I'm thinking of traveling south for a while; maybe I can trade my feathers and shell money for a new bear rug."

Wind bounced off the cedar-bark planks of our new house.

"I may bring a wife back to our lodge. We need someone to cook and keep the fire." I put the skin down and leaned forward. "I'm going tomorrow, Uncle Shup. There's plenty of food in the baskets, and I've stacked firewood outside the lodge."

Shup continued to stare at the dirt floor of our lodge.

"Tomorrow morning I'll leave," I said.

———

The ghost trail stars dropped into my eyes as I emptied my bladder. When I returned to our lodge to stir the fire and rinse hot stones to cook the morning acorn mush, Uncle Shup never moved. I spilled water on the fire in a hissing explosion, but Shup's blanket didn't move.

After my breakfast I called, "Good-bye, Uncle," but there was no response. I cleaned the cooking basket, returned all implements to their proper shelf, and moved quickly through the deerskin door.

On that first day I moved rapidly and chose up-slope routes where level ground would have served. I charged through difficult brambles when unobstructed options were available. Thick fog and pitch darkness stopped my trek beside a very small stream. I chewed a piece of deer jerky into salty spit and then sat against a tree with a blanket wrapped around my shoulders.

I was angry. The bramble cuts felt good. The dirty sweat was cleansing. Uncle Shup was a useless old man—fat, silent, and stupid—so what did it matter, this sojourn of mine? Podnow and Ulati had given me to the wolves, for all they knew, and yet I survived.

Dead leaves collapsed in delicate complaint under the tread of four feet. I whispered, "Coyote? Brother?"

A frantic shower of dirt and small pebbles hit the tree at my back.

"Coyote! Brother! My only friend!"

Rocky soil spewed onto oak leaves for ten heartbeats, then silence of an equal duration, and suddenly a dead rabbit appeared at my feet.

The voice was a harsh growl: "No more slogging through poison oak, you fool. No more tearing up and down hills."

"Brother! Thank you for the rabbit. I shall share the favored parts with you."

The persistent sound of crotch-licking filled the night, and the voice was a muffled, moist whisper. "Listen, my stupid brother, tomorrow I want you to walk down near the Big River." The licking stopped, the voice now sharp as teeth. "Find us an easy path. Do you hear me?"

"Are you back for good, Spirit Brother? I've missed you through these past seasons." I was feeling a bit of panic at sending my brother into hiding again. "Can we talk now?"

"Yes or no on the easy path?"

"Yes! Certainly! I was simply testing my endurance."

"Humph," Coyote said. "I know exactly what you were doing, and I'll have no part of your childish anger. You must think good thoughts of Shup and never talk back to me."

"We're talking already. I want to know. . ."

"Quiet! Stupid boy! I'll fill your head with flames. Smoke will spill from your ears."

"Thank you, Spirit Brother," I whispered.

Coyote groaned, as if changing from one uncomfortable position to another even less satisfying. "One more caution," he growled. "Once more through the poison oak brambles, and the spirit of Traushnah will visit with you every night."

"The first wife of Podnow is dead?"

"Quiet!"

I smiled into the dark night and quickly fell asleep.

◆

My eyes fluttered awake, and I peeked around the oak tree. The shallow nest was still warm to my touch. "Honored Brother!" I called.

A passing skunk raised her tail but withheld any greeting. One brown towhee called to another with the long, thin screech of their tribe. The sun was a red arc through thin mist.

"Brother!" I called. "Follow me on this beautiful day. We will fly like swallows down to the Big River."

There was no wind, but a single leaf in a tangle of poison oak moved.

I bowed my head and called, "Good morning, Brother."

Two leaves moved in succession as if kissed by a single yellow butterfly.

I stepped over a moss-covered snag, pushed through a copse of tangled brush, and broke free onto an oak-shrouded hill. The fog disappeared, and I increased my pace. Near noon, a well-used path in sight of the river encouraged a steady jog. Elk startled at my approach and galloped down into the mass of tule reed. Deer moved uphill and paused to watch my passage. A constant swirl of geese blurred the adjacent marsh. Near dusk of the third day on the river trail, I topped a small hill to gaze at a large village.

◆

The orderly perimeter of earth-and-tule-reed lodges was empty. A few dogs challenged me, and at the fourth dwelling an old woman popped through a deerskin door.

"Young man! Who are you? Why do you disturb our village?"

"I have feathers to trade, honored elder." I held both hands open at shoulder height. "May I offer them in this village?"

She studied me for a long moment, and then said, "I remember you from before." She pointed. "There. Talk with the chief, and he will decide your fate."

I bowed, thanked her, and moved away.

The village chief was making a speech as I arrived. He named a man to lead an elk hunt in the morning, listed those elders and tipne who must meet with him in the sweat lodge to formulate plans for moving to winter quarters, and finally, obtained a group of twenty volunteers for a trading venture to the Pomo. It was a fine demonstration of leadership, and the chief was repeatedly applauded with smiles of approval.

After the final question, the villagers broke into small clusters to move clear of the meeting area, and the chief turned to join in conversation with a few elders. I waited until he finished and then introduced myself.

"Ah! Yes, the feather boy." He shook a finger at me. "I remember your visit from last summer. You are the lucky gambler!"

"Merely a sojourner from the Tachi," I said.

"Well, now we have a problem with those Chauchila folks." He moved his head back and forth, eyes closed. "A band of their young men killed some of our elk and kidnapped two of our young women." His eyes opened. "The Tachi are friends with the Chauchila, so when you talk with my people, stick with the feather trader name and forget the Tachi sojourner part." He turned to walk away and called over his shoulder, "Come, young man—you may ply your trade with my people."

"Thank you, sir. I shall be generous in any exchange that is offered for my feathers."

"Mind you well, young man. I shall quickly hear of any sharp trading."

"You will only hear in what manner your women took advantage of a harmless feather merchant, good sir."

"Ha!" The village chief smiled and then pointed uphill. "Come to the largest lodge of the village for our evening meal. My daughters will welcome such a handsome guest."

The sturgeon steak was crisp along the edges and slipped past my tongue with tender ease. Fresh roasted grasshoppers seasoned the mush, and my basket of manzanita cider was sweet beyond memory. The chief's three daughters giggled and postured as they placed tidbits of steamed green leaves and boiled yellow root on my plate.

Toward the end of the meal, with the two oldest daughters surreptitiously brushing their breasts against my arms and back, I noticed a boy and girl creep slowly through the murky firelight toward the basket of cold mush. They were about my age, sixteen or so. With unobtrusive movements they ladled portions of mush into small, tattered baskets and were five steps into their retreat when the chief grabbed a long wooden staff and struck at the fleeing forms.

"Carrion robbers! Vultures!" he screamed. The daughters and wife joined halfheartedly in the chase, and the lodge quickly filled with curious neighbors. Some few were interested in watching the chief with his cat-and-mouse chase, but most were interested in rumors and gossip that I could reveal from my visits to neighboring villages.

The chief quickly returned to his place near the fire, and soon the games of odd-or-even were in full swing. Fresh kindling brought the flames higher and plastered smoke against the ceiling. Each sister disappeared in a swirl of whispers and smiles, the chief and his wife joined separate gambling frolics, and an old woman fell asleep against my shoulder.

A movement near a large acorn storage basket caught my attention. No one was paying the least attention to me, so I eased the old woman down onto a blanket and moved slowly back to the dimly lit storage alcove of the lodge.

"I see you," I whispered.

Both figures kept their eyes on the floor.

Laughter and cheers and the rhythmic clapping of hands and sticks erupted in ceaseless spurts from the gamblers.

"My name is Kiyu, and I am of the Yokuts." I moved closer. "Are you of this village?"

"Yes," said the boy.

"Are you both of this family?"

The boy humped his shoulders as if he were a whipped dog. "We are outcasts, Kiyu." His head moved in twitches closer to the dirt. "Our mother, who is the daughter of our chief, never married."

The mush and grasshoppers in my stomach churned in rapid turns. "Never married?" A knot formed in my throat. "Yet you sit before me."

The girl held the posture of a dead turtle, but moved closer and closer until we were but an arm's length apart. "We are twins," she murmured.

My stomach heaved to an even greater degree. Both my arms exploded with boils. Twins! Tachi women destroyed such creatures. The females of any double birth, at any rate, are always smothered and buried with the afterbirth of both children. These two creatures were twins, also the product of an illegal alliance. I looked about the dark corner for a weapon.

"Will this serve?" The girl held a long stick in one hand.

A loud cheer turned my head for a moment, and when I turned back to the girl, she held the stick forward with a steady hand. "We are required to keep this stick handy for use by the people of our village."

I cleared my throat of a small green frog. "This is the first time I have exchanged words with an outcast."

"Yes. I understand." The girl made one eyebrow move up into a sharp curve while the other maintained a docile even line. "Tell me, Kiyu, do twins live in your village? Does your tipne doctor tolerate the birth of twins?"

"I'm not sure, but I think they must be destroyed. The girls, at any rate."

The girl leveled both eyebrows. "It is the same in this village." She moved closer. An elusive fragrance tickled my nostrils. Her skin scattered the smell of smoke from manzanita wood and sweet grass, but there was also an elusive aroma that settled my stomach and removed the boils from my skin. Was it the perfume from a night-blooming flower? She came even closer. It was not the flower scent but a smell from the very edge of memory. I smiled at the outcast and her nighttime smell.

The girl put the stick in my hand. "The chief is our mother's father."

"I saw him chase you away from the food. I heard him yell angry words at you."

"Our grandfather sent the village tipne on a long trading mission to the Coast Miwok just before our birth, and now he must placate both the tipne and the spirits." She looked away from my eyes for the first time. "Our grandfather is a good man. He must make every possible effort to beg forgiveness for his error in preventing our death." Again she stared into my eyes. "We are less than slaves, and we are required to serve the tipne as a constant caution to all in the village."

My tongue unwrapped itself like a snake on a cold morning. "Can you ever become one with your People?"

"No," she said

I dropped the stick. "There must be some resolution to a problem that came from no fault of yours. Have the tipne or your grandfather no plan? Maybe your grandfather, at least, has something in mind."

The boy pushed his chin further down until I could see only the top of his head, but his sister maintained her noble posture and spoke with a slow, hard-edged cadence.

"The tipne will never tolerate our assimilation into this family."

I pulled my eyes from hers and nodded toward the fire. "The chief is staring in my direction. I must return to his company."

She lifted the left eyebrow again. "Certainly, but look again. His three daughters have also returned to serve you."

I blinked twice at the twins and turned to scurry through the smoke from wood and tobacco, back to the chief and his family.

"Where have you been?" The chief spoke in a petulant tone. "My daughters feel neglected by your absence."

"I've been watching the gamblers, your honor. I fear that their skill far exceeds mine."

The chief narrowed his eyes. "What a clever one you are." He shook the shoulder of his eldest daughter. "The young peddler claims ignorance of odd-or-even."

The three girls fell against each other in forced laughter while I carefully studied their shape and smell. Certainly there was the pleasant smoke-and-acorn scent about them, but nothing of the ephemeral scent that covered the mysterious girl.

Maybe a game or two of chance would clear my head. "Watch the eyes, never the hands," Ulati had always admonished. "The eyes tell which hand holds two stones and which hand holds only one."

CHAPTER 9

Summer 1793

I WALKED through early morning fog to follow a scraggly line of men to the river. The water was warmer than the air, so I paddled about, diving for white pebbles, and chased a large salmon to the first downstream bend before returning to the lodge. After the youngest daughter of the chief served our mush, I followed him as he moved about his village like a hummingbird in a flower-filled field.

"Hunters, hear me now! Quickly! Go to the northwest and up the triple-humped hill. Yesterday the women saw three elk near the spring in the second canyon.

"Listen to me, you women under the oak tree! Enough with your odd-or-even games! Quickly! The hazelnuts must be gathered in the western orchard. Quickly, before Woodpecker and Squirrel steal the very last one."

He stormed through the village streets toward the sweat lodge, and I followed. A strange prickle irritated the back of my neck. At the second look over my shoulder I saw the twins disappear behind a large, well-maintained lodge.

"Your honor! Please, a moment, if you will."

The chief stopped and turned toward me, eyes blinking.

"Your honor, may I have permission to wander about your village? I have no desire to sit in the sweat lodge at this time."

His face quickly grew into a giant smile. "Wander where you wish, feather boy." Now he waggled his pointer finger. "No gambling! All of my people must work this morning, so no gambling and no trading of feathers."

I raised both hands in surrender. "Certainly, sir. I merely wish to admire your rich village and perhaps join in a soccer match."

The chief laughed from his belly. "I must run quickly to the sweat lodge and warn the men to bury their shell money. Feathers or gambling—either way, my people will end the day with less wealth."

We waved, both of us in good humor, and departed in opposite directions. The twins quickly fell in behind as I walked south along the river. There were no words, and we continued at a slow pace until the sun cleared the last puddle of fog. A grove of stunted oak trees interspersed with large cottonwood trees offered shade, so we sat and maintained our silence. I felt an odd touch of sympathy for the twins. It was nothing much—just a soft whisper, a vague twinge of interest that shuttled between groin and gut.

They stared at leaf litter while I listened to insects forage in the trees. Up on the western ridge a coyote howled, unusual for the time of day. The big redheaded woodpecker rattled a dead cottonwood snag.

I stood. "I'm getting hungry. Let's find something to eat."

The twins followed, still silent, and at my direction moved toward the dry, scrubby uplands. "You two go uphill and gather some chinquapin nuts," I said. They moved off while I remained among the oak trees to hunt gray squirrel with my sling. At noon we met again at our shady spot. The girl started a fire to prepare and cook the three squirrels I'd killed while the boy prepared the nuts. He nibbled a few, but most were passed to me for my pleasure.

The meat was perfect in every manner: crisp on the outside, bloody near the bone. I drank water from a basket, finished a small pile of nuts, and was turning the idea of a nap over in my mind when the girl spoke. "Is there something that I can do for you? Fetch something? Provide a service?"

"What about some tanai?" I asked. "Can you get some tanai for me?"

The boy stopped nibbling small bones as if startled by a large animal.

"I have shell money or feathers to pay for tanai. Just tell me how much I need to pay for a pipe full or two."

The girl removed meat stuck between her teeth, then asked, "Why?"

I felt annoyed by the audacity of her question. Slaves and women had no right to interrogate their masters.

She spoke again in a slightly louder voice. "Why do you seek the tanai?"

I was tempted to get up and leave this annoying creature, but instead I answered with pointed words. "I'm a tipne doctor! I seek guidance from the spirit world with the tanai."

She nodded as if contemplating the merit of my statement. "I'll try to find some, so let us meet here tomorrow and talk again."

"Enough!" My chest felt stuffed with dry leaves. "The chief and his elders have advice for me, and I have questions for them."

As I turned to leave, the girl spoke with a clear voice, like a thrush at dusk. "I will have the tanai tonight. Meet us here after the half-moon clears the mountains."

I walked away, head down and eyes blind to every root on the path.

The chief spooned acorn mush into his mouth with the four fingers of his right hand and the thumb folded out of the way, as was the custom of all noble men. His daughters leaned on my shoulders and anticipated every need. Their breasts moved across my back with slippery ease.

"Now, my young peddler." The chief waved a partially eaten goose leg at me. "What is this sojourn business of yours? The village tipne says something about the white invaders and the Yokuts. It is all gibberish as far as I can determine."

I dipped my right hand in a bowl of warm water and cleaned my lips. "My people fear the White Others, your honor. It is my task to prepare myself to live among the White Others and learn how to defeat them."

The chief threw the goose bone toward his favorite dog. "We've heard about the White Others, of course." He looked to his tipne for confirmation. "Don't they live in the far north among the Walla Walla?"

"And also along the coast with the Ohlone," the tipne murmured.

"Well, in any event"—the chief reached for a piece of smoked salmon—"they've never bothered us here in the upper valley." He chewed and stared at the smoky fire pit. "On the other hand, the Yokuts, especially those Chauchila folks—they have caused many problems for us." He waved the salmon under my nose as he spoke. He pushed one of his daughters away to stare hard looks at me. "My grandmother's cousin recently lost a daughter to those Chauchila raiders."

"I am of the Tachi." I held my right hand toward the chief. "The Chauchila are troublesome even to their Yokuts neighbors."

The chief seemed to grow weary of difficult subjects, and the lines on his face relaxed into a smile. "Ah, well. Our village is strong.

Neither the White Others nor the Chauchila are likely to pose a threat to our prosperity." He moved a bit closer to me. "Tachi, you say? Does your chief supervise a big village?"

"As I remember, it is about the size of yours—maybe slightly larger."

"Hmmm. Tell me, feather boy, what is your lineage?"

"My dead father was an antu doctor, his eldest brother is the village tipne doctor, and we are of the bear moiety."

"Ahhh, that is all good, very good." He moved even closer. "What about some more mush?" He looked over my shoulder. "Youngest Daughter! Quickly! Serve a basket of toasted grasshoppers for our esteemed guest."

"Thank you, your honor. I'll have nothing more." I moved to stand. "Tonight is the half-moon, and I must speak to the spirits before it moves too far above the horizon."

"Nonsense! Stay and drink manzanita cider with my family. The spirits hate tedious petitioners, and my daughters will massage those strong shoulders and whisper small promises into your ears."

I stood and took one step toward the door and uttered a small lie. "Thank you, your honor, but I must train myself to avoid the delights of this world. The White Others are powerful adversaries, and my training requires that I seek constant guidance from the spirits."

"Bah! Nonsense! The spirits will follow those who let joy and good humor flow into their hearts." The chief made a face to mimic a child who had eaten a green acorn picked up from the ground. "The spirits avoid dour fanatics. Stay and enjoy the laughter of my family. I'll even challenge you to a game of odd-or-even." His pained expression was transformed to one of cunning bliss. "I wager an evening with the daughter of your choice against a small pile of those blue feathers you carry."

"A delightful proposal, your honor, but with your permission, I must leave. Tomorrow we can talk about the White Others and the danger they may pose to your fine village."

The chief waved his left hand in dismissal. "Go, peddler boy. Walk down to your Chauchila friends and tell them to leave us alone." He waved both hands. "Go! Go! Tell those spirit friends of yours to teach you how to smile more often."

I made a half-bow and scooted through the deerskin door.

―――――

The moon was tilted just over the western hills, poised to trail after the long-departed sun. My feet found their way along the indistinct path without difficulty, and the twins sat beside a small fire.

"Were you successful?" I asked.

"Yes. There is also a pipe." Her eyes glittered from both fire and stars. "It is the pipe of our tipne."

"How many feathers must I pay?"

"It is my gift to you," she said.

I sat beside the girl while she stoked the fire, and I shredded the dried jimson weed. The fire blazed to waist height, then settled into a pleasant mound of heat and light. I removed a taper and drew lightly on the pipe. "Does your tipne approve of this generous gift?"

"He has many pipes, and he will not miss the tanai that fortuitously slipped into my basket."

"My brother Coyote will approve of your gift, but what about your grandfather? How will he respond to the inevitable complaints from his tipne?"

"My grandfather will not hear a word about the tanai." She passed a basket of water to relieve the hacking cough that followed my first small pull on the pipe. "Calm yourself," she said. "Try again with the tanai."

The second draught of smoke felt like Badger clawing at my throat, but the fifth and sixth were the gentle zephyr of a new memory. During the middle of my second pipe, Brother Coyote sat smiling, first at me, then at the twins. The silly mutt spent an inordinate amount of time reviewing the features and lines of the girl.

"I see you, Brother Coyote." The tanai slipped through my limbs and joints like smoke through a pipe stem.

"I see you, Kiyu." He stretched his paws in four directions.

"I've called to you countless times. Why haven't you answered?"

He shook seeds from his coat and flopped onto the dust.

"Why should I bother with a stupid youngster?" His green eyes stopped my tongue. "Children beg for favors while warriors play with their spirit brothers."

"I'm ready to play, Brother Coyote."

Coyote rolled onto his back, legs akimbo. "Maybe and maybe not, my silly brother. Just tell the favor you desire, the miracle you want performed."

"I need the carnal knowledge of a man. I hunt and fight as a man, only the sexual is lacking. Give me the thoughts and ideas that fit my needs."

"What do I get?" he asked.

"Nothing, my brother. You must simply enjoy sharing with me your exquisite mastery and pleasure of sex."

"Good!" Coyote struggled to turn and stand but settled for a sloppy sitting position. "Is your mind moving in any particular direction, my little brother?"

"Direction? What is there in the act but in and out, up or down?"

"Who is your intended partner in this proposed adventure—the boy or his sister?"

"Oh," I said.

"What exactly does Podnow's nephew desire?"

"The girl emits an astonishing fragrance that I cannot understand."

"Ahhhh, now I understand the essence of your request. You want to participate in the female version of the dance. A good beginning if you want to eventually comprehend the endless vagaries of sex."

"Just get me started with the beginning moves," I said.

"Brother, oh my lovely little brother, you have come to the perfect teacher for such an important task. No other spirit holds a greater command over the sport of sex than Kiyu, your spirit brother."

"When do we begin the lessons, my teacher?"

He scratched his ear and then slobbered at his crotch for an interminable period. Finally, Brother Coyote glanced briefly in my direction and said, "Okay, we'll see how it plays." He stood, again shook himself free of dust, and disappeared into the night.

There are additional memories from that night: the girl's soft lap and her song about owls and beetles and spiders. There were also verses too faint for me to hear, but I remember how vigorously the owls celebrated each captured gopher and how gleefully the beetles clicked among the leaves, and the comfortable manner in which the spiders drew gray thread through my dreams. I felt a tingle of fingers and toes, a smell of damp fur and the odd experience of observing myself from a distance. I stood on a mountaintop or a red cloud to see two boys and a girl cavort in a stream. I blinked twice and saw two men and a woman stand quietly in hip-deep water.

The first glint of sun melted wispy tendrils of fog. I sat up and looked around. The twins had disappeared, but as I blinked away the bright light, I could see the village men ambling to and from the river. I moved to join the parade for my morning bath.

"Wait, Kiyu. We will come with you."

I turned and witnessed Brother Coyote's magic with my new eyes.

They stood side by side: a beautiful woman with wide, thoughtful eyes and thick glossy hair, and a man with the big nose and ears of a powerful man. From the smile lines above their eyes, I knew that I stood before them as a warrior.

"Thank you, Brother Coyote," I whispered.

We continued to the river, bumping one into the other like naked toddlers. I touched her breasts and she pushed the hair back from my eyes. The boy clamped one arm over my shoulder and the other arm around his sister's waist to pull us over the sand and into shallow water. All reason left my head. I waved my arms and shouted: "Woman! You must be my wife!"

She stopped, looked at the clear water, and smiled. "Kiyu, we must walk quickly into the deeper water."

My sense of propriety was a milkweed seed on the wind. "Nonsense, woman. Let the villagers see a man, what do I care?"

The boy, who was now also a man in my eyes, splashed water on us as I put my hands on her shoulder. Drops drizzled down my neck as I pulled her close to feel breasts and hot breath on my chest. I whispered into her ear. "You walk like the winter crane of the Great Valley; your name as my wife shall be Sedit!"

The woman put her hands on my shoulders and held us apart. "Quiet yourself for a moment, Kiyu. I am the same this morning as yesterday." She studied first me and then her brother. "Other than two prominent erections, I see little difference between the two who ate my squirrel meat yesterday and the two who stand beside me today."

The brother stopped his churning of water and stood gazing at us with a huge lopsided smile. "I feel much different today, my sister."

I kicked water at him. "Of course we are different. Dive into the deep water, my brother; find yourself a toothless old salmon to chase."

He charged through hip-deep water, and the three of us fell laughing and clawing, one on top of the other, until we finally stumbled into the depths to jump like fish turned grasshoppers and swam underwater until our lungs turned into tight oak galls. We laughed and played until the river and shore were empty of all others, save for an old woman who walked up and down the beach and spied upon us from behind one large cottonwood tree or another.

We left the water and walked along the beach toward the village, still frolicking, when the boy hit me on my left biceps. "I heard you name my sister Sedit." He punched again. "What about me?"

"Chetic! Your name shall be Chetic, the milkweed seed, because you float from the spirit world as my brother." I stepped forward to embrace him. "Chetic, you are my brother in this world and my brother forever in Tipiknits Pahn."

Sedit joined us in the embrace, and we stood together, crying and laughing, until the old lady walked by us to whisper, "Ugliness! I see slaves cavorting with a tipne doctor!" She stepped closer. "The chief shall know what I have seen. The chief and his wife and daughters, all shall hear my report."

Sedit looked over my shoulder. "We are married, old lady. There is nothing more you can do to hurt me." Her words fell like ice from naked trees.

The old woman stepped back. "You dare talk to me?" She placed both hands on her chest. "You, who should be buried with your afterbirth—yet now as a lowborn twin you speak to our village tipne's wife. Never have I been so insulted!"

Chetic spoke. "We are brothers and warriors." He smiled with the sweetness of one who had just won another man's fortune. "We are brothers forever, in this world and the next."

The woman's mouth puckered open and shut, but there was no sound. She threw her arms up over her head, then down to her side before marching off toward the village.

We collapsed in a heap to giggle and fondle one another. Sedit spoke from somewhere beneath my hip. "Did you speak truly, Kiyu? Are we really married?"

I groped for a soft part of her body. "Yes, certainly, you are my wife and no other."

"When shall we leave this place?"

We untangled and sat in a tiny circle. The twins waited patiently until I was ready to speak. "Sedit," I said, "go to the lodge of the chief and retrieve my clothes and beads and feathers. Carry them back to our oak grove and wait for us."

"What if someone challenges me?"

"Tell them that you are my wife."

Sedit kept her eyes on mine. "Tell me, Kiyu. When shall we leave this village?"

"Tonight, Sedit. We will leave tonight."

She stood and walked away with the slow, elegant gait of the Sandhill crane; Sedit, my wife.

CHAPTER 10

Summer 1793

A WHISPERY BREEZE STIRRED THE rotting-leaf smell of impending autumn. Chetic led the way on a long uphill walk, and at every opening in the trees, we stopped to watch for movement among the lower patches of brush. We saw neither deer nor elk.

Chetic broke our silence. "The old woman will sound the alarm." He placed his bow tip on the ground next to his foot. "The chief will annul your marriage and put me to work gathering seeds with the women."

I pushed him gently on the shoulder. "Don't worry, Brother. We'll bring him a couple of fat deer, and I'll pay the old man a good bride price."

Chetic shook his head but remained silent.

"Look, Brother, I'll even double the bride price just to keep you from the least little concern."

Chetic smiled, but he kept the worried look about his eyes. "The chief had his youngest daughter in mind for your wife."

I put the tip of my bow next to his. "She has the wit of a grouse."

"He'd charge you just half the usual bride price for the grouse."
The worried smile continued. "He might even throw in a couple of
servants if you married his youngest daughter—twins with no
birthright, for instance."

I was annoyed now. The sorry little puppy. "I said, don't worry,
my brother; I'll handle the old man."

Chetic held up a hand. "In the hollow," he whispered. "There,
near the white oak."

I studied the isolated grove. A ceanothus bush shuddered where
there should be no movement. "Chetic, you swing over and move
down the other side of that draw. I'll wait at the lower end."

I squatted behind a boulder and quickly heard two bucks cough a
warning back and forth. They moved cautiously from shadow to
thicket, away from the apparent danger, secure in their ability to find
a comfortable hiding place.

I pulled the first arrow back to my ear, and two heartbeats after
the twanging, screeching thud of pain tore into the lead buck, the
second buck twisted back with two gigantic leaps into my second
arrow. Chetic ran forward with his obsidian-blade knife and quickly
sliced the large neck vein of one deer, while I did the same for the
other. We wiped blood from our arms, sang our praise for the deer,
and thanked them for giving their lives.

"There," I chortled, "nothing to worry about, my brother. Two
baskets of feathers and two fine bucks seem sufficient bride price for
the silly old man."

In the absence of any women, Chetic skinned and quartered the
large animals. Then, proud of our strength, we packed the meat and
skin atop our shoulders. Dead eyes and massive horns pointed the way
back to the Wintu village.

The village chief was waiting for us on a narrow path just west of his village. At his right hand was the war chief, and scattered behind the two dignitaries and into the trees on either side were a dozen armed warriors. "So, peddler boy, what are you doing?" His voice came from low in his gut. "I see that you poach our deer in the same fashion as your Chauchila cousins." The warriors rattled their weapons. "I've heard that you intend to steal my servants and spit upon my hospitality." His body seemed to grow larger. "Is this the way of the Tachi people?"

I dropped the meat and skin at his feet. "The deer have given themselves for your use, honored chief. I have feathers and shell money to offer as a bride—"

"Stop with your lies!" The warriors all moved closer. "The wife of our tipne told me of your obscene behavior. My daughters told me of your inappropriate advances to them." His arms and legs shook with erratic twitches. "You are both a liar and thief—a Tachi liar, a Tachi thief!"

The warriors raised bows and slings and lances.

"Kill this evil foreigner!" shouted the village tipne.

The Wintu were in a close arc before us, not ten paces away. We were all massed in a confined copse of woods, so the Wintu had dropped their bows and arrows on the ground as a likely threat of injury to friends. They moved toward us with clubs and short spears in hand, and now Chetic and I had the advantage of holding the only bows. We moved in opposite directions and together fired our arrows into the massed swarm of men. They had little space to move, and quickly four warriors fell screaming while the rest ran for cover. We continued to pull one arrow after the next and struck two more men.

"Stop! Stop killing my warriors," yelled the chief.

"Stop your attack on me," I answered.

The chief pulled at his hair and glanced at each writhing body. He yelled, "Stop! Stop! I'll do anything! Just stop killing my men."

We lowered our bows and moved cautiously back through the trees.

The village erupted into a keening scream of women. Mothers and wives ran to stop the blood, to force arrow points back through ruptured skin, to bathe loved ones with tears. "Yiiihiii!" they yelled. "Murder, murder! Stop the Tachi killer!"

Sedit met us at the first rise beyond the village. She checked the bruise from a sling-thrown rock on Chetic's forehead and quickly dismissed the small cuts to my arms and shoulder. We trotted back to our little camp, and she quickly heated water for willow-bark tea.

"What now, Husband?" She poured tea into two baskets and passed them to us. "Do we run until they catch us, or shall we wait here for the warriors?"

"We must wait," I said.

"Why?"

"The chief will not attack again this morning. They have time to achieve their end, and I must pay for the harm done to his village."

"But, Husband, it was the chief who initiated the attack. You were innocent of any evil intention."

What had I done? Who was this woman calling me husband? "I killed Wintu warriors and must therefore pay reparations. I injured Wintu warriors and must pay for the pain inflicted. I lied to the village chief and stole what was his to own."

Sedit moved closer and spoke in a whisper. "Do you still call me Wife?"

There was the aroma again. The eyes and lips. "Yes, you are my wife, and Chetic my brother."

"Do you recognize that you have broken other laws in taking me as your wife?"

The breasts and long legs. "Yes."

"What will you do?"

I was a squirming worm on a hook. My stomach felt filled with stones. "We must wait," I said.

A foot drum maintained a steady *thump thump,* and a large fire shimmered under the low fog. Just as Great Horned Owl started his hunt through the stunted oak grove, a winatum from the chief called. "Listen, liar and thief. Listen, killer of brave warriors. Our chief will see you in his lodge at sunrise. You must pay damages for the men you have killed and wounded. You must pay damages for your insults to the chief, and you must return his servants."

I remained silent.

"Do you hear me, murderer of the People?"

"I hear you, winatum of the chief. Tell him I will meet him at sunrise."

"You must bring your entire stock of feathers and shell money." After a long pause, he continued, "You must also bring the twins, Tachi killer of our people."

A night heron croaked. My wife and brother moved into the deep shadows. I sat before the fire and shut my eyes. Clouds and bright spangles passed before the vision of my mind. The misty spirit of my father turned his back on me and walked toward the red mountains.

Brother Coyote smiled with a small turn of his snout. "What now, idiot brother?"

"Could you make the chief and all of his men sleep until the sun burns all fog away?"

"Why?"

"I would gladly make reparations to the Wintu and give them my life, but I cannot surrender my new wife and my new brother to them."

Coyote stretched in a long paw-reaching stance, sat for many moments, then looked up at the bare branches and yawned. "If I understand the situation correctly," he said, "what you want is a decent head start for a race to the north."

"Yes."

I blinked, and my spirit brother disappeared.

I hissed, "Hurry, we are leaving this place."

My wife and brother quickly filled their carry nets with food and blankets, and then Chetic led us along trails west of the village for one hundred paces. Near the Great River he turned to the north, and at a steady jog through the night Chetic maintained the lead. At daylight I took the lead until noon, when we stopped near a small creek to eat dried salmon and cold acorn bread. I walked alone to the top of a small hill and looked southward. A large cumulus cloud sat muttering on the horizon. "Rain!" I shouted. "Coyote! Make the rain fall!"

I turned my head in a sharp twist as a hard, cold burst of rain fell upon my hill. In the time it took me to struggle back to the twins, our trail was mud to my ankles, and the river filled with white foam.

Coyote's rain continued, off and on, for three days, and none from the beautiful Wintu village followed my little band. We three fugitives exchanged few words and slept together under one blanket. Sedit did not ask of laws, and Chetic smiled each time I touched him.

Coyote disappeared with the last drop of rain.

Wood was still stacked neatly on the outside, and at first glance upon entering my lodge, it appeared snug and dry. Shup ignored me until

Sedit ducked through the deerskin door and stood tall at the entrance. His face ignited into a brilliant smile; he jumped from his bed and ran to embrace my wife.

"Daughter! Daughter!" Shup yelled. His entire body smiled.

Sedit returned the embrace, and with her hand still holding his, she took one step backward. "Uncle, please sit by the fire while I prepare your breakfast." She made her eyes wider. "May I prepare your pipe? Brew some tea?"

Shup puffed his chest like the old days, when he had been winatum to the chief and rattlesnake doctor for the village. I joined my smile to his.

"Tea, my daughter; some mint tea would loosen my bowels very nicely."

I removed a pinch of mint leaves from a basket stored in the rafters of my lodge while Sedit stirred the fire to life and made a quick inventory of supplies. "The tongs, honored uncle? Where might I find them?"

"In the dust, beside the water basket, I fear."

"Yes, here they are." Sedit clicked the implement rapidly, like one dog snapping at another. "They will serve beautifully to stir my brother into useful action."

"Brother!" Shup turned his head like an old owl. "Where is this brother of yours?"

Chetic moved from the shadows, folded his legs, and sat close to Shup. "Tell me, honored uncle, how does a man restrain the impetuous words of women? This sister of mine insults me with every click of her tongue."

Shup was speechless. His eyes darted about the lodge. His mouth flailed open and shut.

Sedit moved closer and snapped the tongs again. "His name is Chetic, honored uncle. His back is strong, but he retains the mind and actions of a boy with no hair between his legs."

"There! Have you ever heard such insolence from a woman?" Chetic made his eyes bulge. "The three of us must join forces against such aberrant behavior."

I couldn't hold back the first uncontrolled hoot. Chetic, and then Shup, quickly joined my laughter, and we rolled like bear cubs on the dusty floor.

At the first silence, Sedit leaned over the prostrate form of Shup. "Your tea is ready, honored uncle. May I serve you here by the fire or outside in the warm sun?"

We three he-bears erupted again with uninhibited howls.

———

On the first night of our return to my lodge, Sedit slept on a mat next to mine. On the second night she was a bump beneath my rabbit-skin blanket. I tickled the protuberance, and it giggled in a most delightful manner. Shup snored while Chetic remained quiet on his mat near the large acorn storage basket. Another giggle forced one corner of the blanket open, and I wiggled into the dark, warm void like a snake down a hole.

Sedit embraced me and nuzzled my neck and ear. "Am I your wife or your servant?" she whispered.

I rubbed her from shoulders to firm buttocks with a massage stroke that Ulati had often used on my backside. "Wife," I said.

She rolled over for me to kiss her breasts and lick the nipples into fingers of supple flesh. "Husband! Husband!" Sedit moved my hand to the damp mound between her legs and set it adrift with yet a third quivering finger. Very shortly Sedit grabbed my rigid penis to stroke it up and down with a slow, even motion.

"Wife! Wife!" I croaked.

We threw off the cloak of rabbit-skin blanket, and I entered into her slippery honeypot.

The explosion of our embrace rocked us both from the sleeping mat.

"Wife!"

"Husband!"

"What!" Shup sat up with white hair flying. "What is it? A bear!"

"'Tis a spirit, Uncle," Chetic hissed. "Two spirits: an innocent crane and a randy coyote."

"Aha! They're fucking. Good!" Shup sucked air through his nose as if he smelled the first lupine of spring. "Ahhh, now it comes to me, the beautiful smell of sex. How I have missed that joyous perfume."

I kissed Sedit in an effort to preserve our silence.

Shup finger-combed his hair, settled down on his pillow, and pulled his blankets back into order. "It's good to hear people fucking again." He sighed. "Do it again. I'll pay better attention this time."

I could restrain myself no longer. From the very tip of my toes to my ears I laughed. Sedit and Chetic joined in chorus until we were helpless from lack of breath.

"Very nice, children," Shup said. "But please, I'm an old man, so get on with your fucking before I fall asleep again."

———

During the stretch of warm, dry weather that followed my return to the shadow of the Dream Mountain, Chetic and I built a larger, more comfortable lodge. Shup helped where he was able, and Sedit explored our small valley to collect acorns and nuts and seeds and to smoke-dry the few salmon that gave themselves for our use.

Shup and Chetic became close friends. They pooled their limited fund of knowledge, and each grew apace. Shup learned to hunt; Chetic learned to listen to the spirits and to speak his own thoughts.

"I prefer the snare to the bow," Shup said.

"Your hands are quick with the weaving, and your eyes notice the subtle signs." Chetic paused. "Yesterday I was surprised that you noticed the few hairs caught on that tan oak tree."

"The deer whispered into the wind, and I heard his call."

"What did the deer spirit say, Uncle?"

Shup smiled. "He admonished me to set a snare on the path next to the tan oak tree."

"I saw no path," Chetic said.

"The hair pointed to the path."

"Ahhh." Chetic waited for a respectful moment. "Will you teach me how to speak with the spirits, Uncle?"

"Certainly, my son. I will teach you what I know of both the spirit world and of the other world where I have lived."

"What is the other world, Uncle?'

"It is the world of hunger and silence, my son."

It was a pastoral time in my life. Shup was my uncle once again, and my family was vivacious and fit. Our new lodge survived the early fall rain without a single leak. The spring salmon run was bountiful, and the green vegetables and herbs presented themselves to us in proper order and in great profusion. Spring also brought new life into our camp. Sedit bore our son squalling into the world. When he was old enough to sit and coo to the raucous approval of his universe, I spoke to my family.

"Tomorrow we must leave. Podnow is waiting."

"Where do we go, Husband?"

"To my Tachi village, Wife."

"Will your uncle Podnow show pleasure at your return to the Tachi village?" My wife settled our son on her shoulders. "Will the great tipne doctor count your sojourn as a successful step toward defeating the white invaders?"

Sedit was showing a strange mood at this announcement of our departure. The child was silent, and his uncle Chetic gave me a wan smile that matched his expression at our first meeting. I turned to locate Shup and found him in a crouch, partially hidden by a storage basket. My stomach took a turn.

"What is there in my return that Podnow will not approve? He sent a child on sojourn, a weakling of no account. Now he will receive a warrior, a husband and the father of a healthy son."

Shup did not move during my little speech. He remained silent, frozen in place. He seemed no different to me than during his first year on my sojourn.

Sedit took a step toward me, and my attention turned to her. She was my beautiful brown crane with my healthy son.

"We are packed and ready, my husband. Lead the way and we will follow."

CHAPTER 11

Spring 1794

"I SEE YOU, SON OF my brother."

"I see you, honored uncle."

Podnow stood before me with the stooped posture of an elder.

"Honored uncle, with your permission, I have returned to your Tachi village."

Podnow studied my face for a long moment and then walked past me to embrace Shup. A mockingbird repeated his song twice over before the brothers separated. The greatest tipne doctor of all the Yokuts and Miwok whispered to his younger brother. "Tell me, Shup, how did the sojourn progress?"

Shup shifted his weight from one foot to the other. He made no effort to whisper. "It was very difficult."

Now the brothers spoke so that all could hear them. "Did you follow my instructions?"

"Yes." Shup's body shook as if ice had invaded his blood. "I gave no advice, no help, and few words."

I stopped breathing. Shup had performed his assigned role with perfection.

"Good," Podnow said. "I knew that you were the perfect man for the job."

"He is nearly ready." Shup looked up into the eyes of his eldest brother. "You promised. Do you remember your promise?"

"Of course I remember!" Podnow put his hands on Shup's shoulders and rocked the little man back and forth. "We've missed your huge voice. All in the village welcome back their favorite winatum."

Shup placed both his hands over Podnow's left hand. "Am I still the rattlesnake doctor?"

"Of course you are! The creatures have been a great bother since your departure. Every family in the village welcomes the return of their favorite rattlesnake doctor."

Shup shivered from nose to toes. "It was very difficult, Brother. The silence tore at my gut." Shup's head dropped nearly to his chest. The hump on his back grew larger. "Never again, Brother," he whispered.

"Now, now, all the Tachi welcome you back to your home. I will never ask you to leave this village again." Podnow tousled his brother's gray hair. "Your job is complete, Shup, and the spirits are satisfied with the results."

Podnow pulled his hand free. "The People will celebrate your heroic efforts in story and song. The spirits love you as their son."

"Eldest Brother, the spirits were silent through all the seasons. There were no songs in our lodge until the very end."

The brothers stood with hands at their side. Shup stopped shaking and pointed toward my wife. "She sang to me. She made me smile."

Podnow called over his shoulder. "Kiyu, who stands behind you?"

I could barely speak above a whisper. My heart seemed frozen in my chest. "It is my brother, Chetic."

"Chetic. That is a strange name for a warrior." Podnow turned and took one step toward me. "How did he receive such a name?"

I looked down at Podnow's toes. "His name came to me from the spirits, and he will serve the Tachi as a powerful warrior."

Podnow walked to stand in front of me. "I am getting old," he said. "Often I see people with my eyes when in fact old friends from Tipiknits Pahn have come for a visit. At other times I carry on with a neighbor as if he were dead. Tell me, Kiyu. What do I see standing behind you and Chetic, a shade or a person?"

"That is my wife with our child, Uncle Podnow. She is also the sister to Chetic."

The most powerful tipne of the People waited, but I could think of nothing to say. He finally walked the few additional paces with the slow pomp of his office. "Young woman, you are welcome to my lodge." Podnow made his voice very soft. "What is your name?"

"Sedit."

"Sedit? Let me remember. Sedit. That is the name of the beautiful Sandhill crane of your country, yes?"

"Yes, it is the same, uncle of my husband."

I saw Sedit through the eyes of Podnow: her narrow eyes, large nose, and thin lips. She was nice and chubby, just the way he liked his women. Ulati and Sedit—both were nice and chubby and dark in complexion.

Podnow kept his voice soft as if talking with an old friend. "What a beautiful child you carry. He looks remarkably like the infant Kiyu."

"Thank you, honored uncle."

"He looks as if he is very spoiled"—Podnow added a smile to the kind voice—"which was also the condition of the infant now called Kiyu."

Sedit returned the smile and then looked at the ground.

"The mother of Kiyu, my second wife, will assign a place—"

"Ulati!" I moved three steps and nearly grabbed Podnow by the arm. "Uncle! What position does my mother hold in your lodge?"

Podnow turned from Sedit to face me once again. "She is my wife, of course. Ulati sleeps with me on my mat."

I stepped backward to a respectable distance. "What about Traushnah?"

Podnow stared at me for a long moment before speaking. "My first wife is now in Tipiknits Pahn. It was the white invader's disease, with the red spots and boiling fever."

I lowered my head. "I apologize for speaking her name, my uncle."

"You did not know, so there is no error." He turned back to my wife. "Sedit, take your family and go to my lodge. Ulati will introduce you to the women and assign a place for you to sleep. I must take Kiyu to a quiet place where we will talk."

"Yes, uncle of my husband, I will listen to your wife."

"Shup! Our village winatum! Show the family of Kiyu to my lodge."

Shup stepped off with Badger's gait and Falcon's speed. "Come! Hurry!" he called. "I will show you exactly where Ulati lives. Come! Hurry!"

———

I followed Podnow through tule reed, past oak-dotted slopes, and finally to the top of a small bare hill. We studied the Great Valley with its maze of improbable streams and sloughs and rivers, all interspersed by islands of pale-green willow and stark blue lakes. The brown grass and dead flowers in every corner of the vista whispered warnings of the hot, still days to come.

Podnow pointed to a spot on the ground and sat directly in front of me. "So, you are a man with both wife and child." He moved a bit closer. "My second wife is willing, but thus far we have not produced a child." His smile revealed a few remnant teeth surrounded by black nubs. "She is a constant comfort to this old man."

I followed Shup's approach to wisdom and kept my mouth shut.

"Yes. After the death of my first wife, Ulati spoke with the spirit of my middle brother and then, in a most graceful manner, accepted her obligation as my second wife."

Shup and Coyote both advised more silence.

"So, Kiyu, are you ready to discover the secrets of those white invaders?"

"I will follow your orders, honored uncle."

Podnow moved his body in stiff, slow increments, but he seemed unable to find a more comfortable spot. He gave a long sigh. "Many of the Yokuts and Miwok people are dead. The blisters and fever develop with such rapid virulence that the medicine doctors are unable to treat a single person with any success. Even Ulati's herbs are useless." He stared at a large cloud. "The herbs and tubers that could remove evil spirits are all useless in treating the foreign diseases. Every lodge grieves the loss of warriors and wives and children."

"What does your Eagle Spirit tell you, Uncle?"

"It is the white invaders who send this vicious evil spirit to destroy the People."

"Yes, I am certain that you are correct."

"Are you ready to save the People who still survive?"

"Tell me what to do, Uncle. I'm ready to help the People. My spirit brother and Chetic will also serve. The white invaders are only Others, after all. They are not the People and not best loved by all the spirits."

Podnow studied my face as if it were a deer track in the mud. "When I was your age, I was dumber than a male quail in heat." He shook his head and looked up toward a large white vulture circling among smaller black vultures. It was a spirit bird, a messenger from Tipiknits Pahn, and it was closer to the clouds than our hill but directly over our heads. Meadowlarks sang their tinkling claim to small patches of tall grass. Two red-tailed hawks screamed, clawing each other, midair, for possession of a writhing snake. The wind shushed in quiet, fitful gusts. Podnow studied the vultures and hawks and the file of red ants over his foot. He scuttled closer until he was less than an arm's length away.

"Kiyu! Your body stinks of corruption! Your flesh is the vomit of evil spirits."

I drew back. "What? Uncle, I bathe every day in the river."

Podnow seemed to loom over me, like a hawk over a mouse. "I see a gentle village chief with blood seeping from both eyes and ears. I see innocent warriors carried away to Tipiknits Pahn and wives screaming with despair. Join me, Kiyu. Help me study this vision of treachery and murder."

"Uncle! They were trying to kill us. We did but—"

"Silence!" He grew larger than a bear. "I have answered the Wintu chief's winatum with my own. Ten Tachi warriors carried tribute from the People to those of the Wintu village who suffered from your outrageous behavior."

No! My eyes saw only red spots. "But—"

"Kiyu! You have insulted the People and the spirits of the People with your selfish behavior." His hot breath washed my face. "I have a vision of you that reveals seasons of self-pity, a vision of a wasted sojourn. I see robbery and murder and a cowardly retreat from your pledge of honor."

"I—"

"Silence! Poison drips from your mouth." Podnow uttered a loud shout toward the clouds, pointed his left hand toward the flying curse, and punched me sharply in the ribs. I quelled an upwelling of vomit as Uncle's hand burrowed beneath my skin and bone. His fingers wiggled in violent spasms. Then he pulled a tail-arched scorpion from my body.

"Eeeiii!" I screamed. "It's not my fault. I offered bride-price. I offered presents. I—"

"Stop! Look at this evil spirit." Podnow held the scorpion under my nose. "I must purge you of all evil spirits or kill you." He covered the scorpion with both hands. "Innocent Wintu warriors are dead. Why?"

"The chief would not listen to reason. The Wintu are foolish and stupid people."

Podnow moved his left hand toward the sky and plunged his right hand through my ribs. We were frozen together for ten heartbeats, and when he opened his hands, both held scorpions.

I shut my eyes and began. "In my lodge—"

"Whose lodge?"

"In the lodge of my uncle, it was my duty to honor Shup as the brother of my father. It was my duty to provide whatever Shup wanted. It was my duty to satisfy his every desire." I felt tears for the first time. "I have betrayed my uncle Shup. He was my friend and teacher, and I took no notice of his affection or wisdom."

Podnow put both scorpions in one hand and covered them with the other. "Continue," he said.

"The Wintu were kind to me. The chief welcomed me into his home. He fed me." Tears flushed my eyes. Anger burned my stomach. "I stole his servants and killed his men."

The golden eagle screamed from beyond the clouds. I stopped my tears with tight lids. "Are there more evil spirits?" Tighter yet I squeezed my eyes. "How can I redeem myself with Uncle Shup and with the Wintu chief?"

"Open your eyes."

I watched as Podnow displayed the two scorpions in his left hand. The two spirits shuffled for position until they could each face the other. Podnow moved his left hand toward the sky, and again he pierced my skin and ribs in a bloodless extraction of a third scorpion.

Podnow moved his body slightly to the left and raised his left hand to the sky. The new angle allowed me to catch a fleeting glimpse of his right hand. This time the blow to my ribs was softer and his fingers less invasive. After the sixth scorpion, I said, "It is a trick."

"My magic is a gift from the spirits," Podnow said.

Anger boiled upward into my chest, and the tears vanished. "I see a trick or a lie. Are all tipne doctors tricksters and liars?"

"And you, young man—can you name your spirit brother? Is he a mouse? A butterfly?"

"Must I lie to serve the People? Must I feign a sore paw when all limbs are healthy?"

In answer, Podnow pulled a small basket from beneath his folded legs and dropped the handful of scorpions into their home. He secured the lid and placed the basket at my knee.

I felt as if the sun and moon had exchanged orbits. "Uncle! Stop! Let me watch the eagle burrow into the ground or the gopher fly. Is there no truth in this world, nothing solid to lean upon?" I sucked a deep draught into my lungs and urged my heart to continue at a slower rate. "How are your lies acceptable to the spirits, while mine are not?"

He leaned close to me. "Listen, Kiyu. The Tachi paid the Wintu to make amends for your lies. We are the People best loved by the spirits and cannot allow one of ours to dishonor all."

My questions exploded like eggs dropped from a great height. "What about the magic arrows and your conversation with dead spirits? What about Cuksa flying through the air?"

"They are illusions of my creation or simply friendly jokes that I offer to the People."

"Why?"

"The People require my services."

"That is no answer!" My stomach filled with hot ash. "What about the scorpions and the blood from my body? How did you manage that lie?"

"I remove the stingers and handle the scorpions until they are tame as dogs. I fill frog bladders with deer blood and allow your mind to provide the necessary pain." He maintained a neutral expression with the lines over his eyes straight and even. "I force you to watch my left hand and not the right."

My legs were filled with needles, so I moved to a more comfortable position. "Ulati taught me a similar lesson," I said.

Podnow sat without motion.

"Why do the People accept your lies and tricks?" I inhaled the sweet warm air. "Am I the only doubter among the People?"

Podnow smiled and then blinked his eyes from brown to red and back again to brown.

"Another trick?"

"Of course."

The spit was dry in my mouth. Dust filled my head.

Podnow stood. "I leave you with my tame scorpions and a message from my father and from his father and our fathers into the limits of memory."

I nodded without speaking.

"Only the People are important. A tipne must see through the tricks of God and deflect them for the good of the People. The People. There is nothing in your life but the People."

He turned and walked away.

CHAPTER 12

Summer 1794

DURING THE DUSTY BROWN DAYS I practiced with my scorpions. Often they sat listlessly in the sweat of my hand as I stared blindly toward the western hills. With the departure of migratory songbirds from our tule marsh, I invited Ulati to observe my efforts. She always arrived at my hill in the midmorning and sat quietly until noon. Ulati never gave advice; she merely watched my progress in the skills of my craft. We chatted in animated fashion about the antics of my son and how quickly Sedit had managed to fit comfortably into the fabric of our Tachi village.

"Sedit is a clever woman," she said.

"Do you accept her into our family?"

"She is a good mother and exceptionally smart. The riddles of village status and family intrigue are solved at lightning speed by your wife," said Ulati.

I pulled a scorpion from the left ear of my mother. "Do you accept her into our family?"

"You took a slave as your wife through her machinations, not yours." Ulati pulled a scorpion from my right ear. "Give me a count of the moons passed from the time you arrived at Shup's dwelling and the birth of your son."

I was taken aback by the request and took some time to finger-count the total. "Six or seven, I believe."

Ulati stood. "What have you done?"

I gave Ulati a simple smile. "Do you think me so stupid that I can't count to nine? Are all mothers so quick to diminish the intelligence of their sons?"

Ulati dropped back onto her seat in the dust and remained silent for a spell. "Did you find a woman from a neighboring village to help with the birth of your son?"

"None was needed. Sedit dismissed her three he-bears on a certain morning, and when she called for our return, a newly hatched child was waiting for our approval."

"I see."

"Sedit is my wife and mother of our child. You are the wife of Podnow and stepmother to Hineh." I let the silence spin for a good while, and Ulati neither spoke nor moved.

"As you have already observed, wife of Podnow, Sedit is very smart. You will also find that she has a collection of talents that surpass most women." Ulati bent her head to the left, as if to better hear my words. "Please help my wife help the people of her Tachi village."

"Give me some time, my son. On most occasions you will see my stepmother persona; on rare occasions I may return as your birth mother." Once again she stood to stand before me. "Now I must return to Podnow's lodge and prepare his lunch." She turned and walked slowly down the trail to our Tachi village.

Strange it was how her gait seemed to replicate that of the Sandhill crane. Ulati and Sedit, one crane to fledge me and the other to help me defeat the white invaders. It was strange to finally understand that my sojourn was still in progress, and stranger yet to realize that I was unlikely to improve my skills as student or spy.

◆

During the frost-crunching days and during the time of no sun through the dense fog, Podnow and I whispered secrets and smoked tanai. He taught me to peel bark from trees and explained which could kill an enemy. I already knew from my father which could cure headaches and diarrhea. At certain phases of the moon he gave me over to Ulati, who showed me how bits of grass and leaf and soil became allies in curing both mind and body.

Sedit often joined us in these sessions, and Ulati honored us both with her wisdom. My mother embraced us as one during every season of our Tachi village. It is true that Podnow held the bulk of my attention, yet it seemed equally true that Sedit and Ulati had developed the affection of sisters. The two women of my life lived in a quiet world that allowed them to exchange intimacies with casual ease. Both seemed, at least to my eyes and ears, to maintain a facade of constant good humor that never varied. All in our Tachi village admired my wife and my mother.

Whatever the path my mother and my wife took to achieve their alliance, both seemed content with the outcome. But beyond the most superficial of observations, neither discussed the nature of our family bonds with me.

◆

On a hot, still night, I whispered into the ear of my wife, "Have you noticed that neither Uncle Shup nor my mother offer any tenderness of word or touch to me?"

"Of course I have."

"It was not always so," I said.

Sedit put her hand on my shoulder. "I believe they both still hold affection for you, as does Podnow."

"I remember that before the sojourn I enjoyed their hands on my body, their whispers into my ear. Now there is distance and reserve, not intimacy."

"You are the chosen one, my husband. You must live among the white invaders, not with the People. Ulati and Shup know they must lose you, and their grief is expressed in silence."

"I miss them already."

"Podnow is your teacher in all matters. We who love you must defer to his tactics or put the entire scheme at risk. Podnow is best loved by the spirits, and his instructions to you have thus far proven successful."

"Your grandfather and those of his Wintu village may not agree with your conclusions."

Sedit punched her elbow into my ribs. "Forget those days of madness, my husband. Podnow is the judge of your progress, no one else."

I pulled Sedit into a close embrace. "You show me your love at every moment. Are you immune to Podnow's authority?"

"We serve Podnow together, you and I and Ulati—his entire family. We all must follow his slightest suggestion."

"But—"

"Ulati and I, Uncle Shup and the village elders, we all follow Podnow's guidance in preparing you to infiltrate the white invaders. Ulati is especially anxious for your departure."

"But—"

"Ulati is my teacher in the same fashion that Podnow is your teacher."

"But—"

"Ulati was wife to an antu doctor and can clearly see what is happening to your Tachi village." Sedit held her hand in my face to stop any interruption. "The storytellers are nearly all dead. The women with memories of hidden swales of clover are nearly all dead. Warriors and men of two spirits, all are diminished. Ulati whispers to me that our family may better survive among the invaders than here in our tule marsh."

"No!" What was this nonsense? Was it possible that both women were planning to usurp the power of men?

Sedit pulled me toward our lodge. "Come with me, Husband. I have a small gift for your pleasure."

"This gift is extended on Podnow's command?"

Her eyes twinkled. "Of course, my husband. He described my responsibilities to the smallest detail."

"And Ulati, how do you fare with my mother?"

"Ahhh, my husband. Ulati has taught me a multitude of useless details that will certainly help me master my craft as your wife."

At the end of the second acorn harvest of my return to the Tachi village, Podnow led me and my family to a raft secured among the tule reeds. Chetic and I poled across the sloughs, stirring ducks and geese into whirling clouds that blocked the sun. We walked across the shallow river and up into the brown western hills. At the ridgeline we looked west to low humpbacked banks of clouds and east to a hazy mist. Podnow pointed toward an oak-filled valley to the northwest. "The White Other village is there. If the Tachi are to survive, you must return to the People when you understand their tricks."

I tapped Podnow on his left shoulder to reveal two docile scorpions in my right hand.

Podnow flashed his eyes red and smiled.

Chapter 13

Fall 1796

A THIN CRESCENT MOON, WITH a bright planet in tandem, hung over the abyss of dawn. Two large owls made their last pass of the night over huge rocks and past ancient oaks. I led Chetic and my family toward the rude smell of the white invaders. I must admit that we all walked with stiff-legged fear in our bellies. The youngster peered over Sedit's shoulder, showing large eyes and belching erratic hiccups.

When we were within an arrow-shot of the wood barricade, a gate opened and a small pack of strange people and yapping dogs ran toward us.

"Stand close to me," I said. "Keep still; I'll do the talking."

The child disappeared under a rabbit-skin blanket and burrowed into Sedit's shoulder.

The Indios and dogs surrounded and moved us through the gate and into a village of bare dirt and strange buildings. In quick succession the gate door slammed shut, and an apparition of three brown-robed witches moved in silent parade through Indios and dogs.

The three witches jabbered. Grunts and squeaks spewed from their lips. They seemed ravens fighting over carrion, or possibly brown-feathered jays robbing a nest. An Ohlone man grabbed me and pointed toward his chest.

"Miguel," he said.

"Miguel," I repeated.

He spoke slowly, with a mixed concoction of Ohlone and Yokuts words, and then pointed at the tallest of the monsters. Miguel repeated the same three words over and over until I tried them with my tongue and lips.

"Padre Carlos-Maria," I said.

The tame Indios that surrounded my family cheered and pointed.

"Padre Carlos-Maria," they yelled.

My stomach churned like a fish trapped in shallow water. Yellow eyes stared at me from the depth of a witch's shroud. Insects crawled beneath my skin. Brother Chetic stood close at my left shoulder while Sedit remained a few paces behind, our son now in her arms.

"Kiyu!" I tapped my chest and repeated, "Kiyu!"

The tallest witch stepped even closer, but I stood my ground. Prickly brown hair grew from his ears and nose, and a pelt of the same fur covered the back of his hands. He dipped a metal rod into a basket of water and splashed large drops on my head. "José Jesus. José Jesus," he mumbled. "José Jesus," as he scooped water from his basket.

Miguel stood at my side and whispered his garbled tangle of Ohlone and Yokuts words. "They give new name," he said. "New name is José Jesus. José Jesus."

"José Jesus," I said.

The entire swarm of tame red creatures circled round me repeating the ugly name. "José Jesus," they yelled over and over again.

The three witches turned and walked away, and after a few heartbeats, the red men stopped their absurd shuffling to follow their masters further into the white invaders' village. I was blinded by the flood of strange sights, nauseated by the smell. Miguel whispered in my ear and then grabbed my face so I could see his eyes and mouth. "Keep your head down," he told me. He whispered, "Don't look at the white tipne."

"Who are you?" I asked.

"Miguel. I am the village chief."

I pointed toward a large building that towered above the trees. "Is this your village?"

"No, no. My village is down near the creek among the willow trees."

"Yes," I said, "down below the escarpment." I gestured to the strange buildings. "What is this village? What is it called?"

"It is called Mission San Juan Bautista."

I said the name in my mind, but I could not repeat the strange words with my tongue. After a long moment I asked, "Where do they keep their secrets?"

"There, in the tallest building." Miguel pointed. "It is called the church."

This church was like nothing in my experience, a dwelling of some kind or other. A huge cave carved in some mysterious manner by the invaders.

The crowd suddenly stopped and stood with silent expectation. Miguel looked over his shoulder. "The tipne come again," he whispered. "You must be very careful and drop your eyes and shoulders when they are near."

The three brown-robed men stood in front of me. They pressed hands together and curled their lips over slab-like teeth. They glanced ceaselessly up to the sky, like geese alert for predators, then to the wooden sticks in their hands. Up and down they looked, but never at me or my family.

I ignored Miguel's advice and studied their eyes and the wrinkles above their eyes. Uncle Podnow had admonished me to watch for misdirection feints and said that it was important for me to detect any clue that might mark some subtle trick.

The witches dropped their lips and covered their teeth. All three splashed water at me from separate baskets, but as my instructions from Podnow dictated, I continued to study each discrete motion of their hands and every change in expression on their ugly faces.

A swarm of bees struck me on the face, and I stepped back to see the smallest tipne wave a leather-thonged whip at me. The tallest tipne followed me as I dodged the whip, grabbed the hair on my head, and pulled it in a downward motion. "No!" he yelled. Again he jerked my head and yelled, "No!"

I twisted away from the demon and sent him spinning onto the dirt. The whip struck twice, like a rattlesnake with four tongues. Four tame red men tripped me and forced me down while others held my arms in a sweaty vise.

Bells yammered in a constant jangle. The yelling and pain continued unabated until a tiny black cave swallowed me, and a door slammed with a heavy, distant sound like wet snow falling from a cliff. I sat on the dirt floor and listened as silence spread slowly through the perfect darkness.

Neither moon nor sun could cast a shadow.

There was no Sedit to hold me and melt the ice in my bones. No word or touch from my sweet Sedit, nor was there any hint of chirping laughter from our son.

The sweet memory of acorn mush and baked salmon disappeared. Only the cautious seep of water in one corner kept me alive. If I scraped away the loose mud and packed it around the hole and waited for one hundred heartbeats, there was usually enough water in the mucky bottom for ten laps with my tongue.

I sat with my back to the wooden door.

"Brother Coyote? Are you there?"

"Certainly." He appeared in my mind as a silhouette along the horizon. "C'mon," he barked. "Let's get out of this place. Follow me."

I tried to stand. "Wait," I called.

"Hurry," Coyote said. "Crawl if you must, but hurry."

I managed to get on my hands and knees, but they became tangled, and I collapsed once again into the black void. "Brother! Wait! Please wait for me."

"Are you ready to listen?" a voice asked.

I turned slowly toward the sound. "Who speaks? Are you spirit or man or Brother Coyote?"

"Miguel."

I opened my eyes to the dim light. "How long have I been here?"

"Six days and nights," Miguel said.

"What of my brother, my wife, and son?"

"Chetic is with the unmarried men. Your wife and child live with me in the village." Miguel waited until my eyes stopped fluttering. "Do you remember my village, east of the mission, down the hill and near the stream?"

"Yes, I remember." I shut my eyes, and the spirit of Uncle Podnow smiled down upon me. "Tell me again, Miguel. What must I do?"

"You must forget that you are of the People, the Yokuts."

I flared my nostrils. "Ha!" I said.

Miguel moved closer. "You are a horse, a beetle, whatever the padres make of you. You are nothing or anything." His nose was upon mine. "Do not wake the padres from their dreams. Do not allow your eyes to meet with their eyes."

I studied Miguel. "If I follow your instructions, will I learn their secrets?"

"If you do not follow my instructions, you will die in this cave. They will turn you into a mushroom or a bat. You will never again see the sun or stars."

"I will keep my eyes in the dust," I said.

<hr />

During the first weeks of my immersion into the swamp of evil spirits, the white tipne hid every clue to their magic behind words and tricks that were beyond my comprehension. I felt as if every joint in my body were stuffed with bits of sharp rock. "I can't move," I moaned.

"Drink this soup," Sedit whispered. "The women showed me the proper herbs." She nuzzled my ear. "They warned me of the inevitable pain."

"I cannot go to the field today. I need to sleep for two full days and nights."

"The sun is nearly up." She sat with her back straight. "You must go, and quickly. The padres will miss you at the first ringing of bells. They will put you back in the cave." She shoved the basket closer. "Here, drink the soup. Go quickly."

The fields were located in the flat land below the cemetery. I cleared weeds from the bean plants with a bent oak branch. I pulled weeds from among the sprouting potatoes, first with one hand, then the other. Twice during each day—at sunrise and sunset—young boys filled a wooden trough with thin porridge for us to eat. We pawed at the gruel as a bear pulls grubs from a dead stump. "Hurry!" shouted the whipping padre. "Hurry! God is waiting for his beans and potatoes."

Podnow sat beside me during dreamtime. "Hurry!" he said. "See the blisters of death on the People. Hurry! Feel the heat from their death pyres."

"Uncle! I can do nothing." A lump clogged my throat. "My knees hurt. I'm tired."

Podnow whispered. "You must discover where the White Others hide their magic. You must find the source of their power. You must trick them and chase them away."

I turned away from my dream and held Sedit close. "Hurry," she whispered. "Hurry or they will put you into the black cave."

Padre Carlos-Maria watched me from dawn to dusk. He was alert for any sign of wildness that I could flaunt, and he quickly summoned the whipping padre when I stood to watch a passing eagle or listened intently to a flock of foraging yellow birds. He splashed water on me during every assembly at the church and stood over me as I moved down the long rows of beans. Carlos-Maria prodded me with eyes of a witch.

Podnow watched me during the night, alert for any sign of selfish indulgence that I might flaunt. When I was the least bit lethargic in learning the white invader language or reticent in cultivating an alliance with the foremost white tipne, he prodded me with eyes of a white-tailed eagle.

My knees hurt. Spit dried in my throat. Every morning my shit looked like small black peas.

Chetic, whom the padres had named Tomás, lived in a large, damp room where the young men coughed with the sound of boulders rolling downstream during the spring flood. Every morning stiff bodies were carried to shallow graves and given a final gift of water from the basket of Padre Carlos-Maria.

Chetic worked in fields far from mine. The rule of absolute silence was enforced during morning matins and evening vespers, so we could not talk during the daily assembly of all Indios. Chetic was unable to listen as I recounted my dreams, nor could he offer sympathy for my worries.

There was no one to listen to me—only Sedit and our silent son.

Often she massaged my shoulders until the knots were removed, then whispered, "Come, we will play," and disappeared under our blanket, where she changed into a small mouse that nibbled my toes and crawled carefully up my legs to tease my penis into attention. "Quiet," the little mouse hissed as she licked and kissed and pinched. "Do not disturb the chief and his family with your complaints."

"Stop with the games," I hissed back. "Come up here where I can hold you."

She always wiggled from below to put her lips to my ear and shape her body to mine. I held her close until Podnow stopped with his nagging and Padre Carlos-Maria disappeared. Only then could I fall into the deep hole of sleep.

Our son always remained quiet and close to his mother. Apparently he slept only after we were both asleep. From the small moments that we had alone, I could tell that he was certainly a strange child, but he was always tranquil and discreet in a manner that belied his age of three or so. I tried to show fatherly affection to my son, but he was aloof from my efforts. In turn, I was admittedly impatient for greater verbal contact with him, and eventually I turned my mind to more immediate concerns.

———◆———

One day during the fifth moon of my new name, Carlos-Maria splashed water on my head during the morning work assembly and told me to remain sitting while the others left for work in the field. He made the sign of the cross over my head. "God will have you serve here at the mission." He waved an arm. "The slop buckets. Empty them."

"You, there, José Jesus," another padre said. "Sweep the courtyard. Sweep away every twig and bit of dust. God is watching his red children. He will not tolerate laziness."

"Carry water to the women who twist hemp into rope," the whipping padre said. "God is watching you, José Jesus. He knows what you are thinking. God will administer a hundred lashes for each evil thought. Beware!"

"Empty the cart of those sacks," Padre Carlos-Maria said. "Place them in the storeroom next to the cookhouse." He walked back and forth from the two-wheeled cart to the storage room, always at my side. "There is only one God, José Jesus, and he loves those who obey him. God rewards only those who obey his word." He struck the bag of beans on my shoulder. "Observe! God sends to his loyal servants these beans of Spain. God loves his Spanish servants above all others because we follow his word."

On another day Carlos-Maria sat on a bench while I raked the courtyard. "Listen, my son. God has room in his heart for his red children, but only for those who learn proper obedience to his word." He waggled a finger toward me. "Obey the word of God, José Jesus. Obey him, and he will love you."

———◆———

When Chetic waved to me from across a courtyard or during vespers, I always kept my face forward and never returned his signal. After all,

God, Podnow, and Carlos-Maria were all watching for the very smallest weakness in my nature. On one occasion, however, I turned a corner and found Chetic standing in my path. We embraced quickly and then moved to complete our God-assigned chores.

———

Each day was hot, with no relief given by morning fog or passing thunderstorm. On a Sunday evening, Chief Miguel signaled for me to sit next to him in the shade of an ash tree. "You've got to build your own lodge, José Jesus. My wife is complaining that you moan for most of the night. She likes Sedit well enough, but you're disturbing her sleep, and she's disturbing mine. Your family must move."

During the next six evenings, with torchlight and moonlight, a few neighbors helped us shovel dirt to construct the perimeter of our wall, set the log frame, and weave willow branches into a sturdy roof. On the second Sunday afternoon of the project, we finished the roof with a layer of tule-reed thatch. Our new lodge was small and ugly and soon smelled like rancid beef, but it was ours.

On the first night of our independence, Sedit peeked under the blanket. "Husband! Hold still! We have two mice for company!" She disappeared from view, and immediately my penis was attacked by a startling array of pulls and bites. "Ahhh, good," she called. "One guest is growing in stature."

I cleared my throat. "What about the other invader? Does she need some encouragement?"

"Why, yes. How thoughtful, my husband." She giggled for a moment. "Give me your hand so that I may introduce one to the other."

I found the damp mound topped by the small, lithe mouse. "Slippery little thing, isn't she?" I said.

"Slippery big mouse over here," Sedit said.

"A fine pair," I said.

"I fear they will prevent your falling into sleep, my husband."

"Shhh, less talk. Speed up the chase, little mouse."

"Squeak!" said my lovely Sedit.

———

Sedit worked through the daylight hours in a long building where the women peeled thin fiber from hemp plants and twisted the sweet-smelling string into rope. She made games for our son: to chase after missing tools, for instance, or to bring baskets of water to those women who had no children in service.

Our small son's name day came and went, and now he was called Carlos. It is not a name of the People, but Chief Miguel explained that the name would serve our son until he could send his own son into the world.

"It is a name that will render him invisible to his enemies and to his friends," said Miguel.

"He was born into the name," said Sedit. "My son has been a silent shadow in our lives from his first day. We must thank Chief Miguel for giving him this lovely name."

"Thank you for the name, Chief Miguel," I said. "Perhaps the People will survive and his uncle Shup can then give him a Tachi name."

"Maybe," said Miguel. "For now I perceive that Carlos is the best gift to your son that I can conceive."

———

After her work for the padres, during the dark hour before sunrise and the hour of dusk after sunset, Sedit joined with other women to prepare hot food for their families. Rarely could she satisfy my desire for acorn mush and toasted grasshoppers and sweet clover. Mostly she gave me corn atole; tough, stringy beef; and God's Spanish beans. When she finally crawled under our blanket and whispered into my ear, I often shrugged her away. My lovely Sedit never complained about her work or hunger or my rude behavior. "Sleep, my husband," she said. "Sleep, tipne of the People," she whispered.

I feigned sleep for a while until I heard both Sedit and Carlos breathe in steady, slow beats. I smiled and rolled to match the soft curves of Sedit's body and drop into the void of dark dreams.

Dust motes dribbled from heavy rafters above the sanctuary.

Padre Carlos-Maria spoke. "God has given me a special gift, my son. I can see into the hearts of his red children."

I studied the largest toe of my right foot.

"You came to us as a wild soul of the Devil. Now you love God and listen to me with an open heart. God loves you, José Jesus."

I gave full attention to the smallest toe on my left foot and spoke to Padre Carlos-Maria with a pious lilt. "God speaks to me through your mouth, my father. You are God's emissary, and you act in his place."

Padre Carlos-Maria placed both hands on my shoulders and stared toward the image of my namesake. "Thank you, dear Jesus." His eyes glistened through long wet lashes. He coughed, and the echo bounced three times in the empty church. "Please, Lord Jesus, reveal my gratitude to your Father for giving me this student. He is an Indio who aspires to Christian wisdom, a wild soul who begs for your forgiveness of his natural sins. Praise be to God for his benevolent gifts to me. Praise the all-knowing Lord of all creatures—may he guide this weak vessel along the proper path of Christian instruction."

Carlos-Maria made the sign of the cross over my head and bent to speak. "It is like this, José Jesus. You must keep yourself hidden during the instruction. Stay behind the sixth station of the cross and out of sight from all Christians. The Most Holy Father Lasuén has decreed our red children remain innocent of all scholarship."

I nodded my head in respectful silence.

The padre squeezed my shoulders, then fell to his knees and held his hands in prayer. "God, please hear thy humble servant. I bow to your authority and to the authority you have invested with your servant, the Father Superior Lasuén. I hope that I am hearing your divine instructions and not those of the Devil." He paused, and with no movement of his lips said, "José Jesus, come to the chancel after completion of evening service. Let no one see or hear of your attendance at my school."

———

I remained hidden behind the sixth station. The altar candles gave enough light, and Padre Carlos-Maria placed the slate at such an angle that I could see its letters and numbers. Clear vision of the curriculum was simultaneously maintained for the two soldiers and an occasional villager who also sought instruction from my patron. The smell of wax and sweat and damp adobe bricks filled the sanctuary with a marvelous perfume. My knees stopped hurting, and a feeling of strength permeated my entire body. I did not understand why Carlos-Maria allowed me to watch, but after each lesson I walked down the path to my lodge with light steps and crawled under our blanket like Badger after a gopher. Sedit's nipples enjoyed an extensive lashing by my tongue, and quickly we were as slippery as two river otters on a muddy shore. I was a bull elk, Sedit my entire harem.

"Kiyu," she whispered. "Let's make this the last time. I have your breakfast to prepare in a short while."

"Quiet, sweet crane. God will feed me."

Brother Coyote kept careful notice of my evening romps. He watched us with his tongue lolling and snout set in a lewd smile. "Hey! Spirit Brother!" he'd bark. "When do I get my turn? Remember all those favors I've done for you. Remember who made this wife of yours so nice and chubby. Remember!"

CHAPTER 14

Fall 1797

CARLOS-MARIA TAUGHT ME THE proper technique for preparing the morning hot chocolate. He would have no other Indio attempt the delicate task.

"Listen, my child. First, one must place equal portions of grated chocolate and sugar into rapidly boiling water."

"Yes, my father."

"The sweet froth must cook for two recitations of the beads. Next, one must move the pot to a warm fire and blend the mixture with the scalded milk from a ewe. Add well-beaten eggs, vanilla, cinnamon, and nutmeg, and beat until frothy with a *molinillo*; then we will quickly terminate our prayers and partake of our morning indulgence."

"Yes, my father."

"Ahhh," he said. "The smell of Spain!"

"God is with you this morning, my son," the short padre always said. "The ingredients are perfectly balanced."

"Phew!" the whipping padre always said. "This concoction is hotter than Hades. There's too much cinnamon. Be more careful, José Jesus. God is watching your every move."

From maker of morning chocolate, I was promoted to majordomo for the mission kitchen, and again, Carlos-Maria taught me everything.

"Listen, my son, turn a deaf ear to those who preceded you in this kitchen. My stomach has turned to brittle leather with their efforts."

"Certainly, my father. Instruct me as you wish."

"You will learn the Spanish way, José Jesus. God's way."

"Certainly, my father," I said, and immediately felt another degree stronger within myself. My plan to infiltrate the invaders was beginning. There was no doubt that I was smarter than my teacher, but I had to be patient with the man and let him provide the momentum for his own destruction. First, there was Carlos-Maria to vanquish, and then the path to victory would be obvious.

As my lessons progressed to the preparation of sauces and chowders, the padres and their guests began to fill the dining room with impatient eagerness. Happy belches and redolent farts followed each meal. "Very good, José Jesus," said the short padre. "My mind was transported back to Ibiza with this meal, the sweet Ibiza of my mother."

"*Buurrp*," said the whipping padre. "Too much cinnamon, José Jesus; no true Spaniard can use cinnamon in fish chowder. The Devil loves cinnamon, Spaniards do not!"

<hr />

The spirit of Podnow was unhappy with my exploration into the mysteries of Spanish cuisine, and so was Brother Coyote.

"Your plan is working, Uncle Podnow. I am learning the secrets; I am getting stronger with each day."

"The People," whispered Podnow into my mind. "You must move at a faster rate, my son. Complete your task. Quickly! Quickly!"

"I pee in your chocolate," Brother Coyote said. "I shit on your beans and bread."

"Patience," I mumbled to Podnow. "I must earn the final trust of Carlos-Maria. He is a wary witch and guards the important secrets with great cunning."

"Faster, faster," Brother Coyote said.

"For what reason must I move faster?" I asked Brother Coyote.

"For my entertainment, and no other reason," he said.

"Tell me, Brother, is there any hope for the People to defeat the white invader?"

"A smidgen, I would guess."

"And my son, Carlos—will he survive the white invaders?"

"I won't answer questions about your family, my brother, but you might look to Chief Miguel for answers to questions about your son."

"Miguel is of the Ohlone and not a spirit of the Spanish heavens nor a spirit doctor from the People. What can he know about the future of my son?"

"Ahhh, that is for me to know, my ignorant cook."

At midmorning I served brandy and cake and cheese to the padres. If there were no guests at the table, the noon meal might include bread and soup, mutton stew with beans and greens from the garden, fruit and cheese for dessert, and wine with every course. If visiting padres or soldiers or merchants honored our mission with their attention, then I added a rice-and-bean dish and either ham or beef to the meal. I never made the mistake of serving a roast of beef when foreigners were guests, however. Those White Others from Estados Unidos or England or France complained bitterly about the beef of our mission.

"Tough! Stringy! Tasteless!" they shouted. Only when I cooked the beef over a very slow fire, shredded it into tiny bits, and simmered it for hours in chili sauce did compliments replace complaints.

At dusk the meal was simple: roast pigeon or baked fish, and chocolate.

We were seated in two Spanish chairs, one facing the other. The pleasant sounds of swallows twitting in the eves drifted through the padre's private room. We sat quietly, reviewing in our minds what the likely end of this meeting might bring.

"Tell me, my student of the Holy Bible, why have you called this meeting?"

"My father, I am now able to tell you that I have found Christ our Lord, the resurrected Son of God. I also believe in his virgin birth by the Holy Mother."

"Well spoken, José Jesus. On what authority do you base your belief?"

"Saint Peter, my father. On the slopes of Mount Herman, Christ said, 'Who do men say I am?' Peter responded: 'Thou art the Christ.' This is your teaching, Padre Carlos-Maria, and this is my faith."

"Good, my son."

"Very good, indeed," whispered Brother Coyote.

"Shuss, you fool," I hissed.

I felt the Christian father remove his eyes from my bowed head and saw Coyote slip into a deep shadow. During the extended silence, Carlos-Maria looked idly about the room. There was no window, and a candle burned atop the only chest. Three rough-sawn planks on adobe bricks marked the narrow bed; a single blanket was folded at one end and square adobe bricks marked the other end. He smiled. It was a painful turning of lips. He reached into his brown cloak and withdrew a small book. "How long have you lived with Christ, my son?"

"I entered your mission as a wild savage, my father. During the first year, I fought against your teaching. I sinned in both thought and deed—"

"How long have you lived with Christ?"

"Nearly two years, Father."

"It has always been my arrogant desire to bring an Indio heart to God. I realize that I have defied the teachings of Father Lasuén so that you could learn to read; now I go even further in my iniquitous hope." A wooden pail dropped into the nearby well, and the pulley holding the rope that carried the water-filled bucket howled an anguished squeal.

When there were only the swallows again, Carlos-Maria continued. "This act that I now perform of my own desire is likely a sin without redemption." He held a small book toward me and leaned forward from his chair. "This is a book of catechism, my son. Of all my students, savage or gentile, only you are capable of understanding every nuance, every whisper from God, that this book contains."

My fingers tingled as I touched the soft black cover. "I will do my best, Father. I will pray for divine guidance that I learn every word, every cipher."

"It is yours to keep, my son."

My heart was a loud drumbeat. Was this a book of magic? A tool that might rescue the People from the invaders? Please, Coyote, let it be the magic book. Please, Hairy God and Dead Son and Holy Ghost, let this be my magic book.

Carlos-Maria made the sign of the cross over my head. "Tell me when you comprehend this wonderful book, and on that memorable day I will test your faith."

He signed the cross upon his forehead and shoulders and then whispered, "My faith I must also test on that day."

———

On that first evening of the book, Sedit gave me two stolen candles and her silence. I read the pages until sunrise and followed the same routine through every available moment of the fall and winter seasons. Brother Coyote scratched imaginary fleas and panted huge puffs of air, all in a fruitless effort to lure me into a romp. He moped about and peed on every bush in sight, but I continued to read, night after night.

Sedit managed to keep Carlos quiet, maintain the perpetual weaving of baskets, and restrain the explorations of our pet mice. Her smile disappeared, but not her earthy perfume. My beautiful crane stood guard over my effort to digest the word of God, and she was alert to any desire of mine that she might gratify.

———

Eventually the first-fruits season appeared at Mission San Juan Bautista. Mouse-eared lettuce was scattered through every damp gully, and the young mustard greens were a perfect complement for the padre's spit-turned lamb.

"My compliments to your cook," the visitors from England said.

I steamed a young horse under hot rocks and covered the meat with a sauce of chilies and molé. "This meal is truly magnificent," said a visitor from France to Padre Carlos-Maria. "I must steal this cook of yours."

One night, when the moon was full, I dropped the catechism into the dust and studied the farthest star.

I felt grumpy, like my son without his nap or Podnow without his steam bath. The catechism was a farce; it was neither magic nor useful for any task I might design toward defeating the invaders. Yes, there was a God in the book, a hairy-faced deity portrayed in paintings on the mission wall, and yes, this God of book was partner with the Lord Jesus Christ, portrayed dangling from one cross or another. And finally there was a Holy Spirit of an indefinable nature. Maybe this ghost was designed to lead the fairies and cherubim and devils in perpetual romp. The entire puzzle of three gods in one was merely the beginning of my disgust for the holy books of my teacher. His Holy Bible, replete with unending violence, and this catechism floundering in its tedious effort, provided no solace for me. Neither was a source of magic that could serve the People.

I called to my spirit brother. "Kiyu! Pay attention, mutt. Tell me why those devious gods of the padre leave me in such an utter state of ignorance?"

Brother Coyote's eyes turned blood red. "Did you enjoin them to chase their tails?"

"I am beset by silly gods and a stupid spirit brother." My eyes fluttered open. "I have tried and tried to make sense of both the questions and answers that are provided in this book of catechism, and I find little but a raft of ambiguous statements."

It seemed quieter than usual in the village of Miguel. In my lodge, Sedit and our child were asleep under a brown wool blanket. The neighbors and owls and even the crickets were silent. "Coyote? Brother Coyote? Come, now. What do you think the hairy god meant with his catechism book?"

The frogs went silent.

Coyote ignored me.

I picked up the book. "The three or four gods all must believe that questions hold power, not answers. Questions. Questions." I threw a pebble at Brother Coyote. "Listen, mutt. If you cannot help me, then I must turn for assistance to Padre Carlos-Maria."

"Silliness," Coyote whispered.

"If I can frame the proper questions to my teacher about this book of catechism, he may unwittingly give answers that will help destroy the white invaders and save the People."

Coyote moved ten paces farther from my seat against an oak tree and flopped on the dirt.

I held the book toward the moon. "Gods, whoever you are, speak to me. Tell me why I can't understand this book."

I heard Sedit turn to one side and start the soft snore that always tickled the inside of my stomach. A horned owl made one last cast across the clover-filled meadow.

I shut my eyes in prayer. "Thank you, Hairy God, for this catechism, this lovely little book full of important questions and irrelevant answers. Thank you for your love of the People." Sedit made a small cough to let me know that she was awake, so I spoke in a slightly louder voice. "Thank you, God of all spirits, for your love of the People above all others. Thank you, thank you."

———

We were in the silent church, the padre in a chair with me standing in front of him. I asked my first question of Padre Carlos-Maria. "Dear Father, the book that you have so graciously given to me gives some bits of information that are beyond my understanding."

The padre studied his rosary while giving his answer. "I am your pastor and teacher. What questions do you have?"

"Excuse me for my ignorance, Padre Carlos-Maria, but it seems that the catechism says that the Holy Church need not cite the Bible as the sole source of authority for church doctrine, but that both Scripture and tradition are honored on an equal basis."

I peered at my teacher, and he seemed taken with a fit of drowsiness—his head down and eyes shut.

"Well! Ahem." Now he looked straight at me for the first time in four years. "You must accept the fact that both Scripture and tradition must be honored and accepted with equal devotion." He sat upright in his chair. "It is God's will, nothing else." Now his eyes returned to the beads. "Enough! Back to work. We have three Frenchmen at table today."

I mixed sugar and egg yolks together until they were light-colored and creamy. The padres loved their sugar.

Carlos-Maria had looked at me. His eyes had stared into mine!

Next the salt and flour—just enough—then vanilla to ewe's milk and scald. Quickly now, little by little add milk to the egg-yolk mixture. Stir rapidly! Boil! Remove! Stir in the dark rum, the black cherries, and almond flavor. Set aside, but stir occasionally to prevent a crust from forming.

When I asked a question of the padre, he saw me as a person of God and as his equal. He gave a stupid answer, but he didn't confine me to the black room. What response would my next question of the padre generate for an answer?

The initial step in making a cake required a hole in the flour to place sugar, salt, butter, egg yolks, baking powder, and lemon peel. Carlos-Maria explained that I must squeeze and fold and pound the ingredients until the dough mimicked a soft breast. Then one must divide the bosom into two balls that are rolled flat and placed into greased pans. The first crust is filled with the prepared pastry cream and then carefully covered with the second. As a final step, the top is brushed with beaten egg, a harlequin pattern is scratched with a fork, and then the cake is put into the oven.

I felt invincible. Well, nearly invincible. Soon enough the padres of San Juan Bautista would bend to my will.

I closed my eyes. "Soon, Podnow, very soon, the God of all spirits will again smile upon his chosen people. You shall see, very soon, my honored uncle, how well I have served the People."

Now for the molé sauce. Frenchmen, above all other guests, love my molé sauce.

———

It was Sedit's idea—the tanai tea, that is. She found a swale full of the plants while foraging for clover. "Podnow taught you to dream with the tanai, my husband. Maybe the medicine will relieve some of your anxiety over the questions. A vivid dream might provide answers to your incessant questions, my husband."

"Podnow and I smoked the tanai."

"The tea will not attract unnecessary attention. The tanai tea will warm your head and stomach."

"When is your treat available?"

"Here, my husband, in this small basket of mine. Not a bit will leak through the tight weave."

"Thank you, Wife. The basket itself is a treat to the eye."

"You must drink this tea slowly, my husband."

I drank the tea as if dying from thirst and nodded to Sedit. "Another basket will serve my needs, wife of mine."

"As it happens, I have another basket with an entirely different design, my husband."

"Good." I finished the second basket at a leisurely pace and then studied the intriguing weave of tule reed. Red clouds swirled among the mountains of my mind. "All is well in Tipiknits Pahn," I said.

Sedit began with a slow clapping of her hands. "Ahhhh," she said.

"Are you here, my spirit brother? Speak to me if you will."

Coyote trotted through the red mist and sat at my feet. "What now, troublesome brother?"

"We must talk in a man-to-spirit fashion. I have questions that must be answered by an expert in all matters."

"You seem a bit brusque in your manner, my little pup. Are you upset with your life among the invaders?"

"I am immensely bored with that Hairy God and his servants. In fact, all the padre's spirits seem indifferent to my request for even the slightest help."

"You should pay more attention to your beautiful wife, silly pup."

"Why? She is helpful to me in every way; it is the spirits who deny my petitions."

"Do you realize that when Sedit has questions about your son, Carlos, she consults Chief Miguel for helpful answers or remedies? Further, it is the illustrious chief who counsels your big-bosomed wife on all matters of concern in his village. It is Chief Miguel who teaches your son what he needs to know about surviving in this ephemeral world."

What was this silliness from my spirit brother? I called him to answer serious questions, and he diverted my intentions with prattle about my wife and child. "Now, now, my spirit brother—why would the village chief waste time with a small child?"

My spirit brother pissed on my foot and scratched dirt into both of Sedit's lovely baskets. "Mutt! What is this foolishness with dirt into my tanai tea? Away with you."

The red fog of Tipiknits Pahn disappeared. All was silent.

———

At a small mission such as San Juan Bautista, the padres were required to serve their Lord in every possible capacity. Carlos-Maria was in charge of the kitchen, the vaqueros, and the tannery, and he served as director of the orchestra. The whipping padre managed construction projects and the repair of all buildings. He also served as director of justice and held court every day except Sunday. Those neophytes who offended God, the padres or the soldiers, were punished with a minimum of twenty lashes. At least ten neophytes were whipped each day, so he was very busy with his many duties to God. The short padre supervised those who tilled the vegetable gardens and fields of wheat, oat, and rye, and also the women who made rope and shoes and blankets for sale to the good Christians of the San José and Santa Clara villages.

The mission padres were busy from day to day, just as wrens are busy with their jumping about and telling bigger animals what to do with their lives. Padres and wrens both wore drab coats of brown. Wrens and padres both held anxious dispositions and often jumped into brambles with little provocation. Both responded fittingly to the quiet ministration of flattery.

"Father," I asked Carlos-Maria. "Once again I stand before you as a humble and ignorant petitioner."

The padre sat in the same chair as before, but his eyes were squinted nearly shut, his arms and legs stiff with tension. "What is your question, my son?"

"In Matthew 28:18 the Holy Bible teaches us that Jesus Christ has all authority in heaven and on earth." I gave a long moment for Carlos-Maria to admire my scholarship.

"The question, if you please."

"It seems that the Pope in Rome, and his assigned deputies through the world, have power that usurps God's grace. We may note, in point of fact, the power that Father Superior Lasuén holds over you and me."

Carlos-Maria slumped into his chair, elbows on his knees, head buried in his hands. A hollow windy sound, like that of a doe with an arrow struck deep in her lung, pulsed through the barrier.

"Is my question clearly stated?"

Carlos-Maria again sat straight in his chair. "Satan! The Devil sits before me! The two of you, side by side, in the same chair." He pointed his right hand at me, the first finger fully extended. "The Devil still holds your soul! The Devil has deceived me again!"

"Father! How can that be?"

"Father Superior Lasuén is correct! God is correct! The Devil will never release the soul of a captive red child. Never!" Carlos-Maria struck his chest a mighty thump. "God! God! Forgive me, God! Please forgive me, for I have sinned mightily against your word."

"Father! God loves you, and therefore he loves me."

"Silence! Satan's child! Silence! Leave my room! Now! Wait for me and the other padres at the gate to the mission."

"But why?"

"Now!"

Brother Coyote laughed till tears soaked his snout. My spirit brother howled at the red clouds during the pronouncement of forty days shoveling wet adobe into wooden forms. He cackled like a demented goose when Carlos-Maria declared that I would spend forty nights traveling on my knees from one cross to the next around the mission courtyard.

The whipping padre gave five lashes each dawn. "Devil's spawn," he'd shout with the first blow. "Satan's spy!" he'd yell with the last blow.

After my lesson in humility, Padre Carlos-Maria became distracted in my company. He complained of watery chocolate and stringy meat. He rubbed the back of his neck, massaged his prayer beads in endless contemplation, and on a hot afternoon said, "I have sinned, my son."

His eyes allowed no response from me.

"Tomorrow I walk to Monterey and make my confession to the Father Superior." He stood over me. "Miguel is now your mentor. May God assist him in driving Satan from your soul."

CHAPTER 15

Summer 1798

CHIEF MIGUEL IGNORED ME FROM one full moon to the next, so I studied the soldiers from dawn to dusk. During daylight they did little but annoy tame Indios, but after vespers they gambled or repaired tattered clothing or took their turn with one tame Indio woman or another. "We must stop this filth," I said. "Our women spread their legs for those smelly fools, and then the women pass evil medicine from the soldiers to their husbands."

Sedit looked up from the large storage basket she was weaving. "The women are hungry. The soldiers give them extra food or a child's blanket. It is not so bad."

"The soldiers spew poison from their cocks. The women and children and husbands all die. We must burn the soldiers' den of corruption and keep the women in their own lodges."

"It's nothing," Sedit said. "The rutting of men is inevitable, and the women think their effort is worth the gain."

A red ember burned in my stomach. "Have you gone to the hut with soldiers?"

Sedit put her swath of damp tule-reed fiber on the ground and stared at me with her beautiful brown eyes. "No," she said.

"How can I be sure?"

"I am your wife, not the wife of a tame Indio."

"Last night you were punching holes in a piece of leather." The air seemed to disappear from my lungs. "Where did you get that metal awl?"

Sedit moved her chin upward a small notch. "The soldiers smell like your coyote friend." The chin dropped. "What husband would remain ignorant of such an offensive perfume?"

I marched over to Miguel's lodge.

"Ignore the bastards," he said. "There's a time for the willow tree and a time for the oak tree. Let the wind blow, José Jesus. Let a few branches drop. So what? They'll grow again."

I spit into the fire, and a pleasing hiss filled the dark room. "The White Others will cut your willow men into firewood and fill our fields with their bastards." I spit again. "You, Miguel, can you see that you are nothing but the chief of whores and cowards? Can you see that you do nothing but raise your ass to the Spanish bull?"

Blankets of rabbit and lambskin fluttered in the dark. The wives and children of Chief Miguel sat up in their beds.

"Come, my wild friend. Take a walk with me." Without waiting for my reply, Miguel stood and walked under the low entrance of his lodge. I followed him until he stopped in the center of his village and gestured for me to come closer. "Now we fight. The victor gains possession of the herd."

I sniffed. "I have no interest in your smelly collection of tame cowards."

"Ahhh, a tipne doctor, they say." He moved closer. "Show me, wild man. Let my tame Indio blood flow."

I picked a stout oak branch from the ground and moved with increasing speed toward the chief. He stood still, his crooked smile bent to insult me. I raised my weapon as I ran toward him, but still he did not move. Suddenly, without a cause and for no detectable reason, the stars and dirt exchanged their certain domains. My head struck a sharp stone, and my blood spilled onto the dust.

"Amazing!" Chief Miguel looked down upon me. "These tipne of the wild tules are astonishing with their tricks. Can you repeat such a spectacular stunt, José Jesus? These poor tame beasts of my village are watching your performance." A ripple of laughter surged from the lodges. One man yelled, "Show us the old ways, José Jesus. Turn old Miguel into a snake." Another yelled, "Lead us against the Spanish, José Jesus. Let's destroy those white lizards."

I picked up a fist-sized rock and charged Miguel. As I swung, he stepped aside, and faster than Podnow's hands, Miguel placed his foot between my legs and pushed my shoulders. A crushing blow struck the back of my head, and I fell into a black void.

———

It was barely dawn, and women were rekindling fires and heating the cooking rocks. Miguel sat beside me.

"Can you hear me?"

"Yes."

"Today you will learn how a willow tree survives." He let me open and shut my eyes a few times. "You will learn to live as a tame red man."

I bit my tongue. What was the sense? Words were nothing but filmy snares. Words were questions and answers; both ended in trouble and pain. Neither Hairy God nor Great Spirit could answer their own stupid questions.

"Podnow!" I called into my mind. "What can I do to save the People? Tell me, for the all the spirits are tricksters or fools. Podnow!"

My spirit uncle peered at me from a jumble of tule reeds. "Ask Shup your questions, for only he can serve as your teacher."

———

Chief Miguel put me to work.

He pointed toward a pile of dead cows. "Go ahead, willow boy. Cut those cows up into small pieces and make me some tallow." He waved a Spanish-style salute, yanked at the reins of his horse, and galloped away.

The smell of hot chocolate evaporated from all memory. The bliss of soft breasts conceived from sugar and flour was replaced by the agony of hot oil. Blisters erupted over my chest, legs, and toes. Grease filled my nose and mouth. I stuffed the meat of dead cows into black pots placed over blazing fires. I boiled the animals and then ladled the simmering goo into leather bags. There was no molé sauce on my morning gruel and no mazurka for saint-day celebrations. I was Miguel's minion, the subject of giggles from his women and of crude jokes from the men of his village.

Brother Coyote joined with the tame Indios to tease me. "Kiyu!" he howled. "Come quickly! Save me from a ferocious wren!"

"Shut your yap, camp dog."

"It is an old wren," my spirit brother called, "but very clever. Quickly now, Kiyu, grab your rock and assault the beast!"

After the fifth day of drudgery and insults, I signaled Chetic during vespers, and with the moonrise we met in the olive grove north of the mission.

"I'm leaving."

"Where would you go?" Chetic glanced over his shoulder and then back to the ground.

"I'll return to the People."

"Ahhh, to our Tachi village."

"I shall waste no further time in this smelly swamp."

"Ahhh." Chetic held my eyes for a moment and then looked down again. "Can you describe the magic of the padres to your People? Can you now help Podnow protect the People from the Spanish invaders?"

"The People are best loved by the God of all spirits." I felt like biting a large oak branch into two pieces. Questions! Questions from a slave! "Even the Great Hairy God of the White Others loves the People, so stop with your stupid questions."

Chetic sat straight with his eyes locked on mine. "Just one more question, honored brother." His voice held the supple strength of Sedit, his sister. "Can you explain to Podnow how the White Others use their destructive magic?"

Splinters gouged my tongue. "Fool! Open your eyes! There is no magic here. There is nothing but stupid white men and tame red men and a traitorous spirit brother." I stuck my chin toward Chetic. "What about you, Little Brother? Will you stay? Or follow me?"

Chetic wiggled his toes in the dust but remained silent.

I inhaled a deep breath and spewed it into the dusk. "Listen to me, Brother. The Spanish have a few guns and a few books—nothing else. They are arrogant, stupid witches with nothing to teach. I will work with Podnow to create our own magic. The People are stronger and smarter than the White Others, and we will learn how to survive this invasion of our land."

Chetic picked a dry olive leaf from the ground and crumbled it between his fingers. "Everything you say is true, but it is also false."

"What?" I could barely hold myself still. "What is this noise? Do I hear nonsense riddles from the two-spirit boy who is a warrior only through my intervention? Are both my brothers traitors?" I turned my head. "Bah!"

"I'll stay here at the mission with Sedit and Chief Miguel."

"I'm disappointed." I made a move to stand. "You are nothing but a tame Indio, Chetic. A tame Indio who speaks useless riddles."

"Have you eaten?"

I relaxed my shoulders. "Is this another riddle?"

"Sit with me a while longer, Brother." Chetic pulled a small basket from his robe and held it toward me.

"What?"

"Tanai. I found some jimson weed growing in a ditch." He stretched his hand toward me. "It's probably not much good, but Sedit said that if you have not eaten recently, it may serve the purpose."

"Sedit? How is it possible that you spoke to my wife?"

"Miguel found errands for both of us, and just past noon we three met here in the olive grove." Chetic held the basket as if it were an offering to the Hairy God. "You are our tipne. We ask that you visit with the spirits before you make your decision to leave this nest of evil."

Niggling spasms of curiosity diminished the lump of anger in my stomach. "How is it that you and Sedit can ponder my fate?"

He smiled. "Drink the tanai tea; consider it a gift from your wife and your earthbound brother."

My eyelids fluttered. "I suppose Miguel led you to the patch of tanai."

Chetic remained silent.

"Here, let me try your concoction."

―――――◆―――――

The stars moved like twigs in a whirlpool until one broke free, and soon the rest followed to assume their natural progression across the sky. Brother Coyote sat at my knee and listened carefully as I complained of word snares and feckless padres and inconsiderate gods until my throat became raw from the green tanai. His chaffing hiccup caused me to look beyond my words, and when our eyes met he exploded with laughter.

"You're a silly, witless colt." Coyote bared his teeth. "Tell me, Kiyu, exactly what words will satisfy Podnow on your first night in his village?"

"I'll tell him that neither the People nor the White Others can perform magic. I'll explain that both white and red play with scorpions and both blame the other for every accident of fate. I'll tell him the Californios are dumb, weak, and vulnerable to attack, and that they are as stupid as elk."

Brother Coyote yawned. "Go ahead. Start your journey. Podnow will welcome such delightful news."

I emptied the basket of tanai with one long swallow, and Brother Coyote disappeared into the fog. My dead father rode the horizon on his winged horse, but with his head turned away. The spirit of Shup sighed from behind a bank of roiling red clouds. Podnow, painted with black and white stripes, danced through a meadow filled with dead flowers. The foot drum and clapper sticks maintained the beat for Podnow to circle the meadow, round and round, until dawn set shadows adrift in the mission olive grove.

"I'll stay a bit longer," I said.

Chetic let his eyes smile, and from behind a mound of poison oak leaves, Brother Coyote snickered.

———

Chief Miguel took one step into my lodge. "Report to me at dawn."

I left my staring into the fire and struggled to my knees. "Why?"

"No questions, wild man, just report at first light."

I couldn't sleep; instead I considered the possible tortures Miguel might substitute for his greasy black pot, but I could imagine none with the same ingenious combination of pain and humiliation. I tossed and turned and woke Sedit and our child, and made both suffer my tongue. A male brown towhee squealed into the diminished night, and his mate answered. The powerful perfume from elderberry blossoms smothered the stink of grease and tame Indio shit.

Just before daylight I threw off the blankets and followed Miguel's loud voice.

"Grab those hides and stop smiling, you ignorant wild Indio." Miguel snapped a bullock's whip at my feet. "I'll have you back with the black pots soon enough." He nearly caught me on the shoulder with a lick from his whip. "Move the legs, not the mouth! Get those hides into the *carretas*, you damn wild Indio."

"Yes, honored chief," I said.

His third lick caught me across the back of my legs, and I saw Chetic and Miguel exchange smiles.

When the oxen pulled the carretas uphill, the wheels screamed like twenty men halfway through their castration. On the downhill, the wheels screamed like twenty babies ripped from their mother's teats. During the first night, we slept in a pine forest, and at dusk on the second day we arrived in Monterey. Chief Miguel immediately put me to work loading salt-cured hides aboard a big ship. "Damn lazy Indio!" he yelled. "Put your shoulder into that pile of hides." His whip gouged splinters from the plank under my feet.

A single planet traveled in tandem with a half-moon when Miguel finally yelled, "One more load, wild Indio, then line up with the rest of my slaves." We followed him to the shelter of grassy dunes just behind the beach and quickly built a huge driftwood fire. Shadows bounced from low clouds like puppies from their mother. I whispered to Chetic, "He's smart, that Miguel."

Chetic pulped an aloe plant to rub on his cuts, watched a ragged flock of night herons fly overhead, and said nothing.

"Chetic." I moved a little closer to him. "You're smart too."

He offered the gooey aloe. "Here, get those cuts around your neck and shoulder. They'll start to stink if you let them go."

On the second day in Monterey I began to study the white man's magic. I saw white soldiers marching and white women strolling and black cannon staring down upon us with hungry eyes. We pulled cowhide bags filled with tallow up the gangway and piled them in the ship's bow. We threw our unfinished hides into a quiet corner of the bay and tended them for three days and nights. On the fourth morning we tame Indios stretched the soggy hides on the ground, scraped them clean, powdered the skin side with salt, then dried them on racks and folded them into quarters for hauling onto the same ship.

Amid the drudgery of sweat and smells and saltwater, I watched the White Others. The sailors from a village called Boston were covered with hair and used very loud voices. They kept their cloud boat as neat as Ulati's medicine shelf and were clever with a screw jack and thus able to carry many more hides than other ships. Still, clever and neat aside, the Bostons were the ugliest of all White Others in the village of Monterey.

At first the hubbub was confusing. Gestures and words and smells blurred into each other, but soon I learned to say "He is of the Bostons" or "They are Baltimores" with equal facility. In this enterprise of sorting people, Miguel was of great assistance. "The Bostons never shit," he said. "That's why their eyes bulge out like a snared rabbit." He shrugged his shoulders. "It's the truth. Take it from me. The Bostons never shit and rarely piss."

———

After the green beans were gathered but before the first melons were picked, Miguel again gave me leave from the black pots. We took a detour from our initial route to Monterey and added five additional carts to our convoy at Mission Santa Clara. The day was hot, the noise oppressive, and the dust a gritty shroud. I was ready to reconsider the positive merits of my black pot. "Miguel," I called. "Can we seek water at the well?"

"Quiet, over there. The Santa Clara *alcalde* doesn't want a bunch of wild Indios running around his place."

"How about getting us some food to eat under the carts?"

"Quiet," Miguel said. "We'll get back on the road after the carts are loaded."

I noticed that the Santa Clara carts were already loaded beyond capacity, but the mission alcalde wanted his Indios to load even more. "Three more hides," he screamed. The alcalde pushed and shoved and whipped his charges in a frenzy of venomous commands. "God will send you to the hellfire pits of burning sulfur!" he yelled.

There was something familiar about his indolent slouch and river-rat face. The alcalde had eyes puckered like an oak gall, and he squalled orders like ten scrub jays chasing a daytime owl. He . . . he . . . Hineh! Podnow's only son!

I blinked twice but it was Hineh, and no mistake. He wore a brown wool robe and short black hair, and he carried the alcalde scepter of wood as if he were of royal Spanish blood. Hineh, the only son of Traushnah and Podnow.

Hineh stood near a dour padre who nodded agreement with each command from his alcalde. Twice Hineh kicked tame Indios who staggered past him under a load of heavy hides. "God is displeased!" he yelled. "Faster! Faster!"

He caught sight of me, standing still, like a frozen deer. Our eyes met, and Hineh licked his lips. Another encumbered Indio crossed his shadow. "Get to work, you damn teat-sucker," he yelled. "Hurry up, my little girl." There was no other sign of recognition between us, merely the tongue and kick and the allusion to our childhood feud. We did not speak of the People, nor did we share any secrets of white magic. There were no furtive signals to indicate our alliance and no small gestures of brotherhood. Hineh gave me only the tip of his tongue and the words, "Work, you damn teat-sucker."

———

The muscles of my stomach eased only after our overloaded carts surmounted the first hill out of Santa Clara village. The squeal of ungreased wheels disappeared, and I suddenly felt pleased with the encounter. More than pleased—happy! My enemy from birth was still an evil spirit. Hineh was still my enemy, and now Podnow must finally see the truth. Podnow, tipne to the Yokuts and Miwok, must see his son as a tame Indio, as an enemy of the People. I smiled and tasted the dust with my tongue.

———

We crammed every hide into a single Boston schooner. Up and down I trudged, from gangplank to hold, with no effort or concern. "Hey! Tipne man," Miguel yelled. "Take that damned smile off your face."

On our fifth day in Monterey, a large seabird ship from Mexico sent little boats filled with white women and children onto the beach, and that night I whispered to Brother Coyote and Brother Chetic. "Listen, brothers. These lovely, magical flying-like-clouds ships carry the stories and spirits of long-dead ancestors. These ships are the source of all sustenance for the White Others. These ships carry the magic and power and seed of great ancestors."

"Lots of floppy teats, that's what those ships carry," Brother Coyote said.

"The ships fly in the air like milkweed seed," Chetic said.

"Yes, the downy spawn of milkweed that slips with the wind from one village to the next." I leaned against my hummock of sand and stared at the driftwood fire. "But the white men are not beautiful milkweed seeds. They're ugly nettles. The ships carry seed from the nettle, not the milkweed."

Chetic moved close to my ear. "If we stop the ships, the White Others will disappear—poof!"

"Right," Coyote said. "Good thinking."

The fire swirled in a blustery dance.

Chetic started again with his whisper. "If the ships fail, the Spanish will shrivel and die. They will have no seed for crops nor women to produce their children. Their magic will disappear, and the People will survive."

"Yes," I said.

"Yes!" Brother Coyote said.

CHAPTER 16

Spring 1800

DUSK WAS UPON US. THE black pots were empty and cool. Chief Miguel nodded toward a tame Indio for additional wood on the fire. "Look, willow boy, I understand what you are telling me. I can understand your opinion that the Spanish are weak, but listen to me for a change: the red people are even weaker." Miguel mopped sweat from his body with a handful of moss. "If the Spanish are as weak as a fresh-dropped colt, then the wild Indios are nothing but little brush rabbits curled in a grass nest."

"What about the tame Indios, Chief Miguel?" I sprinkled water from my basket to raise some steam. "Are they tadpoles or something equally ferocious?"

Miguel tossed me some moss. "Here, get that gob of grease behind your ear."

"Maybe we tame Indios are a bunch of tadpoles that can swim out into the bay and chew up a cloud-ship or two," I said.

A few of the older men gave a cough of appreciation for my humor.

"I have to admit, wild man, that you're doing a good job on those black pots. It took a while, but even old Carlos-Maria has noticed how you organized your crew to get a lot more dead cows cooked up." He flicked sweat from his eyes. "Maybe we finally hit on something you wild Indios can do right. Cook grease."

I scrubbed with the moss and kept my mouth shut.

Miguel shifted his weight around until he faced toward me. "I've been wondering, wild man, is it true that you're a spirit doctor?"

Chetic spoke up. "He was trained by Podnow, tipne to all the Yokuts."

"My, oh my, that's very impressive." Miguel leaned toward me. "I've got a little problem with one of the bachelor men. How about giving me a hand?"

The young man cried every night and disturbed the entire dormitory. It wasn't just quiet sobbing, but terrible shrieks from the time the bachelors were locked in their room until they were released at dawn.

I pulled a small tree frog and an orange-bellied newt from his penis and told him that he was free from all evil spirits, but he cried and screamed for another week.

Brother Coyote whispered, "Here, I found this near the padre's outhouse."

I yanked the Saint Christopher medal from the young man's penis and dangled it under his nose. "This is from the Lord Jesus Christ. Kiss it once in the morning and once at night. Carry it close to your heart."

The boy opened his eyes, and I whispered to him, "Jesus spoke to me and said that you are now free of all evil spirits as long as you wear his medal."

The boy sat up. "Truly?"

I kissed the medal and put it around his neck. "The spirit of my name does not lie. Follow his instructions, and you will live a happy life."

Chief Miguel sent the youngster south of the mission to tend a flock of sheep, and after the second full moon passed, Miguel gave me a smile. "I want to tell you, wild man, there's nothing like a cuddly little ewe and a little tin medal to settle a young man down."

I nodded but kept my mouth shut.

"You were lucky, wild man." He dropped his smile. "Try this next one."

———◆———

The woman lay on the dirt floor of her lodge. Miguel spoke with his usual loud voice. "She hasn't budged in three days, and she eats nothing but dirt."

Sedit whispered in my ear, "She's pregnant, not of her husband."

"Take her to the sweat house," I said.

Miguel filled with indignation. "Hey! The sweat house is for men only!"

"It is empty in the afternoon, and the spirits demand this exception to your policy."

"Bah!" Miguel said.

Sedit and two other women carried the limp body and placed her before the steaming rocks.

"Wipe her body clean," I said. "Brush her hair and kill the lice."

When they finished, I had Sedit dress the woman in clean, beautiful Ohlone clothes. We put beads around her neck, and I propped her up against some blankets in front of an enormous fire. She sat and stared at her empty mind.

"Miguel," I said. "We need six singers and six dancers tonight."

He shrugged his shoulders. "Sure, after vespers I'll have them ready."

The singers got everyone in the right mood with their music, and when the dancers started to prance about, the villagers joined to clap and sing and dance and wait for me to do my tipne magic. I sat as still as a heron over a minnow, gazed at the fire, and drank a little tanai tea. Suddenly I jumped up, ran over to the woman, and pulled a damaged awl from her chest.

The spectators cheered and carried on for a bit before I returned to my meditation. A short while later, I dashed over and pulled a wriggling garter snake from the woman's stomach. The crowd clapped and yelled, and dancers jumped high into the air, but the woman remained insensible.

Sedit sat in front of me and offered a basket of warm acorn mush. "Be careful, my husband. The acorns were prepared quickly, and the mush may contain bits of shell or other foreign objects."

"Thank you for the mush, my wife." I leaned forward and whispered. "The father is a soldier?"

Sedit put her nose nearly to mine. "He paid the other soldiers not to stand in line for this woman."

"What did he pay the woman?"

"He gave her Spanish words and Spanish songs."

I spooned the mush with my fingers and carefully removed the unpleasant objects into my left hand. "Thank you, Wife. This mush is very tasty."

The spirit of Uncle Podnow smiled, and the villagers cheered as I pulled a silver cross from the woman's vagina, but the crowd grew suddenly quiet as Sedit placed a very young child in the woman's arms. When the newborn started to squall, the woman sat up and smiled. The child stopped crying. Six times I made the scream of a red-tailed hawk. Six times I led the woman in a silent dance around the fire. All who watched let tears fall into the dust, and when I brought her back to the blankets she felt the comforting hands of friends. The woman who ate dirt accepted bits of acorn bread and grasshopper-flavored atole and studied the face of the sleeping child. She kissed the silver cross and kissed the child on nose and cheek and let tears fall through her smile.

Miguel's villagers ate and danced. Young couples disappeared into the shadows. The old storytellers remembered how the earth was created and how the good spirits always baffled the evil spirits. As stars disappeared, the vaqueros and rope makers asked the old storytellers to tell "one more story. Please, just one more story."

Miguel sat next to me. The sun was nearly full above the horizon.

"No work today?" I asked.

Miguel looked glum, as if overwhelmed by the disclosure of pessimistic news. "I told the padres that a few of the villagers had red spots under their arms."

"What did the holy men say?"

"They told me to keep everyone down near the creek until the red spots disappeared."

"How many times have you used that trick?"

"Not more than ten."

I watched the woman who ate dirt smile as Sedit touched her from shoulder to knee, like a butterfly checking a field of flowers for nectar.

"Miguel," I asked. "What are your people called?"

"The Easalan, by our neighbors, but we call ourselves the People."

I handed over a chunk of dried salmon. "Miguel, what do you remember from the old days?"

He chewed for a bit. "I remember helping my father harvest countless armloads of tule reed and then tying the small bundles until we had created a beautiful canoe."

"Do you still dream about that canoe?"

"Every night."

"Tell me about the dream."

"Is this some kind of tipne trick?"

"No, not at all." I watched the woman who ate dirt touch Sedit on her face, and then I turned back to Miguel. "Podnow taught me that a tipne must serve the People. He danced and sang and gave me a few useless tricks, all in an effort to teach me that the People were everything and a tipne nothing."

"The Tachi villagers called themselves the People?"

"Those from neighboring villages called us Tachi, but we were always the People, best loved by all spirits." I winked my left eye at our village chief. "But then, every child in every village knows that he lives among the People and cannot stop jealous neighbors from inventing unpleasant names for those who are superior to them in every possible way."

Miguel returned my wink, but with the right eye. "I was about to utter the exact same words about the many jealous neighbors of my village."

We sat and enjoyed the antics of his villagers, best loved by the spirits. The People.

"What have you learned from the black pots, wild man?"

"The People are everything; a tipne is merely a catalyst that serves the People. If the tipne serves them well, the People flourish. If the tipne serves himself at the expense of the People, then the People suffer."

"That's it?"

"The People depend upon their tipne for survival."

Miguel belched. "Look, I'm just a dumb Easalan warrior. First you tell me the tipne is nothing, and then you say the People depend upon the tipne." He studied my face for a long moment. "What have you learned from the pots?"

"You are the chief, and I am your tipne. Together we serve the People."

"Are you telling me that this bunch of tame Indios, this sorry gang of dirt-eaters and vaqueros and whores—that they are the People?" The eyebrows bunched right down on the top of his nose. "What happened to those proud Tachi folk and all the rest of your wild warriors from the Great Valley? Are they going to receive my villagers as equal to theirs?"

"Both and all are the People. You and I serve the tame and wild Indios against the White Others."

Miguel ran his tongue over his lips. "Maybe I've kept you on those pots a bit too long. I see a real problem with your thinking."

"What?"

"Well, now, do you actually consider my greasy bunch of mission slaves as the People?"

"Certainly. We are all one and the same—the People."

"Now, now, wild man, this is a momentous change from your previous tirades. Have you been eating some special herbs or found a more benevolent spirit brother than that damned coyote?"

"I credit a secret potion for my transformation, honored elder."

"Well then, just hand over a basket of your medicine or go ahead and tell me what happened. Either way, I'm interested."

I sat back against a tree, squiggled my butt to get a bit more comfortable, and gave a pompous lilt to my voice. "I have come to believe that in the beginning, our red people were given a very special land by the spirits. The invaders can call us Indios, or whatever they want, but all the People must protect our land from all invaders. The white invaders must die or leave."

Miguel was quick to interrupt. "Well, now, esteemed spirit doctor, what if the people can teach the invaders how to share the land and to also teach them how to trade their goods and services for our wealth? You've got to admit, getting metal awls in trade for our acorn meal would keep the women happy. A basket of dried salmon for a gun seems fair."

There was a suspicious wrinkle over Miguel's left brow. Laughter was churning his stomach and about to explode, but I continued my oration with patient reserve.

"I must admit that the strategy of sharing some of our land and developing a system for trade with the invaders was briefly considered in the early days by Podnow. I even remember that the Miwok were especially interested in having the Yokuts serve as the negotiators with the invaders. Nowadays, however, there're only a few drunks and one village chief who hold that silly idea in esteem."

Miguel swallowed some tea and his laughter. "Okay, pot-cleaner, just a few drunks with a bad idea. What's next for the People? What's left of them, anyway."

"First of all we've got to admit that the villages along the coast failed to protect their land from the invaders. Let's just say that they were overwhelmed by the military strategy of the invaders, and let go of all the Kumeyaay and Cahuilla and all the villages up and down the coast of Alta California. Gone forever." Miguel's laugh lines were turned to stone, and I moved on without a chance of interruption.

"Now we get to the difficult part where the spirit doctors—us tipne doctors—must serve all the surviving red men against all the white invaders. The way I see the situation is that the survivors from all the villages must defer to us tipne doctors for finding a strategy that will somehow satisfy both survivors and invaders."

Miguel held his hand up to shut me up, but he waited until I put my head against the tree before speaking.

"I can't say that I've ever seen two tipne doctors from the same village agree to much more than the sun rising or setting." Miguel didn't seem mad or angry at me, just more thoughtful than usual. "Same goes for the padres and dons. They're always dancing around, trying to gain some advantage or other without losing what they have in hand. Fish, birds, or invaders—all critters seem to scramble around to accomplish their own gain."

I moved away from the tree to lean toward my village chief. "Right as rain, Miguel. You'll get no argument from me in any way about how the birds get their seed and bees their honey. No sir. But the way I see my task is even tougher than getting a bunch of ravens to stand in line while I divide up a basket of grasshoppers for them to share. What I need to do is to convince the invaders that they can't steal any more land from the People. The invaders must understand that they will never establish a profitable system of trade with the People while they are constantly plotting to steal more land from them."

"And my people, the Costanoans—they are now Yokuts? Miwok?"

"You must never forget the stories of your village—never. But just as you and I have changed our names from the days when were youngsters, so shall all the people live under a new name."

"What is the new name, tipne man?"

"Indio for the People and Californian for the ones who now think they are Spanish or Mexican or Sonoran."

Miguel merely shook his head and stared into the sky.

"There is no gain in trading with those who dream of living on stolen land. There is no gain is finding a way to trade when held as a slave by the invaders. What is lost cannot be recovered, but the land of the Great Valley still offers a possible sanctuary for all the People. The final victory for the People comes when the invaders promise that they will encroach no further into the land of the People. At that moment of equilibrium between the white invader and the People, negotiations of trade between two nations of equal power can begin." I held my grease-scarred hands and arms toward Miguel. "Such is the lesson from your black pots."

Miguel shrugged as if my declaration had no meaning. "You still want to hear my dream?"

"Sure."

"It's a mixture of dream and memories," he said.

"I have the same problem. It's hard to tell the difference."

Miguel shut his eyes, and with a wooden voice began talking.

"In the dream-memory, my uncle is in his canoe and I am in mine. We're paddling slowly through the reeds and hunting birds with our slings. The sun has barely conquered the eastern hills, and six green-headed ducks have already offered themselves to our family. A wren scolds us with sharp displeasure." Miguel stopped for a long pause. "Suddenly, ducks and geese without number jump into the sky. My uncle stands in his canoe to detect a reason for such a disturbance. His face explodes. Blood spatters my arms. The sky is black with wings."

I waited for a long moment. "Is the dream always the same?"

Miguel nodded but remained silent.

My hand fell upon his knee, as if by accident, and Miguel did nothing to change his position or remove my hand.

"Your sojourn, wild man—is the memory of your sojourn the essence of your dreams?"

"Most of my bad dreams grow from the memories of that damned sojourn."

Miguel put his hand atop mine. "Are there any good dreams for you?"

"My good dreams start with either Ulati's smile or Uncle Shup's huge voice."

"Good dreams are as fresh as the first green clover of spring, as comfortable as a silent sweat lodge."

I squirmed around to look at Miguel. "How did you end up in this place?"

"The murderers of my uncle captured me on that beautiful morning among the tule reeds."

"Soldiers?"

"There were four soldiers and Father Carlos-Maria."

The dancers and singers disappeared. The sun dwindled to nothing. "Miguel," I said. "Can you detect any more red spots on the villagers?"

"Nope. They're all gone."

"I'll get moving to my pots then."

Miguel stood on shaky legs like a fresh-dropped colt. "Sure. The whipping padre is going to wear out his arm today." He rubbed the back of his neck. "I'll tell you one certain fact, tipne man: we'll never get rid of the Spanish with a bunch of wild no-account Indios."

"I agree with you, Chief Miguel. So it looks like we'll have to find some way to get the tame and wild Indios together over in the Great Valley."

Miguel hunched his shoulders up and down. "Okay! Get going, wild man, and make sure you skim that tallow clean today. God doesn't want a bunch of sticks and cow hair in his tallow."

"It will be clean as Sedit's acorn mush," I said.

CHAPTER 17

1804

P ADRE CARLOS-MARIA NODDED TO his alcalde. "The production of tallow has doubled once again in the past twelve months."

"So it seems, Father." Chief Miguel held his hands behind his back.

"The quality of our tallow is also admired by the authorities in Monterey."

"Thank you for telling me, Father."

Padre Carlos-Maria took a step closer to his alcalde. "Who is your foreman on the black pots?"

"José Jesus, Father."

"How has he managed the increased output? Not with more workers, I hope."

Miguel looked down at the carpet of oak leaves. "He works hard, like a Spanish laborer, Father. He inspires the women and old men who tend the pots to apply diligent thought to each small task."

Padre Carlos-Maria repeated his initial nod. "You have done well, Miguel. In fact, your success with José Jesus far exceeds my own misguided efforts."

"He needs firm direction," Miguel said.

Padre Carlos-Maria fingered his beads for an entire cycle. "Tell me—is he moving closer to God?"

"I would judge that he is, Father."

"Good work, Miguel, very good. God smiles upon you."

"Thank you, Father."

"What is next for our young sinner?"

"He will become a vaquero, my father."

———◆———

The first day—after possibly ten heartbeats—I fell from the horse. Pain shot from head to toe but centered near my right shoulder. There was no standing to chase after the beast. Lightning bolts flashed through my chest with any movement.

The head vaquero looked down at me from his horse. "Can you get back up on your horse?"

I tried to stand, but pain forced me to stop all movement. "No," I said.

"Walk back to the village when you are able." The vaquero gestured to the west. "Tell Miguel to send me a vaquero. That damned thunderstorm last night got the cows scattered all over the place."

———◆———

Sedit wrapped the arm in place against my side and kept me quiet until Miguel began with his calling me a "damn lazy wild Indio." I waited another few days until my arm was strong and flexible and then embarked for another attempt with the cows and horses. On this second occasion, I was very careful with the selection of my horse and somewhat more astute in duplicating the activities of the experienced vaqueros.

During the first week of my return, I fell nine times without serious injury. The second week provoked the jeers of my fellow vaqueros only twice. After the third week, the sweat of my body and that of the horse joined in a beautiful scent that allowed me to ride with the others. I was honored that the vaqueros of San Juan Bautista Mission allowed me to join their clan. I became a small fragment of that boisterous group of warriors. We were as one entity that excluded all others.

In the evening we vaqueros told lies and jokes and set every task as a competition between brothers. We were warriors together. We reveled in the eloquent silence of our brotherhood. There were no distractions of women or White Others. We were vaqueros! Brothers! Tachi and Mutsun and Antoniaño and Obespiño together! We were brothers who were stronger, wiser, faster, and tougher than all others. We bragged and lied about whatever suited our purpose. We rode our horses and killed cows so that lesser creatures could dismember them for the black pots. "Death to the cows!" we shouted. "Death to the Spanish!" we screamed.

"Miguel!" I waved him over to the shade of an oak tree. "Podnow sent a winatum to me."

"What did the messenger say?"

"I need to leave in the next day or so for a visit to my Tachi village. Can you protect me from the padres?"

"Sure. I'll tell Carlos-Maria that you're working with a crew over by Tres Piños. There's always a bunch of strays along the streambed this time of year."

"Good. I can't say how long I'll be gone—maybe a week or so. I'll give my uncle the same bunch of nonsense that you loved so much."

"The 'ravens standing in line' bit?"

"Yup. The coast for them and the Great Valley for us."

"A week is okay. Two weeks is a problem."

"I'll do my best."

———

Podnow listened to my words of greeting and studied my posture. He moved closer and touched my face. His voice was like wind through winter grass; his face showed deeper pits and furrows than at our last meeting. "I see you Kiyu, son of my brother," he said

"My name is José Jesus."

He nodded. "I will listen to you, Kiyu. Tell me what you know."

"José Jesus. I am called José Jesus."

"Yes, yes." His nose wrinkled. "Each time you tell me the same name, and it passes my tongue with great difficulty. Tell me again the name, slowly, and tell me what it means."

"José Jesus. I am given the name of a white spirit god. It is the name of an earthbound father who is not truly the father of all spirits. The spirit of my name is the son of the God of all spirits."

Podnow waved his hand in the air. "Stop the nonsense! Stop with the riddles. I'm too old for such madness."

"Yes, Uncle. The White Others pretend to answer such riddles, but even their tipne are baffled by the truth."

"Tell me what you know, José Jesus."

"The Spanish have some guns and a few cannons, but our warriors are smarter, braver, and more cunning. Most of their soldiers are stupid youngsters."

Podnow nodded.

"The White Others don't listen to their tipne. They argue among themselves, and they starve in the midst of acorns and edible insects."

Podnow smiled his old man's smile and spoke with his windy voice. "Tell me, José Jesus—if these creatures are such helpless imbeciles, how is it that they kill so many of the People? How can the few dominate the many? Please, José Jesus, tell me what the People must do to protect themselves from this innocuous enemy."

I had to admit that Podnow was in good form. He was tipne-smart with the feeble smile and the facile questions of an ancient elder. I told him, "The People must keep the Spanish from our land. We must continue to stop them at our border. You must keep the People alert and ready to attack whenever the Spanish appear at our border."

"What are their numbers? How quickly do they multiply?"

"There are more Yokuts than Spanish. Their women have many children, but most die at a young age. A few ignorant soldiers arrive occasionally on their white-cloud ships, but in total, the White Others grow slowly in their numbers. They remain scattered in small villages along the seacoast, and they cower in fear of our beautiful tule-reed marshes. They are ignorant of our small trails and hidden islands."

"Tell me, José Jesus—how long have you lived among the White Others?"

"Eleven times the oaks have offered their acorns to us."

"Eleven." Podnow raised his left eyebrow. "Your dead father gave me better information about the White Others, and he spoke to me when you were still playing soccer with my son."

I sat back on my heels. "Tell me, Uncle Podnow, what counsel have you received from Hineh?"

Podnow retained his benign expression. "None. He refuses my winatum and fills their ears with curses. He refuses to leave the White Others and tell me of their secrets. Those of the People who have whispered into his ear tell me he smells of poison toadstools." Podnow coughed twice and spit into the grass.

Bitter and sweet in combination is a rare treat. Bitter tea with Spanish honey or bitter brown beetles with sweet army worms came to mind. Now here was Hineh dismissed as son, yet unavailable as my collaborator against the invaders. Sweet and bitter, bitter and sweet—there was no difference.

I cleared my throat of Hineh's poison. "The information that I provide to you, honored uncle, may suffer in comparison to what you may have received from the spirit of my father, but it is based upon observations that I have made within the last moon or two." I let my silence slide for the duration of a meadowlark's song. "Tell me if you wish to hear more from the lips of your nephew."

Podnow stared at me as if for the first time. He touched my face again. "Tell me what you have learned from the White Others."

"They argue among themselves." I let my breathing slow to a gentle walk. "In this matter they are no different from the People or any other village that I have observed."

Podnow managed a weak smile. "Yes, just as I suspected."

"Here is something my dead father did not tell you."

"I'm listening."

"They depend upon huge ships for their sustenance. Each year there are fewer ships that follow the wind to the Spanish villages that have replaced the Ohlone villages."

"Pretend I am a simple child, José Jesus. Tell me how these ships are important to the White Others."

"They do not eat our plants or roots or seeds; the Spanish people rely upon those plants and roots and seeds from their faraway villages. It is the ships that bring the seed required to grow their food."

"But once they plant their seed, won't the spirits provide wind and birds and rain to disseminate future crops?"

"Some of their plants, such as their yellow mustard, grow without cultivation, but their important crops grow only from the seed of their native villages, and then only with intense encouragement by the Spanish and their tame Indios."

"You just mentioned that the seed-ships have diminished in number over the years. Why?"

I took a deep breath. "The white invaders who have stolen land from our neighbors to the west have taken to calling themselves Califorñios."

"They torture us with their difficult names."

"The ancestors of those who have invaded our land are called the Spanish."

"Spanish." Podnow shut his eyes. "Continue."

"The Spanish will not send the seed-ships to the Californios unless the Califorñios show greater respect to the land of their ancestors."

At this, light came into his eyes. "Ahhh, now I understand! A feud! We have a war between men of different villages who argue over silly issues."

"Yes, exactly. It is a feud with one white village against another. Now, Uncle Podnow, you must understand that our immediate enemy, the Califorñios, cannot survive without the seed-ships and the labor of red men. If the conquerors of the coastal villages are denied either the seed or our labor, the white invaders will disappear like snow under the spring sun."

Podnow took some time to stare into his mind and then looked directly into my eyes. "Tell me, José Jesus. Why do red men succumb so easily to the white man's magic?"

A queasy shudder wriggled up my legs into my stomach. "Many of the red men seem to lack the courage necessary to stand and fight for the land of their ancestors. They. . ." I let my thoughts tumble to the ground. My throat felt dry.

"Finish, I grow weary."

"The White Others can destroy us only if we destroy ourselves."

"Don't patronize me. Move on, quickly."

I offered Podnow a drink of water from my basket, but he shook his head. "The little moon is fishing tonight," I said.

"The elders tell us many stories about the little moon, and without exception, we are told that it will catch only those fish who keep their mouth open."

I watched the splinter moon move through the ghost path and then disappear. I listened to the large owls and the small owls and to the sounds within my body. "Uncle Podnow," I said. "You are the greatest tipne of the People, the elder brother of my father. If the People follow you, they will die, and our land will disappear. Pokook will call to a land empty of the People."

The night-hunting herons silenced the frogs for ten heartbeats with their stabbing attacks, but soon the quiet birds stood thigh-deep in the booming chorus. Their yellow eyes glittered as they gathered stomach and shoulder muscles for the next assault.

Podnow whispered, "What then, José Jesus? What path will you have me follow?"

"My dead father gave the answer when I was a very young man, before my sojourn. He spoke the truth to you before you took your second wife, my mother."

"Remind me, José Jesus."

"Guard our land. Keep the People and Miwok together. Dig pit traps and lure the mounted soldiers through them. Attack when I say attack, and attack in the location that I describe."

"Yes! I remember." Podnow ran his tongue over cracked lips. "I summoned your dead father in those old days, and he spoke through me. What has changed, José Jesus?"

"Can you still call my dead father from Tipiknits Pahn?"

Podnow blinked once as if to clear a tear from his eye. "No," he said.

"Listen, Podnow. Listen, tipne to the Yokuts and Miwok. I am your winatum from the spirits. I speak for all spirits and also for the Great Hairy God of the White Others. Listen, and follow my instructions."

Podnow sat in silence until the fire lost all heat. Finally, he coughed to clear his throat. "The spirits send their commands in all manner of strange roads." A single smile line above his left eye moved imperceptibly upward. "It seems that now I must listen to an enormously puffed-up toad as my final authority from our ancestors."

"A dangerous horned toad of the desert," I said.

"Prickly and poisonous both, I understand."

I threw a few twigs onto the charred logs, but it was too late for a fresh flame. "There is no other option, Uncle. I hope that I am more poisonous to the White Others than to the People, but still, you must follow my instructions."

Podnow allowed a few more lines to leap from above his eye toward Tipiknits Pahn. "Tell me, Toad Man, what must this old man tell the People?"

"Time is our ally, Uncle Podnow. You must remain patient through every defeat and celebrate the death of our honored warriors. The People must accept all red others into their villages. We will achieve victory over the White Others only if all red men join together against all white men."

"What else?"

"The God of all spirits serves all red men."

"What else?"

"Look for me when the willow bud next emerges. Remain alert for my winatum and follow each of my commands."

"I will practice your new name with my old tongue, José Jesus. You are now tipne of the People, José Jesus. Ulati's son is war chief of the People and savior of the People. José Jesus." Podnow leaned toward me and spoke very slowly. "José Jesus, tipne of the Yokuts and all others who will follow his commands."

CHAPTER 18

Winter 1805

IT WAS AN AUSPICIOUS YEAR. There were earthquakes along the entire mission trail from San Diego to Santa Clara. Not a single thundercloud ship flew into Monterey. The padres sprinkled holy water day and night, yet the rains failed and the cattle starved. There were no salmon in the rivers. There was no seed corn for the farmers or bright red cloth for their wives or gold to pay the soldiers. There were no metal-plated plows to tame the red man's land. Rumors of pirates circled the congregation at each gathering for Holy Mass and evening vespers.

Although Miguel remained alcalde for the Mission San Juan Bautista, I now stood at his side as his assistant. Carlos-Maria verified my status by ignoring me. The whipping priest suffered acute pain in every joint and stuttered each word into garbled nonsense, so Miguel had appointed me to manage the daily punishment of unworthy Indios. The short padre was dead, and no replacement trudged down the road from Monterey. Miguel assigned to me the supervision of all farming activities.

We were gathered in a small circle at the mission gate: two Indios and two invaders. The corporal of the guard, Ramirez, was red-faced with indignation. "Those damn Mexicans! They're nothing but damned atheists!" He turned toward Carlos-Maria. "The Lord should smash those fools!"

We three spectators stood before the senior military representative of the Spanish Crown in residence at the Mission San Juan Bautista. Our heads were down—the better to study toes and twigs.

"Why doesn't he destroy the atheists with bolts of lightning and bring back to us our beloved Spanish king?"

Padre Carlos-Maria continued to stare at the dust, his words as fragile as a spring acorn. "We suffer because the Prince of Darkness has taken control of our land."

"Nonsense," Corporal Ramirez blustered. "We are of Spanish blood, and the true God will always protect us. It is those who call themselves Mexicans who live with the Devil." He stared first at Miguel, then at me. "We are not Mexicans! We must call ourselves Califorñios and continue to live with God and his king of Spain."

"God and king cannot save us here in this remote land. The Prince of Darkness rules our ranchos and pueblos because I have sinned." Carlos-Maria pushed his right hand slowly through his mop of white hair. "I constantly smell the Devil. I whip myself morning and night, yet even at this moment the Devil hovers over my shoulder."

"Nonsense, Padre. We are true Christians! Is God dead that he can allow the Spanish king to desert us and permit the Mexican atheists to direct our lives? How can he allow such a farce?"

"Will the glorious and God-protected king of Spain and the most benevolent Califorñios continue to love their Indio children?" I asked.

Miguel hit my ribs with his elbow.

"Silence, you miserable son of Satan!" Padre Carlos-Maria moved his mouth open and shut like a large cui-cui fish. "There will be no more cursing and no further sacrilege from soldiers or Indios. Silence, all of you."

Ramirez spat.

Padre Carlos-Maria waved a brittle sign of the cross into the spring air. "We must love our Lord. We must celebrate this year of our Lord as a test of our faith." He dropped his arm. "Listen, Ramirez. Do not heed the evil whispers, for we are Spaniards, and God shall always love us. Have faith, my son."

Ramirez made a huge sigh. "Faith, Padre? Where does a poor soldier find faith when his king surrenders to the Mexican *mestizo*? Point to one small gift from God to his orphans stranded in this forsaken place."

"Silence. You must always consider who stands beside us."

Ramirez tried to spit again but instead slobbered onto his bare foot.

I leaned forward but with eyes averted. "Tell me, Father Carlos-Maria, Corporal Ramirez: who must receive God's punishment today?"

They waved feeble arms in my direction. "See to your duty," said the padre. "Pick a few of the most shameless," the corporal said.

I felt the calm excitement of a hunter almost upon his quarry. It was time to notch the arrow, to sing songs of death, for the soldiers wore rags and had little gunpowder and few bullets. They walked with their eyes on the ground.

The two white men shambled toward their quarters; Carlos-Maria worked his beads, while Ramirez scratched his armpits. Both were silent, although their lips moved in slow ripples.

"The time is near, Chief Miguel."

"Slow down, wild man. Let the fish wear his hook a bit longer."

"The spirits whisper to me that the time is near."

"Forget that damn coyote of yours. I'll tell you when to attack."
Miguel hit my shoulder with the flat of his hand. "C'mon, we've got
work to do."

———

Miguel shushed all the villagers and all the mission neophytes. "Listen
carefully." He pointed to a group of bachelors standing off to one side.
"I want you fellows to burn the whorehouse."

They looked at Miguel like spooked horses. One said, "Now?"
and another asked, "What about the soldiers?"

"Start the fire now. If more than two soldiers appear, I want you
to run down to the Willow Grove and hide. Don't confront the soldiers
with any weapons."

The first bachelor spoke. "Can we yell at the soldiers? Tease them
a little?"

Miguel smiled. "Sure. Just don't get any lead in your ass."

The crew moved off like boys to a ballgame in a neighboring
village, and Miguel spoke again. "I want the women to take their
baskets and gather whatever food they can find. Take what is available
from the farms, but also look beyond the mission to find the food of
our ancestors. Let the white people starve, but we must grow strong
again."

The women erupted in a chorus of questions, but Sedit and a few
of the older women moved toward their lodges, and others followed,
like geese after separate leaders.

Miguel nodded to me. "José Jesus will take the rest of the men,
and I want all of you fools to obey exactly what he says."

"No more black pots!" I said.

The men and remaining old women laughed and cheered.

"Vaqueros," I said. "Go and kill a dozen young cows for the villagers, but nothing for the Spaniards."

The cheering surged.

"All the rest of you must walk about as if occupied with tasks assigned to serve the Spanish. Steal what you can without drawing attention to your efforts. Keep your eyes on the ground. Pretend obedience to the padres and their Great Hairy God. Steal the hair from their balls."

Wave after wave of cheers foamed over Miguel and me. "Death to the Spanish," they yelled, as if mindless repetition would accomplish their dream.

———◆———

The heat of summer smothered Mission San Juan Bautista. A second earthquake brought the bell tower down and emptied the central well of water. The soldiers walked about like herons on dry land.

Corporal Ramirez mounted his horse.

"Where are you going?" I asked.

"Your vaqueros claim they cannot find any cows, and my men are hungry."

"It is the wild Indios, esteemed corporal. They steal the young stock and frighten my vaqueros."

Ramirez looked down at me. "So you say, José Jesus. You are full of sad stories, and my men starve."

"God is testing our faith, Corporal."

He struck at me with his crop but missed. "Get to work, you Judas! Get all your lazy Indios to work!"

Ramirez yelled for his soldiers, and from early morning to midafternoon he badgered his army of twelve to load six donkeys with supplies. Just past the hottest moment of the long day, they disappeared through the mission gate.

I waved for my brother to stand at my side. "Chetic, ride out to the vaqueros. Have them paint themselves like wild Indios and chase a bunch of cows through the hills and into the Great Valley."

He nodded. "Do you want Ramirez to chase those wild Indios?"

"Yes. Make it appear that the warriors are consumed with a difficult task and that eventually the soldiers will find victory."

"Do I see Mama Killdeer with the crippled wing?

"Just the same," I said.

"Okay, I will do my best to provide an attractive lure."

"Listen, Chetic. If Ramirez takes the bait, you must ride ahead with a message to the first Tachi village. Tell the war chief that each soldier has three bullets. Tell him that if his warriors harass the soldiers from behind trees, the stupid soldiers will fire their first bullet."

"What then?" Chetic asked.

"The war chief must move his warriors even closer, without the benefit of protection, and after the second bullets are spent, they must attack the invaders from all sides. The warriors must kill the White Others. They must stomp the white mushrooms into the dirt."

"I'll leave immediately," Chetic said.

I signed the cross of the Hairy God toward my brother. "May God go with you," I said.

Chetic laughed. "Just don't send that Coyote Brother of yours after me. Hairy gods I can handle; coyote spirits play the trickster for no reason at all."

"Blasphemer," I shouted. "On your knees; pray for mercy."

Chetic waved his hand, circled his horse twice to raise dust in my face, and rode away at a trot toward the east.

After six days Ramirez returned to Mission San Juan Bautista as corporal to six men, two horses, and no donkeys.

"Mother of God!" wailed Padre Carlos-Maria.

"They were behind every bush." Ramirez pawed at his black beard. "They waited until we had but one bullet each, and then the Indios attacked us in large numbers."

"God did not totally ignore you," I said. "Your wounds are minor, and four of your six remaining soldiers are also likely to survive."

Ramirez stopped pulling his beard. "They were waiting for us, José Jesus. Every step of their campaign was planned with the foreknowledge of our arrival."

"How can that be, Corporal Ramirez? God does not permit his wild Indios the capacity to plan from one day to the next."

Ramirez waved his hand at me as if flicking fingers at a buzzing horsefly, and then turned to Carlos-Maria. "We're leaving tomorrow for Monterey, Padre."

"No! Please do not abandon us, Corporal. Please! God's work requires your diligent help."

"My men need medicine and food." Ramirez shrugged. "We're all nearly naked, and we have neither powder nor lead. Weak men serve no purpose for either God or king."

"I need you." Padre Carlos-Maria fell to his knees in prayer. "Please, remain here at the mission and continue with God's work."

"If the ships arrive, I'll return," he said.

Two days after the soldiers departed, the whipping padre expired. I listened as he uttered a tirade against Indios and Mexicans and cinnamon and then faded away to a silent nothing.

When I told Carlos-Maria that he was the last remaining invader living at Mission San Juan Bautista, he turned his head to the wall and remained quiet.

CHAPTER 19

1805

"STAY AWAY FROM THE CHURCH," Miguel told the villagers and neophytes and bachelors. "No farming or cleaning the mission or working in the rope factory."

On Sundays Padre Carlos-Maria celebrated Mass in the cold, dark rubble-strewn chancel and sprinkled his gift of holy water on a few women and on Miguel, his alcalde, and on me, his assistant alcalde. During the rest of the week the padre stayed behind barred doors to pray and shout orders that we ignored.

After the soldiers deserted our mission, Miguel's village quickly grew as big as any village hidden among the tules of the Great Valley. Smallpox survivors came to us because they were hungry. Widows and children from devastated villages along the coast found protection with us from both red and white enemies. The residents of Miguel's village began to hunt and cook in the old way, while the few who were addicted to brandy and metal tools drifted away to the San José and Santa Clara villages. Cows, of course, were more likely targets than elk for the hunters, and remnant plots of potatoes served as acceptable substitutes for traditional root crops. All in all, Miguel's village prospered.

On the tenth Sunday of our freedom from the Spanish army and the whipping priest, Padre Carlos-Maria appeared at the altar rail. He tried to speak, but his congregation heard nothing. He pawed his ragged surplice and then bent to lift his basket of holy water. The basket spilled in one splash over his bare feet. Tears eased from his eyes, like sap from a tree, and dribbled in solitary procession down his hollow cheeks.

"Here," Miguel said. "Let us help you back to your room."

I fed him acorn mush and water until he could raise his head. "First the Devil starves me; now he keeps me alive." He swallowed spit a few times. "Leave me alone. God is serving me with his just reward. Go. Do not return."

At dusk, one of Miguel's winatums jogged into the village. "A single rider is coming down the Monterey road," he said.

"Do you recognize him?"

"It is the tall private, the one who slouches to the left when he rides at the trot."

"Higuera?" Miguel said.

"Just the same," said the winatum.

"José Jesus, come with me." Miguel spoke to a crowd of men. "Chetic, mount twenty vaqueros and keep them hidden in the cottonwood grove past the cemetery." He waved his arm. "Everyone else, stay here in the village. Continue as normal with your evening meal."

We were waiting when Private Juan Higuera rode up to the mission gate. "I have orders from the commandant," he said. "Take me to Padre Carlos-Maria."

I took the reins of his horse and stood to one side, but out of reach from Higuera's riding crop. "Welcome back, Private," I said. "What is the news?"

"The news is for the padre, not for Indios."

Miguel stepped forward and took hold of the reins on the other side. "The padre is sick, Private. He has large boils under both arms."

Higuera jerked backward, but we held the horse steady. "Does he excrete black pus?"

"Just so, and both padres suffer from the same evil secretions."

"Eiii! I must leave. Let the reins go."

"Wait." Miguel maintained a steady voice and a strong grip. "What is the news? Perhaps we can provide some minor assistance in the service of our Spanish protectors."

Private Higuera looked up and down the road, as if Carlos-Maria were leading an attack of black plague victims. "It is the pirates. A devil named Bouchard is coming to attack Monterey."

Miguel pulled the reins down to provide a direct view of Private Higuera. "Help me understand, Juan. Who is this Bouchard? What danger can he pose to the God-protected Spanish?"

Higuera shook himself like a bear coming from a cold river. "Enough! No more questions." He pulled his shoulders back from their slouch. "The commandant has assessed this mission for twenty-five vaqueros." He held his right hand up and raised his voice. "Indios and Spaniards—together we will stand against Bouchard."

Miguel nodded to me, and we released the reins. "Certainly, Juan Higuera. Tomorrow at dawn I will submit our quota for your review."

"Good." He brushed dust from his rags. "I have orders for a short period of training before we depart for Monterey."

"The vaqueros will mount our best horses." Miguel gave the private a soft smile. "May I suggest, Juan Higuera, that you sleep on the hill west of the mission?" The smile disappeared. "Possibly the prevailing wind will remove the ill humors of death from your nostrils."

Higuera jerked his horse in a full circle. "Yes! Of course!" The horse hesitated. "Tomorrow at dawn, bring your vaqueros to the field beneath the hill."

The elders sat in a tight circle around Chief Miguel. "This fool can barely ride a donkey, and he wants to train us how to ride and fight," Miguel said.

The elders and warriors laughed.

"The end of our slavery is near," I said. "The whites are fighting each other, and the Spanish invaders want our help."

A few of the youngest men stood and danced wildly around the circle, while others clapped and sang.

Miguel raised his hand, and all became quiet. "We will listen to this Higuera, but you will obey José Jesus." He waited until the quiet returned. "I am too old to serve as your war chief; therefore, José Jesus will serve. In all matters of this conflict between the Spanish and the pirates, you must obey his commands."

"Turn the White Others into garter snakes, José Jesus," someone yelled.

The crowd laughed, and Miguel smiled.

"Stuff them into your black pots!" another shouted.

"The Spanish will make good tallow," I answered.

"Yes! Yes!" the villagers yelled. "We'll burn the Spanish for candle wax."

Boys started to dance in imitation of their elders. Women clapped; elders smiled. After a short interval, I raised my voice. "Listen, people of Miguel's village, tomorrow the wars begin. Tomorrow we will begin the first step in the long campaign to eliminate the White Others from our land. We are from many different villages, but we must suffer together. We must celebrate each victory and each defeat together. All of us must burn our hair short with the death of a single warrior."

I lowered my voice because all were silent. "If Miguel's village can unite to fight the White Others, what will the Spanish see as their future in our land? If Miguel's village can join together to fight the White Others, what will the wild Indios see as their future in our land?" A baby squalled and quickly went quiet. "Tomorrow we will begin, so now you must go to your lodges and listen to one another. You must think about your lives after the White Others leave our land."

———

At sunrise my vaqueros rode in two ragged lines to the large field west of the mission. "You Indios are now in the army of Spain," Private Higuera yelled.

"Long live the king of Spain!" we cheered.

That day and the next we spent the mornings shooting at targets with our bows and the afternoons on horseback sticking lances into straw mannequins. At sunrise on the third day our army departed for Monterey.

Before we left, I gave Sedit a folded leaf filled with dried particles of the red-capped mushroom. "Take this special condiment for the atole of the padre," I said.

She nuzzled my throat. My sweet crane.

"We must save the People," I said.

"The People," Sedit whispered.

CHAPTER 20

1805

R ED LEAVES OF MAPLE TREES danced among the lesser yellows and browns on the eastern slope of the coastal mountains. No one spoke. We formed a single line, with Higuera in front. At the top of the last summit we sat for a short spell to study the undulating sea of green pine that dropped suddenly into a blue void.

An old white man on a skittish white horse met us at the outskirts of Monterey. "Hurry! Hurry!" His horse spun twice in a circle. "Higuera, tell your Indios to set up camp down near the river. Once they are settled, come to the commandant's office. Quickly, now, quickly."

Higuera waved his arm at me. "Down to the river!" he shouted. I managed a salute toward the back of his head. My vaqueros followed along a muddy trail to a willow grove next to the river. We slapped together a few temporary lean-to shelters against the evening fog and started the gambling games. Just as I conquered my second opponent, Private Higuera charged into our new camp. "You there, José Jesus!"

He scanned the others. "You there, Oscar, get your horses and follow me."

Oscar was a gray-haired Ohlone from a village along the east side of the great saltwater bay. He moved slowly, yet always killed the first elk. He sang death songs of great beauty, yet always left the greatest number of cattle lying in the dust. Wild colts settled at his touch. He rarely talked, but the vaqueros of San Juan Bautista always listened to his smallest murmur.

Higuera turned his head toward me. "We're going south, down to Point Piños."

"Why?" I asked.

"The pirate ships—they've been sighted to the south."

"Santa Barbara?"

"Yes, so they say. And also near Concepción Bay."

"Good," I whispered.

The ride was short and comfortable. Acrid sea smells followed an onshore breeze to mingle with the fresh pine fragrance. A red-spangled sun settled like a Spanish hen on the horizon, hesitated, and then disappeared. The last seabirds fluttered onto huge kelp rafts, a league or so offshore, to doze and squeal.

Higuera dismounted. "Take care of the horses and then build a fire." He pulled a carry-net from his saddle pack and scrambled down the shallow cliff.

Oscar and I watched him disappear behind a wave-washed boulder. We hobbled the horses and built a fire. The first stars appeared. I fed summer-dry pine branches to the flames and watched columns of sparks spin into the sky.

When Higuera returned, it was full dark. He dropped his net, quickly raked the burning logs with a long stick, and dumped his burden of sea-bearded mussels onto the bed of hot coals. A hissing, salty cloud of smoke erupted, and we stood back to watch the shells slowly open and tantalize us with a sweet, smoky scent. We used sticks to lift them free and then burned our impatient fingers and tongues on the hot orange flesh. We ate until there was no further room in gullet or stomach. The stars sank lower until they topped the trees and white-crested waves. A soft wind hushed the hissing surf.

Oscar belched. Higuera farted. I tugged a blanket over my shoulders. "What's going on, Private Higuera? What's all the excitement?"

"It is that damn Bouchard with his two warships." He poked a stick into the fire. "The governor thinks he may attack Monterey sometime soon."

"Tell me about this Bouchard."

"He's a pirate, nothing more." Sparks spiraled to the first stars. "The padres make him out as a devil, a murderer of women and children, but he's just one pirate among many."

"So, Higuera, this pirate is nothing to worry about?"

"He's nothing—just one of those atheist fools. He and those stupid mestizos down in Mexico—they want to kill all the Califorñios."

I felt foolish in teasing him, one fool teasing another. "Aren't you a mestizo, Higuera?"

"I'm a Califorñio! Stupid Indio! I'm a soldier of the Spanish king and of God." Higuera threw a large branch on the fire. "Go to sleep, Indio. Shut up!"

"How many pirates will the ships carry?"

Higuera scratched his head. "Five hundred, they say."

"A formidable enemy, then."

"We have God on our side, stupid Indio. He will assist us against the atheist fools."

I sat up from my bed of pine boughs and stared into the flames. "This afternoon, Private Higuera, I saw many Califorñios leaving Monterey. Where are they going?"

Higuera emptied a huge orange belch into the fire. "The governor ordered them to go. He told all the families to move inland, along with the padres. Tomorrow those who wear skirts will all leave, and the soldiers will defend Monterey."

"The soldiers and God," I said.

The fire swirled in a sudden eddy of wind, and Higuera pulled his blanket up over his ears. He was satisfied with my surrender to him. I was a stupid Indio, without question, and he was the assigned leader of an important military mission.

"How many men can you bring against the pirates, Private Higuera?"

"We have half the number of the pirates here in Monterey, but we are equal to the enemy if our soldiers from the south arrive in the next few days."

The wind settled to a stealthy whisper. Oscar began to snore, and Higuera's breathing settled into a steady march rhythm. I called, "Brother Coyote! Are you out there? Do you smile on the People? Do you lift your leg on the White Others?" The slight wind disappeared in a blanket of fog, and I plummeted through clouds of black feathers until the sun and Private Higuera's shouts restored shadows to the world.

———◆———

We established our routine on the first day. At daybreak two of us watched the horizon while a third checked snares for quail or tiny bush rabbits. During low tide we gathered moon snails and snagged eel or fish in the isolated pools. When night came and Bouchard was no longer our responsibility, we gorged ourselves with roots and berries and the flesh of fish and quail and rabbit. We sang songs. We farted. We danced and we waited.

At dawn on our tenth day I stood contemplating the western horizon. A distended ridge of clouds approached from the southwest. I watched as two giant white-winged birds detached themselves from the gray-blue thunderheads, and I admired them as they strayed closer and closer to the shore. The sun moved higher in the sky, and suddenly the birds transformed themselves into ships. "Private Higuera!" I yelled. "Juan! The sails are here! Bouchard is here!"

Private Higuera shouted, "To the horses! The atheist is among us!"

———◆———

A soft rain fell during the afternoon and larger drops through the night. Dawn saw the dust of yesterday reborn as viscous mud. Two-wheeled carts pulled by teams of four oxen, loaded with children and chairs, squealed toward the eastern hills. Women clad in black dresses rode mules next to the carts and ordered servants to run back to the house and retrieve one more precious tool or cup or ivory comb.

All was muddy chaos in Monterey. Soldiers screamed contrary orders to my men, but we merely drew further into the soggy remnants of our lean-to shelters and dozed. Near noon I called to Chetic, and we walked to an isolated clearing. "Take two horses and walk them south, through the woods, until there are no white men. Then ride quickly to Podnow and give him my message."

"I'm listening," Chetic said.

"Tell him the time has come. Tell him the whites are fighting among themselves. Tell him to attack the missions and ranchos and to kill the White Others. Now! Kill the White Others now!"

———◆———

The last cart pulled out of Monterey, and the rain diminished to a light mist. Tiny frogs celebrated the new wet season with a pulsing chorus of approval. Near noon, Higuera rode into our camp. "Saddle up, you Indios—follow me!"

We tethered our horses east of the dunes and carried bows and bundles of arrows to the beach. Higuera pointed toward a soldier wearing a blue and gold jacket. "Corporal José Vallejo commands this beach. If any of you Indios surrender to the pirates or run away, the corporal will shoot you with his cannon. Follow his orders, and we will defeat Bouchard."

He made a cutting motion with his hand. "This half, follow José Jesus over to Corporal Vallejo's cannon. The rest, follow me."

Fog and clouds melted to reveal a small ship close to shore. We heard an exchange of shouts between ship and shore but could make no sense of the words. A much larger vessel emerged through the mist and quickly dropped nine small boats into the water. A dozen lines of rope served to lower sailors and two small cannons into the boats, and after a short interval, the flotilla pushed off toward our beach.

Corporal Vallejo yelled, "Get ready to fire!" The corporal beat his dazed subordinates with the flat side of his sword. "Left! Left! Move the cannon mouth to the left, you idiots!" Two soldiers struggled to lift the tail of the gun carriage and swing the muzzle toward the left. Vallejo stabbed his sword into the sand and joined with the effort.

"Steady, now!" He quickly retrieved his sword and raised it into the air. "Steady! Fire!"

A soldier from each group put a burning taper to the touchhole and then joined the others in a wild scramble through loose sand. Two thunderous smoke-filled explosions sent squadrons of gulls screaming in panic. Eight boats, not nine, dipped oars toward the shore. Vallejo pointed his sword. His soldiers stared wide-eyed toward the sea. They jumped and cheered and thumped each other on the back.

"Idiots! Attention!" Corporal Vallejo pointed toward me. "You there! Come here!"

I stepped forward and motioned for Oscar to join me. "What will you have us do?" I asked the corporal.

"Those boxes over there"—he pointed—"They hold grapeshot, so bring one box for each cannon."

We followed his instructions, then stood silently as the soldiers prepared the next load of powder and rammed a twelve-pound ball into the cannon's maw. "Ready to fire!" Corporal Vallejo yelled. "Fire!"

This time we watched two large splashes appear well beyond the small boats.

"Grape!" Vallejo yelled. "Load the cannon with grapeshot!"

I helped rip lids from boxes and carefully observed as the soldiers loaded powder and small metal pellets. "Lower the elevation. Left, now, left a bit more. Ready to fire! Fire!"

The sound was different this time—more like bees in a thunderstorm. A rain of small spurts erupted around one of the boats. Several men stood, raised their arms, and collapsed out of sight.

Vallejo yelled affectionate obscenities to his men and moved them forward in the routine of loading the two cannons. Slowly the rate of fire increased, and the small boats hesitated at the surf line, sat briefly in a twirling swell, then reversed course back to the large black ship.

"Load the twelve-pound balls!" Corporal Vallejo yelled. "More powder! Ready! Fire!" The explosion from the extra powder made blood leak from my nose. Each of the next six balls crashed into the black ship with a splintery crash, but no apparent damage could be observed.

A sergeant galloped down the beach toward us. "Cease fire!" he yelled. "They have raised the white flag. Cease fire!"

"Never!" Vallejo replied. "Not until every dead pirate floats onto our shore!" His men loaded and fired three more rounds before another sergeant rode up to us. "My son, stop at once. Do not disgrace me with your insubordination!"

The black ship eased away from shore and moved south a small distance toward Playa de Doña Brigida, and once again it released the little boats to swim back and forth between the shore and mother ship. Their action was beyond the range of our cannons but within our line of sight. Soon, pirates beyond number stood on the sand; then they formed columns and marched down the road toward Monterey.

—————

The Califorñios were gophers running from a flood. Private Higuera led my vaqueros along a path through the woods, over the first ridge to the east, and down to a creek. The horses rested and drank their fill of water. "Where are we going?" I asked.

"I'm not sure," Higuera said. "We'll follow the crowd for a while."

"Were there no contingency plans? No meeting place in case the pirates proved invincible?"

"Atheists cannot defeat Spaniards!" Higuera kicked at the mud. "God is playing tricks on us." He shrugged. "I heard a sergeant say something about Rancho del Rey. Over the next ridge, I think."

"Yes," I said. "We pass the rancho on every trip to and from our mission. There are a number of good springs scattered around a nice little valley."

Higuera mounted his horse. "Let's go, you Indios; enough with your loafing."

"You lead the way, Private, and I'll make sure there are no stragglers."

"Damn lazy Indios," Higuera muttered.

———◆———

Just before dawn, at the beginning of the second day after Bouchard's invasion, Chetic covered my mouth with his hand until I recognized who he was.

"What!" I whispered.

"I spoke to Podnow's winatum. The one stationed up in the hills east of Paicines."

"Did Podnow send his warriors?"

"No." Chetic waited quietly as Oscar and a dozen other vaqueros gathered around us. "The People are dying. Every village obscures the sky with smoke from their funeral pyres. Many of the People are dead. Many suffer from the yellow boils and burning sweat."

I moved closer to my brother. There were cuts on his face, and his shirt was in shreds. My mind refused to comprehend the words of my brother. My sanctuary! Where could we rally the people without the Great Valley as our sanctuary? "What else?" I asked.

"I gave the winatum your message to attack." Chetic shook his head. "But the winatum told me of the sickness and said the People would not listen to such foolishness. He said many of the People are moving to the east, away from the tule marshes and into the hills. He said no one would follow your orders."

Over my shoulder and up the hill I heard Pokook call, *"Coo-cooo. Coo-cooo."*

"Pokook tells me that the eldest brother of my father is dead," I said.

"Yes." Chetic nodded. "The winatum gave me the same information. It must be true."

"My uncle now lives with the earth and seeds and animals," I said. "His spirit will always help the People."

"The People are dying," Chetic said.

"The White Others also suffer, and they can survive only if the ships return. The People will live forever." He must have flawed information. Chetic was not lying; he was simply giving me information based upon his inadequate skills. "You are wrong, my brother. The people you met were timid or ignorant of their duty."

Chetic shook his head. "The People die like grasshoppers on a fire. Your uncle is dead."

I felt a rope tighten about my chest. "Chetic, go beyond the first winatum. Speak to every village chief you can find. Tell them that we must attack the White Others now. Go to the next village and the one after. Go to the Miwok and to the people of the desert. Tell them they must join together and kill the white parasites."

My vaqueros started with a soft clapping of their hands. Oscar chanted words of encouragement. "All the warriors must attack with the next sunrise." I spoke with a louder voice as the rest of my vaqueros gathered around. "All red men must attack with every sunrise until all of the White Others have disappeared. Take two fresh horses, Chetic. The white invaders must die!"

CHAPTER 21

Winter 1805

RANCHO DEL REY WAS A MESS. Sergeants bellowed, "Retreat! Go north! The pirates are here!" Corporals countered, "Attack! Go south! Save Monterey!"

The screams from horses matched those from men. Mares slashed sharp hooves at any man that dared approach. Stallions squealed and led small harems into the woods.

I told my men to follow me in single file, uphill and away from the turmoil. When we came to a little glen filled with fruit trees, I ordered, "Build some shelters and keep quiet."

Oscar whispered to me, "What about food? Water?"

"You help get the shelters up, and I'll poke around."

It didn't take long to load two bags of Spanish beans over a docile donkey and a beef quarter on my shoulder. I smiled and waved at any inquisitive eye and moved apace back up the hill. A second trip found two iron cook pots and a few large water baskets for our use.

The misty rain thickened, cook fires smoldered under beef and beans, and most of my vaqueros started gambling. A few gazed from their meager lean-to at the scattered pine and apple trees.

Higuera stuck his head in from the rain. "Hey! Indios! I've been looking for you."

"We're trying to stay dry," I said. The clapping and belligerent shouts of contestants continued. "Why don't you come back tomorrow if the rain finally stops?"

He looked about the crowded shelter. "I'm feeling lucky today. How about making room for one more?"

"What about the pirates? Do they leave us in peace?"

Higuera shook water from his hat. "Nobody knows about the damn pirates. I'm keeping out of the way until the dons decide what they want to do."

The vaqueros went silent.

"Do you know the odd-or-even hand game?" I asked.

Higuera moved into the shelter. "Sure. Sure, I've played the silly game since I was a kid."

"Then come here, Juan Higuera. We play poorly, but join us in our silly game."

He shoved his way through the men to sit knee-to-knee with me. "Good! Here, give me the stones. I'll begin."

Juan lost his nice Spanish knife and three copper coins before Corporal Vallejo pulled the blanket door open.

"Higuera!" he yelled. "Get out of that shack!" Vallejo's horse pulled rope reins backward in a prancing dance. "Get that smart Indio of yours and follow me. Now!"

Vallejo snugged the horse still, vaulted onto his saddle, and disappeared into the mist at a full gallop.

"The boy rides pretty good," Oscar said.

"Not bad," I said.

◆

Four young Californíos joined Higuera and me to chase after Vallejo until he stopped at the ridge overlooking Monterey Village. Our horses gulped air and stood with sides heaving. Saliva covered each animal like sea foam over rocks.

Smoke boiled from one building to the next and then drifted south in a dense brown cloud. Small boats struggled through the surf and out to the anchored ships. The steady clang of hammer on metal marched up the hill and then disappeared into the rush of fire-scented wind.

"The bastards," Vallejo hissed. "Atheists."

The young men made short feints toward the pirates. "Look! They burn the church! My father's house! The customs house!" The Californíos ripped hair from their heads and turned tired horses in circles.

"Corporal!" I pointed to three men chasing a bullock into the woods. "The animal will make his stand in the next clearing."

"Yes! You're right!" Vallejo turned to his army. "The Indio has sharp eyes. Now, my friends, we'll have a little sport."

Corporal Vallejo led us on a path just inside the tree line and adjacent to a small forest meadow. We gathered in the heavy shade of a pine thicket and watched as first the bullock and then the hunters burst into the clearing. A musket exploded, and the bullock fell to his fore knees.

My first notion of the only pirate I could see at the moment was of a burned corpse—a spirit leaving a funeral pyre. The bullock's ghost distracted me for a moment as it drifted up from the tall grass and through the pine branches. I sang one of Oscar's short songs to honor the beast, then turned back to study the largest of the three pirates. He was surely cast from black adobe mud. The second was formed from beach sand, and the third, the one that held the still-smoking musket, was the perfect replica of a red-capped mushroom.

Vallejo eased his horse into the gray light and began clapping his hands in a slow, sarcastic beat. "Hurrah for the brave atheists!" he called.

The bullock twitched legs and head.

Vallejo walked his horse further into the clearing and waved his arm as if greeting the children of servants. "Such heroes!"

The three pirates turned to face us. Two screamed, "We surrender! We surrender!" The black man glanced around the clearing for an escape route, then yelled, "Shit!"

Corporal José Vallejo dismounted. "Dignity," he said. "From the Califorñios you shall receive the honor of dignity. You are undoubtedly atheists; still, I shall grant you the solace of dignity."

He took the musket from the poison-mushroom man. "Tell me, atheists, who are you? What do you want from the citizens of Alta California?"

The black man—that improbable creature—stepped around the other men and spoke. "I'm Norris, a free man of Guinea." Phlegm rolled along the surface of his purple lips. "My name is well known to you, I'm sure."

Vallejo compressed his lips. "I'm rarely bothered with the names of niggers. I assume your owner's name is Norris."

"I'm Bouchard's lieutenant," he said.

Vallejo sneered. "You, a lieutenant? Truly, before God as my witness, you are a nigger lieutenant?" He turned to his friends. "I could possibly imagine an Indio lieutenant, but never a gorilla lieutenant." He turned slowly back to Norris. "Not even an atheist, a godless pirate, would promote a nigger as a commissioned officer."

Norris balled his fists. "Nonetheless, I am a free man, and I fight with Captain Bouchard for the freedom of all subjected people!" He made a bow. "I am Lieutenant Norris at your service!"

Vallejo stared and nodded his head with a tiny rocking motion. "Tell me, black man, why do you attack us?"

"Attack? We simply wanted water and wood. When we called for permission to anchor in your harbor, you opened fire with your bloody cannon." He took a step forward, and two of Vallejo's young men moved quickly to block him with guns at the ready.

Vallejo held up a hand. "Hold." The corporal adjusted his hat and nodded to the second pirate.

A tiny man, whose head was not much above Vallejo's chest, stepped forward. "Thank you, sir! I thank the Holy Mother for your rescue from this black monster!" He dropped to his knees with both hands held toward Vallejo. "Please, sir. Protect us from this black heathen."

"Rescue?" Vallejo peered at the little man as if he were an exotic bug. "What is your name?"

"Esteemed sir. I am Nicolas Cavarria of Peru." He gave a quick nod of his head to Vallejo; "A clerk who survived the destruction of. . ."

"Enough." Vallejo turned from the groveling Peruvian to the third pirate. "And you? An Americaño, I presume."

"Yes sir. How could you tell?"

"The speed of your surrender was my first clue." Vallejo gave a small sardonic bow. "Also, those lumpy shoulders, green eyes, and the size of your hands all provided the necessary information. So tell, what are you called, my Americaño—another lieutenant?"

"Joseph Chapman." He ventured a small smile toward Vallejo. "That Bouchard fellow—he took me from where I was working in the

Sandwich Islands. I'm a blacksmith and a carpenter." His smile became more insistent. "Could you be using such skills?"

Vallejo shrugged his shoulders. "It is for the old men to decide."

Chapman spoke again. His Spanish was abominable. "One other thing you fellas should know. This Bouchard thinks you Califorñios will join him in fighting against the king of Spain."

José Vallejo was truly puzzled. "It is not possible for Christians and atheists to join together against God's king."

"Well, now." Chapman extended his right hand toward the ocean. "It seems like a lot of folks want to cut free from Spain. Bouchard's got people from Brazil and Peru and Argentina, and they all talk like they want to start up their own country."

Vallejo was speechless.

Chapman leaned forward. "How do things stand between you folks and the Spanish king?"

Vallejo hissed. "Never will we oppose our God-protected king!"

"Good, that's what me and Cavarria was hoping. You fellas not throwing in with Bouchard, that is. We've both had about enough of him and his niggers."

Norris moved two steps and struck the redheaded man with his fist. "Bouchard will eat your balls for breakfast!"

"Enough!" Vallejo pulled a pistol from his belt and held it at Norris's head. "Bring some rope, quickly now."

We bound Norris with three turns about his arms and waist and then secured the rope to Higuera's saddle. The other two were tethered loosely about the waist, one to the other, and Vallejo led our troop up the first hill at a slow walk.

It was dusk before we gained Rancho del Rey. The white soldiers still yelled into the wind and pulled swords to slash at phantom pirates, but the bells and horses were finally quiet. The rain had stopped. Stars emerged between scudding clouds with the brilliance of candles at a midnight Mass.

—◆—

I met with Lieutenant Norris on the first night of his captivity. It was a simple matter. The guard slept soundly, the moon was full, and Norris spoke Spanish.

"Black man, can you hear me?"

"Yes," he answered. "Pull the blanket from my head. I can barely breathe."

I tugged the wool blanket from his head, and we stared at each other. Norris's nostrils emerged like gaping holes from his widely spaced cheekbones. He had mustard eyes and lips as thick as ship's rope.

"Thank you, Indio." He smiled, and his fat yellow teeth absorbed the moonlight. "Now, Indio, cut the rope from my hands."

"Not yet." I moved closer. He smelled like a stillborn lamb covered with blood and wet wool and afterbirth. "Say again. Why are you pirates here in Alta California?"

The smile disappeared. "Bouchard will free all slaves. He will destroy the Spanish and . . ."

"Stop!" I waved my left hand before his face and pulled a scorpion from his cavernous nostrils with my right. "Answer my question."

Norris laughed at me. "Untie my hands, Indio. I'll show you better tricks." He spat against the wall of his chicken-coop prison. "Even in this dark shed I can see your hands. You need a better teacher."

"Why are you here?"

"We were hungry and thirsty."

I took my knife and cut a clump of black wool from behind his left ear. "Why are you here?"

"To find allies in our war against the Spanish."

"The Californios? You wish to enlist these white men in your war?"

"Bouchard decides who is friend or foe—only Bouchard."

"The Californios support the Spanish king, and they would never join Bouchard in such a venture."

"Fine; so be it. Bouchard will find more suitable allies."

"Bouchard has defeated the Californios at Monterey. Now what will he do?"

"We'll take what we need and leave. Bouchard has no interest in this place; he only wants food, water, and allies."

"I can serve as ally to Bouchard."

"Cut my rope, Indio, then we'll talk of allies."

"Together, Bouchard's pirates and my army of Indios, we can destroy the Californios." I felt my good plans flying astray. "I must show my ideas to Bouchard. I want to find an agreement between two allies that will benefit both of us in this war."

"Cut my rope, Indio, not my hair. I'll take you to see Bouchard." Norris squirmed around to hold his bound arms toward me. I'll make sure that he listens to your plan, Indio."

"Not yet, Norris. First I'll speak to Bouchard, then we'll discuss your freedom."

"Ha!" Norris squirmed closer to me. "Captain Bouchard will never talk with you if you approach him without my support. He keeps four Kanaka around him, and those warriors never sleep. They'll kill you, Indio."

"I am tipne to the People."

"You're a puffed-up savage."

"Tell me where Bouchard sleeps."

"Bouchard never sleeps. His Kanaka guards never sleep. They both love to kill, and your blood will make them very happy." Norris studied the willow-pole wall of the chicken shed and then looked up through the torn ceiling to the moon. "You'll never meet Bouchard unless I come with you."

Norris had the flat black face of the white owl. It was an exceptionally ugly face, a devil face. Maybe the Californios weren't so bad after all. They were stupid and lazy, but possibly a better choice than this devil and his evil spirits.

"Listen, black man—I'll release you from the ropes."

"Good. I'll tell Bouchard that you are a very smart savage. An ugly savage, but smart."

I cut another gob of wool from his head. "Do exactly what I say."

"Certainly, Indio; you are tipne to the People, whatever that means." He gave me a snort.

Brother Coyote counseled against the act, but I ignored him and cut the ropes. Norris sat quietly for a long moment.

"We'll crawl through the door," I said. "Then we'll move to the left. Keep low and follow me through the apple orchard."

"What of the guard?" he asked.

"He's asleep. Full of brandy."

"I'll kill him," Norris said.

"No. He's young and stupid, and he'll sleep until dawn. He's a rabbit, not a warrior."

Norris made one rub of his wrists and then slipped past me as quickly as a weasel. The soldier lay with his face on a pile of straw. Norris put his foot on the soldier's neck, grabbed the man's hair, and snapped the head back. There was the sound of a stick breaking but nothing more.

"We often snare rabbits in Guinea," Norris whispered. "It's pleasant to hear the neck break so quickly." The black devil pushed a hand through his ragged hair. "Now, let us go and see Captain Bouchard."

"Follow me," I said. "I have two horses waiting."

———

Two Kanaka warriors stood behind a white man. The three men stared at me with bright-eyed intensity, like three prairie falcons hovering over a single lark.

The leader spoke—a skinny white man with bright white teeth. "What's his name, Norris?"

"Tippy-something. Ask him yourself, Captain; he speaks good Spanish."

"I am José Jesus, war chief of the San Juan Bautista Indios and tipne of the Yokuts."

The white man, the Kanaka, and Norris joined in a humorless bleating.

"Which is it, José Jesus?" The captain fiddled with a small dagger. "Are you with the Spanish dons, or what?"

"Are you Bouchard?"

Norris spoke for the white man. "This is Captain Peter Corney, commander of the frigata *Chita* and second to Bouchard."

"I will speak with Bouchard."

"You'll speak with Bouchard, will you?" Captain Corney struck the table with the flat of his hand. "Enough, Indio! No one speaks to Hippolyte de Bouchard unless I seek his indulgence. He would feed both of us to his Kanaka if you rushed into his office unannounced."

Corney's two Kanaka warriors stuck out their enormous tongues at me. "Blaat!" they said.

"What do you want, José Jesus? What can you offer the great Bouchard?"

"I want the Spanish out of our land. I offer the pirate Bouchard the service of my warriors. We can provide both warriors and supplies, now and into the future."

"What about honey?" Captain Corney asked.

"Yes. Spanish honey from Spanish bees."

"Tell me, how many warriors are there under your command?"

"I can provide at least five hundred, maybe twice that number."

"A good-sized army." Corney combed both hands through his sand-colored beard. "We've routed these miserable Spanish outcasts with three hundred troops and a few dozen cannons. Tell me, war chief, what's keeping your big army from doing the same as our little army?"

"We need cannons and guns," I said. "My warriors need a single victory over the Spanish, and then they will believe in themselves. If Bouchard will give us guns, we will destroy a common enemy, and the red men will reclaim their land."

Corney gave a bitter laugh. "I see. I see," he said. "You want Bouchard to chase the Spanish from Alta California, and then you want Bouchard to give the cannons and land of the white man to the Indios." He pulled himself from the chair and placed both hands on the desk. "Am I correct, Indio?"

"Certainly you are correct, Captain Corney. But listen to the benefit for both of us. It is our land that we will reclaim. Together, Bouchard and my army of Indios, we will chase away the Spanish and establish a permanent alliance."

"I think not, José Jesus. The Indio will never conquer the white man. The Indio will never fathom the complexities of civilized existence." Captain Corney turned toward Norris. "Indios and Guinea men—they're all savages. Slaves or savages, that is."

The black man moved slowly, like a cougar through tall grass. The smile remained on his fat lips until he was nose-to-nose with the white man, and then there was no smile from either white or black. "This is your first voyage with Bouchard." Norris's voice had no rough edges, only a soft purr. "Do not presume that his ignorance runs as deep as yours."

The Kanaka giggled like two Spanish girls. Captain Corney motioned. "Follow me," he said.

———

Bouchard was a small, thin Frenchman with a scraggly black beard and black eyes. He tried his rattlesnake stare with me, but I held his gaze.

"Do you know Ortegas, the smuggler?"

We continued our battle of eyes. "South of Point Concepción," I said.

"We will leave Monterey in five or six days. First we'll stop off and relieve Ortegas of his misbegotten gold, and then we'll sail south to Santa Barbara. I invite you to join us, José Jesus. If we defeat Ortegas and his band of outlaws, then I will talk with you about a partnership."

I dropped my eyes to the floor.

Bouchard snickered like a skinny horse that had just thrown his rider. "So, Indio, shall we see you at the Ortegas rancho?" He looked over at Norris. "I'd bet not. How about you, Guinea man? What do you think of this man?"

"He's an ugly little demon. Ugly and prissy, I'd say."

"Now, now, my handsome lieutenant, what is there about his face or character that offends you so much?"

Norris studied me for a long moment. "Notice the thin, bloodless lips of the Indio and the nose better suited to slice bread than draw breath. He seems more a bad dream than a person with any spark of life."

"Hmmmm." Bouchard joined in the study of my face. "The eyes, Norris—are they indeed piss-yellow?"

"I'd say they're more the yellow of a cowardly fox or that wild dog of this country."

"The coyote?" Bouchard suggested.

"Yes." Norris replied. "Coyote eyes, for certain."

Bouchard gave me a slight nod. "So, Coyote Eyes, will you bring an army of wild dogs to the ranch of Ortega?"

"My men will attack from the east and north," I said.

"So, my Indio, do you know the lay of the land?"

"Yes." I let the little man rustle some papers on his desk. "First, my men will scare Ortegas with some yelling and a few arrows over his stone wall. As soon as my scouts see your ships, we'll attack in force." I sat down in a large wooden chair across the desk from Bouchard. "My army will secure the southern road so none can escape, then we'll apply constant pressure along the entire perimeter. Ortegas will see only my men, and yours can land unopposed and with dry feet."

"Not so bad for an Indio."

"My vaqueros will herd cattle and horses for your use." I turned to Corney. "We'll bring five hides full of honey."

"Excellent," Bouchard said. "Ortegas's brandy and Spanish honey. Fine companions on cold, wet nights."

"You take the brandy," Norris said. "I'll take the daughters of Ortegas."

"Fair enough," Bouchard said. "If the Indio shows up with his army, I'll have an ally, my men will have a fiesta, and you, my esteemed lieutenant, will have first choice of the women."

"First and second choice both," Norris said.

"Granted," Bouchard said.

I stood from the uncomfortable chair. "We're agreed, then. In five or six days, we'll meet again." I took a step toward the door. "Our armies will meet at Ortegas's rancho."

"Don't be late, my ugly friend," Bouchard said. "I don't want to hunt through the tule reeds for any Indio rabbits."

Norris brushed the back of my neck with a gentle flick. "Those Spanish ladies are waiting for me, José Jesus. Don't disappoint them."

CHAPTER 22

Winter 1805

"HIGUERA!" I DUCKED UNDER THE cowhide door of his shack. "The black man escaped last night."

"I know! I know!" He slapped a hand on his leg. "The bastard killed young Pablo Olaya! The nigger bastard!"

"Ahh, you heard the news." I squatted on my heels. "These are difficult times for you Californios."

Private Higuera flared his nostrils. "Trouble follows after you, José Jesus." He squinted his left eye. "Where've you been? Twice I chased around and couldn't find you either time."

"My men told me you were looking for me."

"Where've you been? The black man is missing, and an innocent boy is dead."

"I've been praying, Private Higuera."

He hit me along my jaw with his fist. When I stood, he hit me in the face with alternate blows from both hands, and then he pushed me to the ground to kick my ribs. "Where were you praying?"

I rolled into a shell of arms and legs and spoke to the dirt. "I was west of here, sir, on a small hill."

Higuera kicked me again. "Liar!"

I uncurled and sat upright to look at Higuera. "From the hill of my prayers I saw flames to the south. Possibly it was a building of the Califorñios, sir."

"It is the refugees—their cook fires, nothing more." He moved to kick again.

"No! It was a building, sir, and no mistake." I wiped blood from my face. "Some of my vaqueros were talking this morning of many ranchos burning." I struggled to stand. My ribs and face hurt, but there were no broken bones. "Tell me, sir, how many rumors have you heard about such crimes?"

Higuera picked up his wool poncho. "Listen, Indio. I'll put you in the ground, right next to Pablo, if I find that you helped the nigger." He pulled it down over his head. "No matter what the facts, Pablo will go to heaven, but you will go straight to hell!"

I spit in my hand to clean blood from my jaw.

"There are only your rumors of rancho burning, Indio, and none from men of God."

My head and ribs and gut throbbed with pain. There was nothing Higuera could hear from me, and I stood before him as a silent observer.

"Let's go." He stepped toward the door. "I've got some bread in my saddle."

On that second day of the pirate victory, Higuera and I sat on our horses and watched as they butchered sheep and cattle. When the west wind started to gust, we watched the pirates roam through the buildings to steal what they could, then burn them to empty shells of ash. On the third day after my meeting with Bouchard, the pirates anchored both ships above Playa del Brigida, and during the next three days they ferried water, food, wood, and loot from shore to ship.

The pirates saw us clearly enough, up on the hill, but they ignored us. From dawn to dusk Higuera noted each act of destruction and reported to his commander from tallies made of rope and straw.

"What are the rope knots?" I asked.

"They are trips taken by the little boats to the frigate."

"The pieces of straw?"

"Buildings burned."

"Would it help if I compiled a written report for your commander?"

Higuera flicked his fingers toward me and bulged the muscles of his jaw. "Quiet, Indio. No more with your ideas from the Devil."

⸺

Each night I rode down to Trés Piños, but neither Chetic nor Oscar appeared at our designated tree. Nothing from my messengers, so at each dawn I knocked on Higuera's shack to hand him a basket of acorn mush and then find and saddle his horse. On the sixth night, with Monterey destroyed and the pirate ships ready to depart, both Chetic and Oscar sat waiting for me near the second of the three huge pine trees. Fog obscured the stars, and there was no wind.

"The Paleuyami sent a few warriors, but no one else," Chetic said.

"They are good neighbors to the Tachi," I said.

"The Paleuyami burned a single rancho to the ground."

I waited for more information and finally asked, "What happened with the other Yokuts villages?"

Oscar spoke to our little fire. "The swamps are bad," he said.

Tears streamed past Chetic's new cheek tattoos. "The white man's fever has taken people without number." He coughed. "Many of the villages are empty."

Nettles filled my balls. "The Tachi?"

"Empty. There is no one in the village to mourn your elder uncle."

Stones clogged my throat. "No women or children hiding nearby?"

Chetic moved to touch my knee. "I'm told that some of the Tachi are living in the eastern hills. Many of the People have moved to higher land."

"The swamps are bad," Oscar said. "The white man has turned them into a haven for evil spirits."

"No! The wetlands are beautiful and nourishing in every season and through every moment of the day."

"Bad," Oscar said.

Chetic leaned between us. "He may be correct, José Jesus. Those who live near the slow-moving water die in greater numbers than those who live in the hills."

"My brother and friend, is there no end to your bad news?"

"There are only a few warriors remaining in the Great Valley, my brother, and none will attack the invaders. Neither the Yokuts nor the Miwok are able to attack the Spanish or pirates or invaders of any description."

I joined Oscar in moving my head and shoulders in a rocking motion. "All is lost," I moaned.

"Now the Great Valley people and the Ohlone can cry together." Oscar tossed tobacco crumbs into the air. "Our ancestors wander about with no home." A single tear coursed the ruts of Oscar's face. "All is lost."

I followed the tobacco trail up into the stars. "The pirates will leave, and the Spanish will stay," I said.

"It makes no difference who stays and who leaves," Oscar said. "We are lost souls with no guides to Tipiknits Pahn."

———◆———

On the final day of their occupation, the pirates destroyed the gardens and orchards and torched every remaining building in Monterey. They waved to the Californios as they rolled through the surf in their tiny boats. A sharp northwest wind came up during midafternoon, and it carried the beautiful cloud-ships quickly into the incessant fog bank.

On the evening that Norris lost his bet, I sent Chetic to Mission Santa Clara. "Find the alcalde and give him my message," I said.

"What's his name?"

"Hineh. You know him as my cousin."

"What do you want of him?"

"Describe what has happened here in Monterey and ask him if we can talk together."

"That's it? You want to talk with your cousin?"

"When you return, I also want you to tell me everything you see at Santa Clara."

———◆———

Chetic returned after one day.

"Any message?" I asked.

"No message and no kindness of any sort."

"What did he say?"

"Nothing; he sent one of his neophytes to chase me away." Chetic shrugged his shoulders. "With merely a quick glance, I can't report any changes in Mission Santa Clara from the last visit we made."

———◆———

Chief Miguel sent a winatum to see me.

"What does the chief want?" I asked.

"He wants you to do nothing; just shut up and behave like a tame Indio."

"Miguel wants me to do nothing?"

"No more acting like war chief and no more bothering a busy alcalde in Santa Clara."

"Is he talking about my cousin Hineh?"

"Yes."

"Tell me, sir—is there anything else from our village chief?"

"Miguel says to tell you that the Califorñios are capable of doing something extraordinarily stupid. You must be patient with them and nudge them gently in the correct direction." The winatum was a stern-faced old man. "Chief Miguel says don't do nothing. Just watch the silly fools and do what you are told."

"Anything else, sir?"

"Keep your eyes down and don't make the Califorñios nervous."

<hr>

All was lost. My Tachi kin were lost in a remote land. My ancestors were lost without the comfort of their beautiful tule country. It was also true that the Califorñios had lost their most important village to an ephemeral band of pirates. And that Norris had lost his opportunity to make sport with two women. But nettles again filled my stomach because the most significant loss was Bouchard, an ally in our war against the Spanish king. All was lost because of my stupidity in dealing with Bouchard. Five hundred warriors promised when five was stretching the number certain to follow my orders.

Coyote poked his snout into my crotch. "Listen, stupid Kiyu. Talk with me before making any further promises."

My dead father whispered, "Kiyu, you must talk with me before making any further promises to the invaders."

The oldest of my uncles whispered, "Kiyu, you are the chosen one. Save the People. In order for you to save the people you must talk with me before making promises to the invader."

Shup remained silent.

On the morning after the pirates left Monterey, I sent Sedit and our son, along with two dozen village women and their children, to the eastern hills of the Great Valley. Chetic and two of my vaqueros served to guide and protect the women.

"Find some of the Tachi and join them with Chief Miguel's villagers. Make sure there is a good source of water and oak trees available for this new village."

"What shall I say to the Tachi chief?" Chetic asked.

"You and Sedit make all decisions together. Make an effort to encourage other Indios seeking refuge to linger in your village. Let them rest until they decide to stay or continue to search for a safe home."

"Sedit is a good antu doctor and can provide solace for the problems that trouble most travelers."

I frowned. "Your sister is not an antu doctor, but she does have kind words and a few herbs. Tell her that the women of Miguel's village will prepare food and feed those who are too weak to help themselves. Tell these women that except for Sedit, they will provide children for those warriors without wives."

"How long shall I stay with my sister and her village?"

"Help them survive for the next few seasons. Also, Brother, keep me informed with every change that you observe among the villagers."

"We will leave today."

"Stay in the lodge of my wife and son. Protect them with your life."

"Certainly, without second thought."

"Take a string of extra horses, and use the most gentle to carry the older women and young children."

"What will you do, my brother?"

"I will keep my eyes on the dirt and do exactly what the Californios tell me."

CHAPTER 23

Spring 1805

EVERYONE WORKED FROM GRAY WET dawn until gray wet dusk. Even the soldiers and merchants and priests worked. The white invaders and tame Indios worked side by side. The governor and his old men and their sons all turned their hands and faces black with soot. Within the first hour after sunset, we all collapsed into sleep.

On the third day after the departure of Bouchard the pirate, the same fussy little sergeant who first met us in Monterey sent Higuera and me to retrieve Chapman and Cavarria from Rancho del Rey. During the trip I queried soldiers who were guarding missions and ranchos, but none were worried about any attack from the wild Indios. I asked a few refugee women if they knew of any trouble caused by the Indios, but they all waved their hands and said, "Look with your own eyes, Indio slave. Here at San Carlos and over at Mission San Antonio there are no problems. We have no problems whatsoever."

When Higuera and I returned with the prisoners, the fussy sergeant told Chapman to set up a forge and for me to act as his assistant. He pointed to Cavarria. "Come with me, little man. The governor has need for a clerk."

"What about me?" Higuera said.

"Report to Corporal Vallejo. He needs help setting the foundation for his father's home."

"Send the Indio to haul rocks. I'll work with the red-haired American."

"José Vallejo wants your strong back for the rocks and the clever Indio to work with this foreigner."

Higuera turned red. "What! Do you reward Indios and foreigners with the easy work, while a true believer hauls rocks? Never!"

"Move, all of you," the fussy sergeant said.

I pumped the bellows as Chapman made hinges from syrupy red metal. We pulled the whipsaw through pitch-oozing pine logs and took turns in the pit, with wood dust and bark tumbling into our eyes. We teamed to produce clean straight planks and squared timbers for the reconstruction of Monterey. At first, Chapman stumbled along with a few Spanish nouns and pointing with his hands, but soon he took comfort in teaching me the American words for tools and opinions.

"Where are the wives and children?" Chapman asked.

"They find comfort with the padres at the missions or with relatives who owned ranchos in the area."

"Ahhh," said Chapman. "So it is the absence of feminine comfort that requires the old men to sleep with the young Indio women? Yes?"

"They steal women from the missions of Santa Clara, San José, and San Juan Bautista," I said.

"They seem remarkably attractive young women." After a glance into my eyes, Chapman added, "And they are also remarkably good workers."

———◆———

Chief Miguel gathered an additional forty women and children from his village and sent them off with a few vaqueros as protectors and guides to find Sedit and her village. I sent Brother Coyote to serve as Sedit's helpmate.

"I'm a good server." Coyote chuckled.

"Be careful with your intentions," I warned. "Sedit carries a very sharp Spanish knife and would shorten your penis if you made the wrong move."

"I'm very quick," said Coyote.

"I'd bet on Sedit's smile at your bloody cock," I said.

———◆———

Shortly after the New Year, the Mexican government sent a new governor to Monterey. Manuel Sola was his name, and he quickly ordered everyone to stand in front of his nearly completed mansion. With a fine clear voice and Castilian accent, he made his first speech in Alta California.

"We are civilized men of Spain," he said. "We are the administrators of God's will on earth. Therefore, we gentlemen of Spain, with my authority vested from the all-powerful government of Mexico, hereby declare that all the bestial tasks of life must be delegated to the lowborn."

With his simple proclamation delivered, the stone walls and foundations for Monterey were thereafter completed by the mestizo privates of his army, who delegated to the Indio slaves every mean and difficult task. The tame Indios cut and hauled wood and raised the walls of Monterey. Chapman and I made locks for the doors of Monterey and locks for the arms of the prisoners of Monterey and also metal braces for the buildings of Monterey.

The gentlemen of Monterey drank brandy from clay pots and filled their whiskers with beef fat, and they ran giggling to the huts of silent girls. The gentlemen cheered the proper horses at the races and cheered at the victory of bulls over bears. The mestizos complained of their food, watched the sporting events, and kept their eyes on the Indios.

When, at long last, the white women and children returned to Monterey, I led the remaining San Juan Bautista vaqueros back to Miguel's village. The whisky spirit was powerful, for he enticed some of my men into his clutches before we topped the first rise of hills. Some additional number of my warriors sat their horses as vacant-eyed shadows of their days at Mission San Juan Bautista. All my remaining men still called themselves vaqueros and struggled with the proper jokes, but now there was a difference, for few were truly vaqueros anymore. Those special few, the ones who rode with squared shoulders and still called me Tipne Man—together, we surveyed the land as would any of our black-eyed predators.

Chief Miguel was sitting in the first row of benches. A slight breeze moved through the open door and stirred dust that moved past Miguel and deep into the church sanctuary. I stood at his shoulder until he moved to make room for me to sit.

"We've got to get out of this damn mission," he said.

"What do you have in mind?" I asked.

"Let's look around the east side of the Great Valley, and if there's no other option, then we have to find someplace up in the hills."

"Why?"

"The padres are dead, and there's a bunch of farmers coming here from down south. They're going to take all the mission land." Miguel stared at Christ on the cross, upside down and on the floor. Good, dry firewood for the new tenants. "My winatum tells me these men are mean and stupid. Worse than the damn padres." He waited until another dust devil settled. "What about you, José Jesus? Are you coming along with me or not?"

"I've got a few ideas to think about, so I'll stay around here for a while."

Chief Miguel looked at his toes. "What about Sedit?"

"My wife and brother are trying to get a new village going."

"Okay. Good. Those two are busy with a big job." Miguel looked over to my toes. "What about you, Tipne Man? Where are you headed?"

"I need some time to smoke tanai and call Brother Coyote back to my side."

"The tanai is okay; that Coyote is trouble."

"He is my spirit brother."

"Spirit trouble."

Miguel was anxious about something. Eyes all over the place, with straight lines on his head where they didn't belong.

"How's your stock of tanai?" I asked. "You got any left from those Utes?"

"Sure, I'll send some over tomorrow." Now he finally looked me in the eye. "Just stay away from that damn whiskey, my friend."

I gave Miguel what he wanted. "Why don't you join what's left of your flock with Sedit's village? You and Chetic and Sedit could make some good things happen up there in the hills."

Miguel nodded as if the thought had never passed his mind. "It's not a bad idea, Jose. I'll study the situation." His eyes went to wandering again. "If I can find her little village, that is."

"When you do find Sedit, and if it is okay with her, why don't you just send Chetic to find me? I'll hang around either here or over in the pinnacle caves for a season or two."

"What about you and Sedit?"

"We understand each other. Sedit has her job with the new village, and I have mine with the invaders." I looked Chief Miguel in the eye. "We'll see each other when we can, and we'll exchange winatums when we can't."

"And you, José Jesus—will you and your boys get yourselves into more trouble?"

"No need to even ask, Miguel. My men are all vaqueros, after all."

Miguel smiled. "What do you have in mind, you and those three other idiots?"

"Six idiots in sum total," I said

Miguel gave a small nod of his head. "Let me know if you need some help," he said.

"Don't worry," I said. "We're vaqueros."

CHAPTER 24

1806–1807

I DRIFTED SOUTH OF SAN Juan Bautista, south through bizarre pinnacles and caves, and then further south to the marshlands surrounding a small lake at the very end of the Great Valley. Just me— I was down to an army of one. Blackbirds in raucous chorus invaded the gray fog of my mind. The delicious smell of red and white *hoco'm ci-tat* sifted through both nostrils. I found a shaded cove upon the lake and slept each night in dreamless comfort from one full moon to the next.

During the day there were frogs to gig or ducks to snare and sweet water to drink. The season, dominated by a blanket of molten heat, was followed by pleasant showers of rain, then cold rain, fog, and eventually brilliant mats of flowers, all in proper order.

When the first dreams interrupted my sleep, I walked north into the lovely Great Valley. The sheltered gullies were still green from the rains of late spring, and the heat was tolerable. Chetic was waiting for me at the first river of any consequence, as if by some previous agreement, and we traveled northeastward toward Sedit.

"I see you, my wife," I said.

Sedit stared at the packed earth of her lodge. "Our son is dead." Her head leaned on my shoulder when I sat next to her, but she said not another word.

Through the day and into the black night we sat quiet and still. Mice poked about the roof thatch with their quick movements and niggling sounds. I took Sedit's hand and held it. Wind whispered through the walls. In the far distance a child cried, and my wife echoed the lonely sob into my shoulder. Pokook remained silent, and Brother Coyote stayed curled in a tight ball at my feet.

The sun was well above the eastern mountains before Sedit stirred. "I'll start the fire," she said. "We'll have tea and mush."

"Are you ready to tell me about the death of our son?"

"Yes."

"I will listen, wife of mine."

"As you know, my husband, our son Carlos was an odd person, nothing like any of his peers."

"Tell me about our son Carlos, my beautiful wife."

Sedit stared at my knee and let each word fall onto the packed earth of her lodge. "He did not play soccer or learn to gamble."

"How did he spend his time, my wife?

"He read your book from the padre, over and over until he received three other books taken from an abandoned Spanish rancho."

"Carlos studied my book of questions, and then he acquired three additional books. Am I correct in this sequence?"

"Yes."

"How did our son learn to read?"

"There were passages that you read aloud to me during the time of your cooking for the padres." She continued as I remained silent. "I practiced reading the same words when you were absent, and when

Carlos showed interest, we teamed to expand the words that we mastered."

"What then?"

"It was not long after his name day that Carlos began teaching me new words, and soon I was distracted by my duties, and our son continued on his own. He spent every moment of daylight with his heaven-sent treasures, puzzling them out and cherishing them."

"Did you encourage such behavior?"

"It was Chief Miguel who provided the new books, and it was also Miguel who gave our son the protection he needed to study the books."

"I must thank Chief Miguel for his kind service."

"Miguel is also dead." Sedit lowered her head. "One morning he was busy with his duties, and at dusk Miguel was covered with red pustules."

"Is there no end to our misery?"

Sedit was silent for a long stretch and then continued with the story of our son. "The women called him witch, and the children teased him as a boy with two spirits, but Miguel called a halt to their bad manners."

"Did Chief Miguel spend much time listening to our son read the books?"

"Almost every day the chief listened to Carlos read, and often he interrupted our son with questions or requests for information derived from the books."

"I must thank the spirit of the chief for his protection of our son."

"There was no sense of duty in his actions, my husband, for Miguel was always warmed by the charm of our son."

I emptied my basket of tea. "How did our son die?"

Now Sedit looked at me for the first time. "He was lost in a blizzard this past winter. We searched for him through the winter and spring, but never a hint of his body did we find."

I leaned toward my wife. "Warriors frequently survive winter storms. Do you see a possibility that he somehow survived the cold and was rescued by strangers?"

Sedit managed a wan smile. "Our son was not a warrior. Your Uncle Shup would have an edge over Carlos in surviving a horrendous storm. Snow accumulated at a depth unknown by the Miwok elders of these hills."

"Our son is dead, and I am alive?"

"Yes."

The earthy odor of spring flowers, far past their prime, seeped through the door of Sedit's lodge. "How many people survive in this village of yours?"

"A handful of your Tachi survive here in this village, and there are possibly a hundred more kinsmen scattered within a three-day walk."

"Do all the villages suffer?"

"Some count fewer dead than others, but most are poor remnants of their past."

"Do the People share their grief with the strangers among them?"

Sedit turned to stare directly into my eyes. "Each village is afraid of the other. Each family judges a neighbor as responsible for sending evil spirits to kill a husband or child." She held my hand and kissed each finger. "Many of the village elders are dead. Those who live seem to drift through life like sticks on a river."

"The People must celebrate a Lonewis," I said. "Our son is dead, and we must celebrate his life."

Sedit sniffled, and Chetic turned away from me.

"Listen to me, both of you."

Sedit blew her nose while Chetic crawled on hands and knees to sit in front of us.

"Those of the People who survive in this world must help those who have died. We must help the dead find peace in Tipiknits Pahn."

Sedit put her head on my chest. "They are afraid of every neighbor and will never leave the security of their lodges."

"I am tipne doctor for the People. The God of all spirits demands that I help both the dead and the living." A large obstacle clogged my throat. "I left my son in the care of others when he was alive, now I must assist my son in death."

"They will kill you, just as they killed your father," Sedit said.

"My father was killed by the People because he was unable to heal them of the white invaders' diseases. It was a death that he accepted, and if the People and the strangers among us decide on my death, I shall follow in my father's steps."

Chetic began to clap his hands as if he were a village elder. Sedit moved from my chest and joined her twin brother with a slow and steady beat.

"The People will die if I fail them. The Great Hairy God of the invaders will rule the Great Valley if I fail them. A Lonewis will secure peace for both the living and dead."

"We will help you," Sedit said.

"We will die with you," Chetic said.

CHAPTER 25

Fall 1808

IT WAS THE SMALLEST LONEWIS IN the memory of all elders. Pokook cooed and cooed and brought remnants from bedraggled villages of the hills and valley to Sedit's village. A melancholy stupor covered the entire encampment. Visitors wandered about the village lanes and vast oak groves in a listless manner. None could laugh or work, and an awkward number died the death of a sudden and ferocious fever. The antu doctors were helpless to provide a viable cure for either death or despair.

The Yokuts and Miwok complained of witches and evil spirits and bad magic. The tame warriors who had escaped the padres or ranchos stood apart from the rest. Many strangers among us carried whiskey in goatskin containers and red pustules on their penises. They did not know how to grieve for the dead, and they smiled through stiff lips at our songs.

On the first day of the Lonewis, I told Podnow's story. It was the long, complicated recital of how he had organized the Yokuts and Miwok against the White Others. At first the People and the Miwok and the tame warriors gave me only their polite attention, but slowly, as Podnow's skill became evident, the elders added tentative smiles and small hoots of encouragement.

After I finished describing the first Lonewis of our alliance, all the men and women and children beat the ground with fists until I raised my arms for silence. I felt the Lonewis fire burn away my own sadness for Podnow's death. The flames purged my eyes of tears for my son and for my dead vaqueros, so I danced about the central fire. The participants saw me imitate Podnow's big belly and big ass. They saw his black and white stripes from head to toe and heard his boisterous laughter.

"You are the chosen People! The God of all spirits adores his People!" Podnow spoke through my mouth. "Listen to me, for I am the greatest tipne doctor of the People. Listen, for I speak to you from this land of spirits. Listen to a message from the spirits. Listen!"

The Yokuts and the Miwok and the strangers among us all shouted, "Speak! Speak!"

I lowered my voice so all were forced to listen carefully. "Yes, the white invaders are strong, but listen! The Yokuts, together with the Miwok and the strangers among us, are stronger."

Now the foot drum boomed, and the cocoon rattles shook. Young men joined, with wild gyrations, to circle me as I danced slowly about the great fire. After six turns I stopped and waited for the silence to return.

"The spirits of our dead relatives live in Tipiknits Pahn, but deep in the nether world, in the world below, live the crumpled, twisted spirits of the invaders. They limp through scorched hills, and there is no water for the shades of the invaders. There are no oak trees or tule reeds in their blasted world. The spirits of the invaders never smile, and they are unable to shed tears. They look about in the deep shadows of their minds for guidance. 'Where are my ancestors?' they wail. 'How can I find peace?' they scream."

I stepped back into the shadows to watch the young and old dance and hug and sing. The pall of melancholy evaporated. The possibility of life bubbled into the cadence of foot and voice. The brightest planet of the heavens fell beneath the horizon before I stepped forward and again raised my arms for silence.

I felt Podnow move my lips. "The white invaders must leave our land or they must die." The People cheered. "Listen to me, for I am the voice of Podnow, who was the greatest tipne of the People." The People cheered. "The invaders cannot survive in the land of our ancestors because they travel without the spirits of their ancestors. The spirits of our ancestors created the Great Valley for the Yokuts and the Miwok. From the time beyond memory our ancestors have fashioned the essential harmony for us to share the Great Valley. Now the Yokuts and the Miwok and the strangers among us must chase the invaders from our land. We must feed those invaders who stay in our land to the magpies."

All cheered.

I walked slowly around the perimeter of the fire, first at a normal pace and then with Uncle Shup's rolling badger gait. Six times I toured the circle, running, stumbling, and walking on my hands. All assembled howled with laughter as I told them of Shup and his great triumph with the Wintu others. I described his prowess with young women, his hunting instincts, and how he could knock leaves from the trees with his voice. All were lies, of course, but doubly appreciated by the elders who remembered my little humpbacked uncle. I stared into the blue flames and told everyone that Uncle Shup was a great teacher and that I had been his inadequate student.

When the flames flickered into empty blackness and a caul of smoke covered the People, I looked up toward Tipiknits Pahn. "Shup," I said. "I did not hear you through the silence of our sojourn."

Silence, then in the far distance Pokook called in his sweet voice: Once. Twice. Six times Pokook called. *Coo-cooo. Coo-cooo. Coo-cooo.*

Six times Uncle Shup called in his boisterous yelp, "I forgive you, I forgive you. . ."

———◆———

On the next morning of the Lonewis, during the quiet time when all must listen for direction from the spirits, the Yandanchi chief and his surviving elders sat with me.

"The People have no leader." The chief sipped willow bark tea. "Your eldest uncle is dead, and his son Hineh lives with the White Others."

"You speak the truth," Sedit said.

"José Jesus, you must serve all the villages as supreme tipne," Chetic said.

"You are Podnow's voice," Sedit said.

"You are the only one," the young Yandanchi chief said. "The others who seek Podnow's position will misuse his awesome power."

The elders thumped the hard dirt in agreement.

———◆———

There were six other tipne who aspired to leadership over all of the Yokuts and Miwok and strangers among us. Some were powerful personages from the largest of the decimated villages, but clearly my performance on the first night had made me the favorite. No other candidate could match my relationship with Podnow, and none had much experience with the invaders. The older surviving village chiefs were familiar with my youthful sojourn to the north, and all of the war chiefs knew of my experience in fighting at Monterey.

I assigned Chetic and the Yandanchi chief to talk with those who did not know me. Sedit spoke with the important women of each village. Both men and women received the special gift of my attention. The elders listened to my thoughts and said, "Yes, it was the same with Podnow" or "Yes, you have Podnow's tricks."

On the third night of the Lonewis, the night of the doctors' battle, phantom arrows rained among the combatants. We powerful tipne used our strange voices and our wondrous screams as we jumped around the six fires. We used tricks of misdirection and sleight of hand to impress our constituents. We twirled Cuksa round and round the gift pole until the rope wound up and he disappeared into the darkness. In the end, as dawn struggled over distant mountains, I stood alone, surrounded by the fallen bodies of my comrades.

Podnow and my dead father and Shup had overwhelmed those spirits marshaled against me by my opponents. The three dead brothers had guided my spirit arrows through impossible barriers. They had marked each opposing tipne with deference to my power. Now the brothers smiled as I toured the circle around the Lonewis fire. The dead brothers smiled as I collected adulation and small gifts from the Yokuts and the Miwok and the strangers among us.

———◆———

On the last day of the Lonewis I sat in the circle of spirit doctors and village chiefs. On my right hand was Estanislao, a Miwok chief.

"This is what we must do." Estanislao looked first at me and then at the others. "If the Spanish come into our territory, we will lure them as we do the antelope. We will wag our butts in their faces and then lead them through the tule swamps and into the gullies full of poison oak. They will follow us until they shake with frustration. When the whites are exhausted, we will make a stand on a hill of our choice. We will taunt the White Others with their stupidity, and force them to enter our snare."

"A good coyote trick," I said.

Estanislao smiled. "Both of us are guided by the coyote spirit; José Jesus and Estanislao—we are coyotes together." He stared into his basket of tea, drank a small sip, and continued. "When we have the whites surrounded by our hills and swamps and warriors, we will kill them. None who assault our territory will live."

A Chulamni village chief spoke. "Estanislao, you were a child in my village. Your mother was a child in my village, but your father was a soldier of the Spanish. Your father was the enemy, a white invader."

"Yes, honored chief, but my loyalty is to my mother and to her blood. I am Miwok, loyal to the Miwok and to our allies, the Yokuts and the strangers."

The old chief was persistent. "You are one of the strangers, Estanislao. You served as alcalde at Mission Santa Clara. How can we possibly trust such a person of mixed blood?"

Estanislao stood with feet apart and hands extended toward his challenger. "Yes, old man, I am indeed a half-breed." He puffed himself like an ardent rooster. "I am the perfect leader for the people of our Great Valley. I have absorbed the white invader's magic and can turn their poison back against them. My Miwok blood is sacred to me, while the invader's blood has no significance."

The chief would have his final word. "Here is José Jesus at your side. He served the Spanish at Mission San Juan Bautista, and I contend that the brown-robed witches have corrupted both of you with their ugly words."

Estanislao walked toward the chief, drew a long Spanish sword from a scabbard attached to his belt, and stabbed it into the ground.

"Drain my Spanish blood. I serve only the Miwok."

The Chulamni chief smiled. "No one doubts your bravery, Estanislao, only your heritage. Today there are Miwok and Yokuts and strangers around this council fire. My question is simple: What will happen to your blood when the Spanish yell insults at you? Will you stab a sword in the ground and ask them to drain your Miwok blood?"

I moved between the two. "Watch and listen, chief of the Chulamni; you must watch and listen and judge if we two coyotes act for the Yokuts and Miwok or for the Spanish invaders. But remember that without us, there is only death for the People. You must watch and listen and not speak against us, because we stand as the last opportunity the People have for survival."

"There is indeed no doubt that you both are coyotes." He stood in slow, arthritic spurts. "I'm too old for coyote games and too stupid for clever words." The Chulamni chief turned to shuffle through the circle of his peers. "My villagers are too weak and too sick to play with the coyote, so we will leave this place. The ancestors buried in our beautiful hills cry for our return."

There was a vague shuffling of feet and arms, an attack of coughing, and a long spell of silence interrupted only as three additional elders left our circle. After a short interval, two returned to sit with newly filled baskets of tobacco tea. Only one other than the Chulamni chief refused us.

Estanislao turned and spoke to me as if there were no others present. "We must not merely wait for the invaders; we must also attack the Spanish invaders."

"Attack?" I pretended confusion. "I thought we were the fire builders, and the invaders were nothing but grasshoppers striving to jump onto our hot coals."

"We are fighting white witches, Brother, not grasshoppers. Certainly we will punish the Spanish if they attack the Great Valley, but we must also attack the white grubs in their own nest."

A few of the leaders applauded, but most merely refilled tiny wooden pipes with tobacco.

"You, José Jesus, must attack the ranchos while I organize the defense of our land."

"I see. So you will send my arrows against their muskets." I smiled along with most of those gathered. "I believe that I like your grasshopper plan better."

"Now, now, José Jesus, do not diminish your talents. You can capture horses and trade them for guns. You're a smart tipne, and therefore you must procure muskets and cannon for your bandits and also for my defense of our Great Valley!"

I stood and faced Estanislao. The pup, the pretender. He had the smell of Hineh, to my thinking. More likely a bully and threat to the well-being of the people, and certainly never available at times of their misery. "In my younger days such praise would drive me into battle without pause. Now my grey hair demands patience. I agree to your division of power between us, and yes, I will gather my vaqueros to assert their skills. But we must move slowly."

Estanislao stood and spoke to my left shoulder. "Throw caution aside, my brother." He spoke to the assembly of notable people. "It is only through quick and decisive action that we can hope to defeat the invaders. There is no purpose in wasting the dry seasons."

"The spirits of our dead ancestors will guide us." I turned slowly about the circle, memorizing the blemishes and tattoos on each face. "Time is on our side," I said to those who remained in the circle. "We must be patient in conducting this war against the White Others. Our villages are weak, but the Yokuts and Miwok and strangers among us must be strong. Many of our storytellers are dead, but we must remember every ancestor. We must protect our children as if they were oak trees that produce only sweet acorns. We must be very patient in discovering how we can survive in this world of brown witches and evil spirits. We must embrace the strangers among us as our own blood. Together we can achieve victory over the Spanish or French or whatever collection of white witches come against us."

A voice spoke from behind a large pine tree. "The Chulamni are always patient, José Jesus."

The Chulamni chief stepped from the shadow. "I will watch the twin coyotes. I will listen to what they say and what they do not say, and soon we will see how patient are these two coyotes." He coughed. "I think we have one coyote, maybe, and one camp dog, but only time will tell which is the dog and which the coyote."

He spit into the dust. "I doubt if I will live long enough to see the truth of the matter."

CHAPTER 26

Summer 1809

THE VISITING YOKUTS AND MIWOK and strangers left Sedit's village that morning after the Lonewis. Flat grass and oppressive silence replaced the noisy celebration of death. From one new moon to the next I agonized over Estanislao's plan to defeat the White Others. Nothing about the plan was new; nothing about the plan gave a hint of success.

"Not true, my brother," whispered Coyote. "I believe that you have finally finished your sojourn. Finally! Maybe I can finally leave your side and let you make those decisions that surmount any resources I may bring from the spirit world."

"Do I hear a promise or a threat, my brother?"

"That is for you to determine, Brother. You and your worldly mentors appear to have rendered any advice I could offer superfluous."

"Maybe my hand to another hand of flesh will provide me with greater comfort than my hand to your ephemeral paw."

"You refer to my mangy paw, of course, my silly brother."

"We have been estranged in the recent past. Maybe it is indeed the appropriate time for our separation."

Coyote shook himself with great vigor but remained silent.

I knew the old fart was teasing me in the same fashion that a sulky child might deliberately annoy a parent. So be it; the silly game must be played. "Tell me, Brother—do you have any parting advice in the matter of Estanislao?"

"No, no, no! I am nothing. You are now a man of the spirits, and therefore all decisions are yours to embrace."

"I'm the tipne man for all who say I hold that position. I'm a creature of flesh, and more likely to miss the correct path and choose the false road at any moment of choice."

"I guess that you have finally finished your sojourn, Kiyu," whispered Brother Coyote. "Who and what you are is no longer my responsibility."

"Brother, what am I to do with Estanislao?"

"No more with the questions. This ancient spirit needs a nice long nap."

"Stop with the teasing, Brother. Stand faithful to your obligations to me."

There was no answer.

"Brother?" I called. "Brother?"

<hr/>

Sedit interrupted my thoughts only with food or the names of men who waited for my orders. I told the men to meditate in the sweat lodge or sit in the deep shade of a pine tree. I gave Sedit a small smile in return for each basket of mush or manzanita cider. After a full moon was diminished by half, she took me by the hand and led me to a quiet spot where the thrush sent prayers winging to Tipiknits Pahn. We slept side by side but never touched the other with fingers or tongue or soft lips.

At sunrise, Sedit put an arm over my shoulder and whispered into my ear. "Go!" she said. "You are tipne doctor for all the People, and you must lead them in this war against the invaders."

I turned my head away from her lips.

Sedit moved to her knees and massaged my neck and shoulders. "You are the chosen one," she whispered.

"I'm afraid of another defeat," I mumbled. "I have not changed in any manner that I can comprehend. My spirit brother has resigned his post, and you are more an ephemeral dream than my wife. Our son Carlos is dead. The Yokuts and Miwok are a shadow from the days of Podnow, and we are now immersed in a forest of strangers who are led by pretentious half-breeds of suspicious character."

Sedit rubbed my back and buttocks and whispered, "Every night we will speak to each other. We will meet in our dreams and embrace the other. We will share every secret." She kissed my ear and wiggled her fingers past my hips to tease my dormant cock to life. "You must lead your vaqueros, my husband."

I rolled over and embraced my sweet brown crane, my Sedit. Our sweat joined, and then our lips and bodies, and finally we were both cranes, moving slowly through the brown grass, attentive to the other, willing to share the sweet grubs at our feet and the feather softness of the other.

"I will leave at sunset," I said.

"Shhh," Sedit said. "Hold me."

The sliver-thin moon gave no light, but my feet followed the path from Sedit's village toward the war against the white invaders. At first there were two warriors: Chetic, who agreed with any pathetic plan I could conceive, and Benito, who debated my assumption of authority in every instance.

Benito was a Chauchila war chief, whose past was marred by his theft of six magnificent horses from Vallejo's rancho near Petaluma— and getting caught for it. In direct consequence of this tactical blunder, Benito was chained hand and foot by General Vallejo and then given as a slave to my cousin Hineh, who was then serving as majordomo at Mission Santa Clara. Such were the perils of Chauchila genius.

"That damn cousin of yours," Benito shouted at our first meeting. "First thing I do to him is break every bone of his fingers!"

"Why?"

"The sonuvabitch held me in a small black cave for days without end."

"He was your alcalde at Mission Santa Clara; I would expect nothing less from him."

"It was your damned cousin who gave me this despicable name and the dirtiest jobs. The sonuvabitch."

"Welcome to my army," I said.

"Since when did a Tachi get to tell me what I should do?"

———◆———

We three stole a few dozen saddle-broke horses from a rancho near San José Village and found a hairy-faced trapper who accepted our horses in exchange for three muskets, a small cask of powder, and a handful of flints.

In the early fall, during a time of hot easterly winds, we rode east of the first tall mountain south of the west-flowing river and set an upwind grass fire to destroy Don Tarabél's rancho. We saw the old man try to save his favorite stallion. At one moment he was holding a lead rope tied to the white horse, and the next he was quiet in the dust. His wife and two vaqueros ran to his side, and they squatted next to their don with tears flowing onto the dust. The rest of his family scurried to heap a plow, some bags of seed corn, and a few chairs into a two-wheeled cart.

"C'mon!" Benito yelled. "Let's see what they're stealing from us!"

Chetic gave his horse a soft pat on the neck. "You'd better keep quiet, Benito; those old women would die from laughing if they saw us coming down the road."

"No! C'mon. We'll yell like those Comanche warriors."

A single ox pulled the cart piled with chairs and small children. A vaquero and two boys moved a small herd of cows trailing behind a half-dozen women, a few big girls, and one stoop-shouldered young man. The entire muddle of people and animals moved at a slow pace, and all stared west without a single backward glance. The young man had an awkward gait, almost a shamble, and he followed the oldest woman at a single pace. The remaining women and girls protected the rear and both sides like a gaggle of geese might move to shelter an injured member to a safe shore.

"Too bad about the old man," I said.

Benito settled his horse and nodded toward me. "You knew the old man?"

"I heard a few stories here and there. He raised good horses and always had some water and bread for any passing traveler."

"He'd give some comfort to you and me?"

"Me and Chetic, anyway."

Benito gave a growl. "He'd been around for as long as I can remember. Where'd he come from?"

"Baja is what I heard. My uncle Podnow had a few words with him when they were both young men."

"He was a mestizo, right?"

"Maybe; can't really say. I do think that Podnow always had Tarabél in mind when he was talking about finding a way for both the Yokuts and the invaders to survive. When I think back to those days, it seems that Don Tarabél and Uncle Podnow shared dreams that made no sense to anyone else."

"Well, he's a dead sonuvabitch now, and that's no lie."

"They're both dead, Benito, so let's find a place to bury the don."

"What about those women and cows? Let's chase them down before they get out of sight."

"I need your help digging a hole, Benito. With your back and my brains, we should find a place with not too many stones."

"Are you trying to tell a Chauchila war chief what I should do, you damn Tachi coyote?"

"Tachi tipne man," I said.

◆

Two of my vaqueros from Mission San Juan Bautista and three neophytes from Mission Purisima joined us after the Great Tarabél victory, and we moved to the Monterey area and burned a few more ranchos and captured another batch of horses. We traded for more muskets and some beans, and gained a few additional volunteers for my army.

With the second acorn harvest, most of those isolated ranchos located north of the saltwater bay and down to Monterey were either burned or abandoned. Now fifty men followed my orders. They were mostly former mission vaqueros and therefore skilled horsemen, but some were hill-country Miwok and high-country Paiute who rode their mules like fat padres. There were also three Sonorans who offered themselves as volunteers, and they were different from all the rest.

"What are you called?" I asked.

The tallest stepped forward. His hair was straw-colored, his eyes were witch's blue, and he bowed in the Spanish manner. "I am Joaquin Murietta." He turned to the oldest of the trio. "This is my brother, Tomàs, and the other is my cousin, Three Finger."

"Three Finger?"

"He will accept no other name."

Benito stepped between the Sonorans and me. "Hey! What are you thinking, Tipne Man? Three white men in our army?" He spit toward the Sonorans. "Didn't your dead uncle tell us to chase the damn white man from our land or kill them?" He pulled a long steel knife from his belt. "Let's kill the sonsabitches!"

Joaquin Murietta kept his hands in plain view and smiled at Benito. "We are Sonorans, my friend, not Spanish or Mexican. We are an ancient tribe and allied with red men, not white men."

"I hear nothing but lies from these damn spies! White men are all invaders, nothing else." Benito moved his horse toward the tall Sonoran.

"Hold, Benito!" I moved between the two and turned to study Murietta's eyes and the lines above them.

"Will you three Sonorans accept my orders?"

"If you lead us against the Spanish, we will follow. If you kill the Spanish and take their horses, we will follow."

"I suppose you'll be no different from the rest of my army," I said.

Joaquin smiled with his eyes and teeth. "How is that so, tipne chief? What are the differences between Sonorans and those of your army?"

"Well, sir, I would guess that at our very first defeat, you Sonorans will head south, while the rest will head north. The only difference will be direction, not devotion to our task."

"We'll soon see the truth of the matter, my friend."

The creases over his eyes slanted sharply toward his nose, a sign I liked even more than his smile.

The straw-haired man spoke again. "I think that it is possible that this army of yours will find the stomach for more victories than setbacks."

"You imply an awareness of my previous disasters."

"I have studied your previous schemes from those rumors heard here and there." Joaquin Murietta gave a pleasant shrug of his shoulders. "I am an ignorant man interested in joining your band of warriors, nothing more."

"Rumors always carry the kernel of truth. What do you see that may improve my chance for a final victory over the white invaders?"

"You now have our support, Tipne Man."

The winter storms were infrequent in 1810, and I was able to continue almost daily raids against the Spanish. I divided my army, and Chetic became a war chief with nearly one hundred warriors to advance against the ranchos and small villages, from Don Tarebél's rancho to the Monterey area. Benito became the captain for a similar group, and he operated to the north and south of San Luis Obispo. I was initially captain of the southern war, but soon I turned the title over to a tall, skinny Luiseño with the name of Lugardo. Thereafter, I maintained only a detachment of twenty vaqueros and the three Sonorans under my direct command.

It is true that my war chiefs stirred up a lot of dust with their stealing horses, killing cows, and chasing the White Others into their dirty little pueblos. My spies told me that the Spanish were pulling their hair and telling their beads and swearing that the Indio José Jesus was the Devil incarnate.

"We must have bullets and soldiers!" called the pueblo leaders. "Hear our prayers, O forgetful Lord," called the women. "Send us bullets and soldiers, for we must kill this fiend and his demons," said the men.

———— ◆ ————

Sedit came to visit me whenever I managed a stay among the caves south of San Juan Bautista.

"Listen, Husband," she whispered. "It seems that recently more of our babies survive than die in all the villages that I have surveyed."

"What about leaders of the villages?"

"Many of the old leaders are dead." Sedit put her head on my shoulder. "Some of the new chiefs are strangers and some mestizo, but many are well intentioned." Now she looked into my eyes. "Most of the village leaders lack the experience necessary to guide the People in the way of our ancestors."

"What about the women in the new villages?"

"They serve the men." She moved a soft hand along my leg. "Even the dullest man eventually learns how to fulfill his duty."

I put my hand on hers in an effort to stem any further progress. "Go slowly, Wife. The sun is still above the trees. Two messengers await my—"

"You must quiet yourself, my husband. Turn yourself into a docile war chief and tender tipne doctor. Let my hand roam, and you must remain quiet, my dear. Quiet."

———— ◆ ————

All my vaqueros rode quiet, fast horses, while the rest of my troopers rode quiet, slow mules. Both fast and slow found great pleasure in chasing cows and women in carretas. My army was boisterous with their behavior after each inevitable victory and always forgiving of their comrades' imperfections. They gambled and played rough ball-kicking games. They kicked an oak gall from one goal to another, and they ate their fill of both Spanish beans and sweet acorn mush. It was a happy army. They were fat and healthy and pleased with their power. The Sonorans did everything I asked of them, and even Benito stopped grinding his teeth when I gave orders. I was José Jesus, the war chief for this diverse army. I was José Jesus, the supreme tipne doctor to the Yokuts and Miwok and all the strangers who followed my lead.

———

I called a meeting for Chetic and Benito and me at a freshwater spring near Paso Robles. Cold water in the hot valley. All my men were with me, and both my captains had a few vaqueros with them. A little fewer than forty men sipping water and exchanging jokes around a very small fire. I clapped my hands to get their attention.

"When I was very young and very thoughtless, Uncle Podnow was the supreme tipne, and he taught the Tachi to listen while he talked with the spirits."

"Dammit to hell," Benito said. "Did you drag me all the way down here to go on and on about the damned Tachi people?

There were a few titters, but no significant support for Benito.

"Settle down, my war chief friend. Listen for a while."

He made a show of filling and lighting his pipe, so I continued.

"I remember the time that my dead father flew down from Tipiknits Pahn on his winged horse and argued with Podnow and explained to him why the White Others were more dangerous than grizzly bears or an extended drought.

"It is true, my friends, that Podnow taught me many tricks, and I in turn taught my friends in the same fashion how to listen to me."

None of my men seemed surprised when Benito stood and shook his head like some old grandmother about to teach a lesson for the tenth time in one day.

"Listen, you Tachi fool, I've got fleas that bother me more than this sorry army of yours disturbs the white invaders."

"Very funny," I said. "Why don't you go chase up to Sonoma and capture a few of Don Vallejo's white stallions?"

Benito blinked his eyes at me—first the red and then the yellow eyes. "Why don't you go load yourself on top of that big stallion over in the next canyon? The one that manages the big bunch of docile mares."

I sipped my tanai tea. At least Benito had the eye-blink trick in hand. "You got something useful to say for a change?"

"Stop having so much fun," Benito hissed. "You and your ball-kicking boys have got to put a mean expression on your faces. You've got to bite those white boys on the balls and hang on even if they hit you on the back with their fists."

"I can tell you're all puffed up with some brilliant ideas for us stupid Tachi."

My vaqueros and Chetic joined me with a benevolent chuckle.

"Why don't you just go ahead and tell us all that we need to know to destroy the invaders?" I said.

"Not me!" said Benito. "You'll get no big-time ideas from me." He smiled that pompous smile of his to all about the circle. "Hey! You have this great Sonoran war chief in your service. What could I possibly offer by way of assistance?" Benito spit into the fire. "A Sonoran war chief, and you as the supreme bull-shitter of this sad collection of fools and cowards—what can I possibly add to that wonderful combination?"

Three Finger choked on his laughter.

Benito walked over to me, sniffed at my shoulder, then exposed his penis to pee on my bare feet.

Joaquin Murietta and Tomàs and Three Finger and Benito all rolled on the ground laughing and poking each other. Chetic and my vaqueros joined me in a silent observation of the ridiculous puppies.

No one said anything for a long time. We smoked tobacco and listened to hoot owls. Benito kept laughing and laughing until he finally went quiet. I passed around a few big baskets of tanai tea, and we all traveled to our own secret places. My captains and vaqueros sat and dreamed and listened to the frogs peep and the black-crowned heron croak.

Joaquin spoke first. "Those Mexican people have plenty of guns in Santa Fe."

"Where's this Santa Fe?" I asked.

"You go east a full moon or two, then north for a while," Tomàs said.

"First the Colorado River, then the Gila River, and then north up the Rio Grande," Joaquin said.

"Hot! Hot! Hot!" Three Finger said. "There's lots of bad mountains and not much water anywhere."

"Can we trail horses over to this Santa Fe?" I asked.

"Sure," Joaquin said. "Mules too."

"Maybe," Tomàs said.

"Lots of pretty mean Indios along the way," Three Finger said. "There's Shoshone, Paiute, and Mohave one place or another." He held his hand up to reflect the firelight. "It was those Mohave boys that got my two fingers."

I let the last of the tanai tea drizzle down my throat and let my stomach gurgle for a while. "You Sonorans ever traveled to this Santa Fe?"

"Nope," Tomàs said. "But I got two cousins who traded in Santa Fe. Three, four times they went up there."

Joaquin smiled his beautiful smile. "Both of our cousins were killed by the Apache."

Two of my San Juan Bautista vaqueros started laughing, and soon the entire army was rolling on the ground, wiping tears from their eyes.

Joaquin yelled into the din. "Those Mexican fellows have plenty of guns in Santa Fe!"

"Lots of guns," Three Finger yelled.

"They've only got a few ponies and mules, I hear," Joaquin said.

"On to Santa Fe!" I yelled.

"Santa Fe!" my army screamed.

CHAPTER 27

1816–1828

WE STOLE MORE THAN THREE hundred well-trained horses and sixty mules from the ranchos east and south of Los Angeles pueblo. My vaqueros moved them through the snow-topped mountain pass east of Los Angeles pueblo and into the desert. Small purple flowers and green grass covered the sandy soil, and there was ample forage for our beasts. We moved at a steady pace, first along the Mohave River, then southeast toward the Colorado. I stayed two days ahead of the horses and mules and met the Paiute and Shoshone elders in their tiny villages.

"We need to trespass on your land," I'd tell them.

"Go to the north or south with your beasts. They will eat all of our clover and all of the spring forage for our own horses."

"We need to trade the beasts for guns to destroy the white invaders," I'd say.

"You are the invaders," they'd say.

"The grass will quickly return," I'd say, and wave my vaqueros to the east. None were friendly, of course, but all permitted us to move through their territory with the loss of only a dozen or so horses and a few mules.

The Quachan people held a large reach of the Colorado River under their control, and they were different from those Indios of my experience. Most of the Quachan used the Spanish language with great dexterity and also spoke many languages that were commonly held by my Yokuts villagers. The chief of the first village I encountered invited me into his lodge and fed me squash soup garnished with bits of fish. He listened carefully to the details of our defeat at Monterey and nodded his head in approval of my new army. After my stomach was full and my tongue weary, he motioned for me to follow him.

"Here, near the river and also upstream at the foot of the big yellow hill, is where the Spanish built their missions. This one by the river they named Purisima Concepción; the other was San Pedro." The chief waved his arm downstream. "There was also a pueblo near the ferry crossing where the Spanish carried supplies from Mexico to Alta California." He peered at me through bushy eyebrows. "Their mules ate our grass down to the roots, and soon the rains ripped barren gullies toward our river."

A black hawk with a red tail circled high overhead and remained silent as it spiraled out of sight. "Honored chief," I said. "I see only Quachan and a few Mohave here in your village. Where are the Spanish now?"

"The men we killed; a few women and children we kept." The chief made a gentle motion with his right hand. "The women are much happier with our warriors and wouldn't return to the Spanish even if we gave them the opportunity."

"On my next trip I'll bring a few Yokuts women for your pleasure," I said. "Your warriors will find them as docile as the Spanish women, but without the witches' eyes."

"We would be honored with such a gift, José Jesus. The Spanish women produce vigorous Quachan warriors, and your doe-eyed Yokuts will doubtless serve the same purpose for our villages."

"Tell me, honored chief, have your villages suffered losses from strange new diseases?"

"The spotted fever has killed many of our people."

"It is the same with all villages who have contact with the White Others."

"They have an infinite supply of evil medicine," the Quachan chief said.

"If we combine the forces of our ancestors, maybe we can defeat the white witches."

"We Quachan and your Yokuts could be valuable allies, José Jesus."

"Our cousins, the Miwok, would gladly join us in an alliance. Together we could control the Great Valley and this immense desert. We could share our resources and destroy the common enemy."

The village chief seemed to consider the possibilities of my unlikely proposal and then returned to his original story. "In the beginning, the Spanish gave us gifts, and we accepted them into our territory. We treated them with dignity, and yet they beat our men and ate our squash and corn. The grass and deer and fish and women they stole." He inched closer to me. "We crushed them—all four of the padres and fifty-two soldiers. We spilled their guts to the vultures. We took their women and children. Six times they sent soldiers to seek revenge for our victory, and six times we crushed the new invaders. They will never again whip another Quachan warrior or steal a single squash from our farms."

I nodded my head in appreciation of the Quachan people. "Good, very good," I said.

The chief returned my nod and asked, "How can the Quachan help the Yokuts and your allies?"

"If you give me three guides to the Santa Fe pueblo and twenty of your warriors to expand my army, we will exchange half the guns that we procure from the Mexicans."

He gave one quick nod of agreement.

I stood and shouted, "Death to the Spanish invaders!"

"Death to the Spanish!" the Quachan chief whispered.

———

By the winter of 1820 I had friendly contact with most of the villages scattered across the desert to Santa Fe. The Quachan had surplus weapons to trade up and down their river, and Estanislao was happy to receive twenty muskets and three barrels of powder for his fort.

In the early spring of 1827, Chetic, Benito, and I met at our favorite cave above Santa Barbara Mission. A cool wind blew against the ridgeline, and soft air drew toyon-blossom scent around us in a comfortable embrace. Green-backed hummingbirds chattered and fought noisy looping battles over their coveted bitter cherry blossoms.

Chetic leaned up against his leather saddle with relaxed grace. My brother of this world no longer smiled nervously when I spoke to him. He no longer jumped to anticipate my needs. Chetic was a captain, a war chief, not a winatum.

"How goes it?" I asked.

"We've burned two more ranchos." Chetic tapped tobacco into a small clay pipe and then reached over his knees to snag a twig from the fire. "We've killed one Spaniard and picked up another two hundred horses. Most are good for eating but nothing else."

"Benito, have you got anything worthwhile to say?"

"Why sure I do, Tipne Man. I've always got a good word or two for you simpleminded Yokuts fellows."

I sat silent, waiting for the birds or breeze to move Benito into action.

"I spoke with Lugardo's winatum. He says that all the isolated ranchos east from San Diego pueblo are deserted, and that it's the same situation east of San Luis Obispo." Benito spat into the fire. "The Spanish are running from us like rabbits from the fox."

A hawk circled above the craggy coastal hills, then drifted slowly south. "We're ready for the next step." I sat with my back against a warm rock. "The outlying missions and ranchos are destroyed, so now we'll move to our next objective." The hawk disappeared behind a large cliff. "We must pick one major Spanish pueblo and destroy it."

Chetic sat straight up, away from his saddle. "You're mistaken on this matter, José Jesus." He pointed the stem of his pipe at me. "What are we going to do about that Mariano Vallejo fellow? Remember him? He's José Vallejo's younger brother."

"He's nothing but a young fool," Benito said. "Every spy describes him as a book reader and confidante of the old men."

"He's the one who sent you to Santa Clara Mission," I said.

"Damned lucky sonuvabitch he was," said Benito.

Chetic waited for the fire and Benito to settle. "We've talked before about Mariano, and now you both must listen. He has destroyed the Pomo and Wappo villages. Only in Mariano's domain are the Spanish expanding their territory, and that also, I judge, is where they remain unmoved by our assaults."

"Bah! The true Spanish power is in the south, not the remote and useless north," said Benito.

"Let me tell you something new that Mariano is developing. He's organized a group of lancers up in his Sonoma pueblo. They're all young men with fancy dress, fast horses, and long, long spears."

"So what are you trying to tell us, Chetic?"

"Twice my men have fallen into snares set by him. He's captured three of my best vaqueros, and another dozen have deserted into the tule marshes. My brave warriors are less brave now that Mariano and his lancers are a threat."

"Just kill the bastard," Benito said. "If you need any help, I'll be happy to join with you in the sport."

Chetic dismissed Benito with a wave of his hand. "Tell me to kill the next circling hawk; it's an easier task."

Benito spit and stared off toward the ocean.

"We can't let one man intimidate us," I said. "Estanislao is making progress with his fort. We've got to step up our attacks, not run away."

Chetic pulled his knees against his chest and leaned steady against the saddle. "We still have some good men." He placed his chin on his knees. "I'll check on Vallejo's servants. Maybe we can poison the witch or put a burr under the saddle of his horse."

Benito spit. "Maybe your vaqueros can turn their butts to Vallejo and fuck him into the grave."

Chetic laughed and stood in one smooth motion. "I'll send Vallejo down south, Benito, and maybe this time you can take his measure."

"He was lucky. Like I said before: lucky, not smart, the sonuvabitch."

"Enough from you two; we've got to attack and then attack again. Those are my orders. When the cattle and horses are gone, the Spanish will disappear."

"A simple strategy," Chetic said.

"We need more men," Benito said.

I shut my eyes against the bright sun. These were my captains, and they had the wit of a Spanish private. Red clouds bloomed on my eyelids. "Go to the villages in your area and recruit young men. Find the hot-bloods and half-breeds; the smart-asses who think they are invincible, and train them into your army."

Chetic gave a single hard laugh. "Ha!"

"You must think we're both pretty stupid," Benito said.

"White-man stupid," I said.

Neither captain answered.

The wind diminished. Two sparrows bounced in erratic chase through the underbrush until the hawk returned at treetop elevation. Chetic walked a few steps to sit in front of me. "Are you okay, Tipne Man?" He studied my eyes and mouth. "You don't look so good."

"I thought you were a warrior, not an antu doctor."

"You've got black circles around your eyes, and your skin has a slick gloss." He tapped me on the knee. "What dreams are keeping you from sleep?"

"Nothing is wrong; I merely suffer from the complaints of two dumb captains."

But my brother of this world knew me too well. "Are you repeating the dreams again—the dreams with pirates and oozing black blood and hiding in miserable caves?"

"Every man has dreams."

"Tell me," Chetic said.

"Every night my stomach shrinks into a smaller and smaller ball. Hineh laughs and laughs as he whips the neophytes under his command."

"Damn troublemaker," said Chetic.

"I haven't had a good loose shit in weeks."

Chetic inched closer and put both hands on my knees. "Listen, Tipne Man. We won't run this time, not like at Monterey. Nobody will run. Not you and not that damn half-breed with his big fancy white-man's fort."

"That's no fort—nothing but a white man's fart for all its use," Benito said. "The damn thing is nothing but a snare, and we're the bait."

Chetic stared into my eyes. "Don't worry so much. Benito and I will find a few simpleminded boys to ride with us. Vallejo will break his leg dancing, and everything will be okay."

Benito scratched his butt. "Whatever did happen to that damn sonuvabitch Hineh, anyway? Maybe he's ready to change sides again. Maybe he's got two thousand vaqueros hidden someplace, all ready to join our army."

"He's a pet dog for Commandant Gomez in Monterey." Chetic kept staring at me. "I heard that Hineh walks around sniffing white crotches most of the time, begging atole from white women."

"Maybe your cousin Hineh will save a spot in his shack for our half-breed fart builder," Benito said. "Those white witches can always use another pet dog to lick their hands." Benito pawed fingers on his face. "I guess those half-breed fellows enjoy the stink of Spanish beans."

"Estanislao won't run," I said.

The hawk circled back over our heads, screamed a long, thin warning to us, and then dove toward a patch of green between two red rocks. The bird and a small bush rabbit met in an explosion of dust.

"There's our sign," Chetic said. "We're the hawk. We'll fall from the sky and kill the Spanish rabbits."

"Maybe those witches changed Hineh from a hawk to a rabbit," Benito said. "My guess is that they'll change our half-breed too. I don't trust either one of the sonsabitches."

The hawk pulled a long string of intestine from the rabbit and gulped it down.

"We're not rabbits this time," Chetic said. "Estanislao will lead us to victory. He has lived with the whites, and he retains their medicine through the spirit of his father. He's a good man, I believe, and a brave man to boot."

The bird ripped the rabbit into small bits. Even as fur and bloody flesh went into his craw, he kept his eyes upon us in a persistent stare.

"Estanislao's mother was raped by two soldiers." Benito shrugged his shoulders. "Who can tell one father from the other? They were both witless privates, outcasts from their own village. Criminals, from all the gossip told to my winatum."

I nodded toward the hawk. "Don't worry, my friend. He'll pull the guts from the Spanish, and the Great Valley will be safe again for the People."

"The only thing worse than a white man is a half-breed," Benito said.

"He's our last chance, Benito. If he fails, we'll lose the Great Valley and end up like Hineh, smelling crotches and begging."

Benito sat down between Chetic and me to form a tiny circle. "Listen to me, Tipne Man. I'll follow you. If you follow Estanislao, that's your affair. I don't trust him, and I sure as hell don't like the miserable mestizo."

Chetic put his pipe in a soft pouch. "Let's get going." He stood and walked to his horse. "I've got a bunch of warriors sitting around with nothing to do."

"Watch out for that Vallejo fellow," I said.

"Send the bastard down to see me," Benito said.

"Good idea," Chetic said.

CHAPTER 28

October 30, 1829

*T*O *MY DEAREST AND MOST* Esteemed Padre Narciso
Duran:

Most loving father,

I am not returning to Mission San José. I renounce my honored position as alcalde. I renounce my commitment to your Christ and to the father of Christ, whom you call God.

We people of the tules and the hills announce our rebellion. We will drive you back to the land of your ancestors or we will kill you. No longer will we tolerate the murder of our people in your missions and ranchos. No longer will we tolerate the rape of our women and the destruction of our villages.

We have no fear of your soldiers. They are but few, and most are mere boys. None are sharpshooters. Against these incompetents we will

*bring skilled and dedicated warriors. Tell your
people to leave our land before many of them are
killed. You who love all creatures must work to save
the Califorñios from destruction. We give you fair
warning, although you gave us none.*

We are rising in revolt of your tyranny. Beware!
Estanislao

Estanislao peered over my shoulder. "Interesting letter," I said.
"Listen, José Jesus."

I stood and faced the half-breed. We were an arm's length apart,
but Estanislao spoke so that his assembled warriors could hear every
word.

"José Jesus," he said, "I want you to take your best twenty
warriors and protect the winatum who carries this document."

He avoided my effort to stare into his eyes. I fluttered his letter in
the air. "Do you expect an answer from Duran?"

"No, no, certainly not. Duran will send a message to Martinez,
and Martinez will send one of his sergeants to deal with the misguided
Estanislao."

"I assume you have spies at Mission San José."

"Only one or two, and not nearly as well placed as your spies,
José Jesus. I would appreciate the favor of your keeping track of my
letter to Duran."

I stood two steps backward. "Okay, my sagacious commandant,
I'll have the letter delivered." The man was actually finger-combing
his beard and arranging his uniform with little taps and slaps of his
hand. A damn green-head duck would have more sense. "And I'll also
hang around San José and Santa Clara for a few days, just to see what
happens to your letter."

"Good," Estanislao said. "Hurry back to my fort when you have
a copy of Duran's letter." He fussed with the shoulder brushes for a

bit. "I'll make my plans according to what Duran and Martinez cook up."

"I imagine a week or two for an answer. It shouldn't take longer."

———

November 6, 1829
Commandant José Martinez
San Francisco Presidio

> *My Dear Friend and Protector,*
>
> *My heart grieves for the loss of my alcalde, Estanislao. He has deserted his post at Mission San José and taken a position of leadership in an insurrection of Tuleaños against God and king. In a letter to me, and in announcements to all who will hear his proclamation, Estanislao has declared himself the leader of a revolt.*
>
> *I beg you to send us the aid of ten soldiers, if possible, under the command of Sergeant Soto. The troops should leave here by Sunday the 16th of November in order that the ringleaders are arrested before the heavy rains begin. It is important that a punishment of sound thrashings be administered to Estanislao. The cursed José Jesus, and Benito, late of Mission Purisima, must suffer both the whip and a spell of incarceration. We must cut out this cancer of rebellion before it spreads.*
>
> *We of the mission will provide your troops with all supplies, including carts and muleteers, but excluding gunpowder. You will recall that the barrels of gunpowder last shipped to the mission are*

all worthless—pure carbon. The troops must also
bring their own cartridges.
 Please act expeditiously on this matter. God will
reward you with His guidance of your soul.
 Father Narciso Duran, Q.B.S.M.

Estanislao wore nothing but his tattoos and a belt. He sat on an ornate mission chair with his knees under a desk made from rough planks and willow-tree stumps. A line of young warriors moved slowly, in orderly fashion, to the lodge entrance; each took a quick peek and then ran to join the multitude. They laughed until their hiccups caused painful spasms. The warriors kicked feet in the air and yelled the same questions over and over. "Did you see the chair? Yes! Yes! What about the desk? Yes! The quill and paper? Yes! The whiskers? Wonder of all wonders, whiskers! Yes!"

It did seem odd that an Indio could sit in a mud-plastered lodge and casually apply pen and ink to paper. Beyond odd, seeping into the realm of dangerous subversion, was the fact of throne and Spanish whiskers. Certainly, and beyond question, was the fact that all such accoutrements were indecent for a Miwok war chief.

"Estanislao," I said.

"What?" He looked up from his work.

"They're laughing at you."

"Certainly. I'd laugh also."

"You'll lose their respect. Our warriors will fall in with those who demean you for your white blood."

Estanislao put his quill on the desk. "You're wrong, my tipne friend. They take heart that I own the white man's medicine. They see the strength of my fort, and soon my warriors will understand the meaning of victory. My whiskers and throne will serve as symbols of my power." Estanislao shook his head at me, then picked up his pen and resumed writing.

———

I found a deserted grove of trees west of Estanislao's fort and sat with my back to a large box elder tree. On the third night Sedit brought me a large basket of tanai tea and then disappeared without word or touch. The red clouds of Tipiknits Pahn swirled about my mind, but no spirits came forward to give comfort or counsel. Long-dead uncles and cousins remained insensitive to my petition for help. In the end I leaned my head back to bark and yip and howl as if my paw were caught in a white man's trap.

"Okay! Stop! Stop that caterwauling nonsense. Shut up!"

I opened both eyes to stare at Brother Coyote. "Finally!" I announced. "Is there any hope for a little attention from my spirit brother?"

The hazy image of Coyote sat before me, legs scrambled, the perfect image of a harmless camp dog.

I leaned toward him. "Listen, you miserable mutt, give me the truth of the matter. Is this half-breed braggart one of us, or is he another Hineh?"

My four-legged vision collapsed into a boneless heap and started to patiently lick his forepaws. Suddenly, he sat up to scratch ferociously behind his ear and then sat down just as quickly to stare into my eyes.

"He's okay, I think."

"You think he's okay? No details of fact, nothing more?"

"Listen, my annoying brother, I suggest that you decide what is best for the people." He stopped with his licking and looked at me. "You don't worry about that white papa of his."

"I do worry, and with great justification."

"The Great Hairy White Spirit never entered the child's body," Coyote whispered.

"No child can deny the spirit of his father," I said.

"The infant Estanislao's mother sang the songs and whispered the stories of her people into his ear. She gave the boy over to her brothers for instruction. His clan is of the White Eagle, and they have trained him to see everything from the high clouds and to strike the enemy with loud screams." Coyote paused to sniff the air. "He's okay, believe me. Estanislao is a Miwok chief and someone you can follow without too much concern."

"Brother. I hear strange voices whispering in my dreams. Long-dead ancestors charge Estanislao with a lack of constancy to their authority. They hint of his fealty to white gods, not to us."

Coyote sat in the dust and stared at me with yellow eyes. He yawned. "You worry too much," he said.

I shut my eyes to better observe the dream.

Coyote stood and shook with frantic vigor. He winked at me with both yellow eyes, then turned to jog down the foggy path. Once again he disappeared from my view, like a shooting star on a moonless night.

"You damned worthless mutt!" I yelled.

The tree seemed to settle comfortably along my back. A cuckoo called three times. My apprehensions drifted upward until they dissolved into harmless white clouds. Sedit put a light blanket over my shoulders and then sat at my side to put her head upon my shoulder. My eyelids fluttered briefly and then shut.

———

Estanislao looked up from his desk. "Another twenty recruits arrived this morning. They brought ten horses, three mules, and a hundred baskets of beans."

"From which mission did the recruits escape?" I asked.

"They arrived from Santa Clara, and they tell me that the alcalde there, Yozocole by name, will bring hundreds more baskets of beans in the next few days."

"Wonderful," I said. "A few hundred baskets will feed our army for possibly two days."

"Yozocole will also bring horses and cattle from Santa Clara."

I nodded. "We'll send the women he brings up to the hill villages. The men we'll keep here at the fort."

Estanislao turned a piece of red sealing wax over and over with his fingers until it formed a perfect worry bead. "There's something else."

"Tell me."

"I know this Yozocole from when we were neophytes together. He's agreed to serve as my chief aide."

"Do you mean as *our* chief aide?"

"He will serve as my aide." Estanislao put the bead on his desk and looked at me. "I want you to continue with your horse thieves and to keep Chetic and Benito working up and down the coast. Give them the supervision they need and keep a steady stream of cattle and horses arriving so I can feed my men. A fat army performs much better than one that complains of hunger."

My first sensation was pleasant. I felt a smile in my stomach and let it creep up onto my lips. "This Yozocole—his mother is an Ohlone and his father was a Spanish soldier. Am I correct on that issue?"

"He's a good man, and he knows how to fight the Spanish."

"That may or may not be correct, Estanislao, but the fact is that you need me here in the fort. I'm the greatest tipne of the Yokuts. The villages hold me as both tipne and war chief, not you." I shook my head at the half-breed. "Remember the Lonewis council, my commandant; the People won't fight unless you and I fight side by side as equals."

Estanislao pushed his chair back and stood to face me. "Name your victories, tipne. Tell me of your success in defeating the Spanish." He walked around the desk and glared at me. "I'm the commandant. You must obey me as I speak, or you may desert the army to mope in some remote cave or other."

"You'd make a good padre, Estanislao." I smiled my broadest coyote smile. "You've got a witch's eye and a witch's tongue."

"Obey or leave."

The good feeling left my stomach. Little stones grew in my throat. My deceitful brother, the four-legged one, giggled from the deep weeds of my mind. "What will you have me do?"

"I told you once, and I'll repeat myself only one more time." Estanislao puffed himself a size larger. "I want you and your vaqueros to continue with pressure on the ranchos and small pueblos. Bring us a daily supply of cattle and horses to supply our cooks. Also, as important as food for the army, you must make sure that you keep the southern Spanish soldiers busy." He leaned forward at the waist. "You must especially keep that Vallejo fellow occupied."

I looked at him straight on. "Now it is your turn to listen to me, Estanislao. Your construction of this fort is a novelty for the villages of the Great Valley, but my war with the Spanish is part of every storyteller's recital. It has been my vaqueros who have accomplished victories without number, not yours." I was getting furious with this puffed-up half-breed. "When I was fighting the Spanish at Monterey and trading in remote Santa Fe, you were growing your beard. Now that you have this fancy fort, you want me to keep Vallejo and his lancers down south where they can do you no damage." I took a step closer. "My captains will continue to take my orders. The war chiefs of the Yokuts villages will continue to take my orders. If we hold any chance for success over the Spanish, you need to share all plans and all decisions with me. No one else—just me."

Estanislao retreated a few steps until his desk blocked the way. He raised his right hand as if speaking from a pulpit. "Think for a moment, José Jesus. Think of your failure at Monterey and your constant reliance upon the white Sonorans for information and support." His voice projected over my shoulder as if he were speaking to an unseen audience. "The old ways are finished, José Jesus. None will follow you beyond a few old vaqueros. Your pitiful army causes little damage to the Spanish and generates little respect from the Great Valley villages. You stand alone, José Jesus. The old ways are dead, so you must follow me or suffer unpleasant consequences at my hand."

"Ahhh, so the old dog is threatened with a boot on the tail." I stepped forward and pulled a scorpion from the half-breed's ear. "Beware! This Indio dog still has a mouth full of teeth."

Estanislao slapped the scorpion from my hand. "Enough with your silly tricks. Listen carefully, José Jesus: if the People don't follow me, they will die. We must ignore the old ways. We must fight the Spanish with their own weapons, not with scorpions and village storytellers."

"No! No! You must listen, Estanislao. The old ways are the ways of our ancestors. What reason is there for living except to please the dead?"

Estanislao laughed his white man's laugh and pushed past me to regain his throne behind the desk of planks. "You prove my assertion, Tipne Man. Leave this war to those who are confident of victory. If you follow my orders, we will chase the Spanish from our land. If you follow my orders, you can spend your remaining days with stories for the children of our villages."

My stomach felt as hollow as any drum. "What then, Estanislao? After the whites are gone, what then?"

Again he laughed and then spoke from his mouth hidden by whiskers. "Our victorious army will take over the ranchos, missions, and pueblos of the Spanish. We'll trade with Mexicans and Americans as equals. The ships will bring those items that we desire in exchange for our hides and tallow and grain."

"And you will serve as governor to the many Indio villages of this imaginary nation?"

"All will call me King Estanislao." He made an awkward bow from his throne. "The Indios are too ignorant for the rule of a mere governor." He sharpened a turkey quill with his penknife. "I will serve those who obey me with benign good will. White men shall kneel before my throne in the same manner as the Indios. All will lower their eyes as they approach me, and all will follow my orders."

"The People. . . shall the People lower their eyes and kneel before you also?"

He opened his right hand toward me. "Listen, José Jesus. You are my lieutenant. You will serve me in this war, and later, as minister to a king." He dipped his pen, wrote a few words, and then looked up again. "What are you waiting for, Lieutenant? Go quickly." His voice was quiet and precise. "Sergeant Soto will arrive soon to sample my hospitality. I want him worried about the ferocious José Jesus, the famous horse thief and murderer of innocent Christians. I want you to stir little tremors of fear into the dreams of Sergeant Soto."

There was no help from the spirit world. Sedit was off in her village doing her good deeds. Chetic and Benito were blundering about their assigned territories with constant messages calling for my help. "I'll do as you order," I said.

"That's good, my tipne friend. It is a choice of action that is both good and sensible." He moved the pen with a flourish. "Thank you, José Jesus. I must thank you for your tenacious loyalty, Lieutenant."

I left His Royal Highness, and within the first deserted stand of oak, I sat on a comfortable boulder. There he was, at the blink of my eye, curled in relaxed repose upon my feet. I wiggled my big toes, but the mutt simply readjusted his limbs, as a bag of Spanish beans might settle over the shift of two small rocks.

"Traitor," I hissed.

He turned his head toward me in a most languorous fashion and whispered, "You called for my assistance?"

"I would plead with my cousin Hineh for help before listening again to your duplicitous advice."

"Listen, brother—"

"Disappear, mutt. Scram."

His carcass dissipated, but his words lingered. "There is no truth in life, my brother—only jokes."

"Jokes?"

Silence.

"Jokes?"

Silence.

CHAPTER 29

1829–1830

*E*STANISLAO STOOD ON THE CATWALK *of the top rampart, cupped his hands around his mouth, and shouted, "Soto! You're a coward! You're afraid of Indios! Coward! Coward!"*

A chorus of shouts from our warriors echoed Estanislao's taunts. Infrequent musket explosions from the Spanish troops disappeared into the thick mud of insults.

"What a fine celebration, Lieutenant!" Estanislao tapped me lightly on the shoulder. "Soon we will have a frolic." He smiled. "The poor Spaniards—they still believe that a few ignorant soldiers will defeat an army of Indios." He touched the underside of my throat as a man might caress his young nephew. "But the old days are over, aren't they, Tipne Man?"

A winatum huffed up a ladder set at a sharp angle against the palisade wall. He maintained feet and hands on the ladder and spoke in a calm, well-modulated voice. "They've split into two groups, master. The six on saddled horses are moving east around the woods and toward the river. Soto and six men are walking through the northern oak grove toward this very wall."

"Good work, my friend!" Estanislao turned and shouted. "Captains! Come here at once!"

I stepped back to allow Yozocole and four others access to Estanislao. They stood quietly and waited. "Yozocole, take your warriors out the north portal and into the woods. Wait until the soldiers are ten paces from your arrows, then shoot at their faces. Aim for the eyes." He waved his arm toward the enemy. "Go!" A group of fifty young men followed Captain Yozocole into a tunnel under the palisade wall, and one by one they disappeared, like pebbles into black water.

Estanislao and I walked up and down the fort's catwalk and listened to the sounds of men moving about until a second messenger found us. "The soldiers on the east side of the fort, master—their horses are stuck in the tule marsh."

"They are in the marsh between the fort and river?"

"Yes sir. It is the marsh east of our fort."

Estanislao pushed me toward the winatum. "Here's your opportunity to destroy the Spanish, my tipne lieutenant. Take your men and show no quarter to the enemy. Hurry!"

We arrived in time to see saddled horses hump and scramble and work hock-deep in the mud. Spanish soldiers screamed and yanked at reins until they saw us move to surround them. They struggled to load and fire their muskets from atop the thrashing beasts, but soon beautiful quills waved with careless gaiety from leather armor and bloody faces. The horses floundered in helpless agony as arrow after arrow tore into rider and beast.

I left my vaqueros to hack trophies from the dead and walked back to my post. Estanislao pretended that he did not see me approach.

"Estanislao." I made a slight bow from the waist as he turned toward me. "The six who were stuck in the swamp are all dead," I said.

Commandant Estanislao smiled with this confirmation of his genius. "Of course they are all dead!" He turned to the clutch of captains and warriors who waited at his back. "All of you must cheer a victory for the Tipne Man! Cheer our victory for all Indios!"

"Victory! Victory!" they responded.

"Enough!" Estanislao turned and pointed. "Look! Soto is next!"

Sergeant Antonio Soto and his six men walked steadfastly through the lovely oak grove. The soft, rich soil caressed their tattered boots as swarms of arrows thwacked into trees and Spanish soldiers. When Soto reached the margin of trees and the meadow that spread before the fort, he turned and retreated with the remnants of his army. The sergeant stopped for one brief moment to pull an arrow from his face, and while the shaft pulled free, the obsidian point remained embedded beneath his cheekbone. Two slightly wounded soldiers covered the retreat while a squad of muleteers, cooks, and woodsmen scrambled to pull their equipment and heavily wounded soldiers northwest, to the safety of a large wooded stream.

"Victory!" yelled Estanislao.

"Victory!" yelled the officers and warriors of his army.

At dawn of the next morning, Sergeant Soto led his men to the west and away from Estanislao's fort. I watched Soto's stumbling gait and wondered if the Christ child would lift him from pain or if the Madonna would smile upon his soul and escort the poor, dumb toadstool into the white man's heaven.

I watched vultures gather in a massive swirling throng and slowly descend from the blue sky onto those men and beasts left on the field of battle. I imagined that the spirits of red men flew smoothly toward Tipiknits Pahn but that the spirits of white men lay in the mud like fish thrown on the bank of a summertime river.

The first black clouds of winter produced short periods of blustery wet storms, and these were followed by weeks of dry, windy weather. I established two more bands of raiders north of Don Tarabél's old ranch and south of Monterey, and we maintained constant pressure on the ranchos and small pueblos as far south as Mission San Diego. We sent many of our captured horses, together with a few cattle, to the kitchens of Estanislao's fort, but we sent the best horses south into Mexico and exchanged them for weapons and food that we stored in my secret caves.

Joaquin Murietta continued to serve as my agent in all supply matters, and he maintained cordial relations with the desert nations and the Sonoran villages. It was Joaquin who traded our stolen horses and mules for wheat and corn and beans and exotic bolts of cloth and needles and pots. Of course, Joaquin became very rich as my agent, for he was a thief, after all. But he always treated me fairly and always gave me his big smile whenever we met.

It was just before the first-fruits ceremony, the time when the oak forests of the Great Valley were sprouting new leaves, that Joaquin Murietta sent a winatum to me.

"More mules," said the winatum. "Joaquin says his Sonoran clients need mules for the spring planting. Quickly, you must send more mules to the south."

Benito captured a great herd of the sterile beasts at ranchos near Santa Barbara and Santa Paula, and I followed their dust until we reached the Mohave River. It was there, with mules milling about, that Joaquin introduced me to a gimpy, garrulous Americaño.

"This white man has offered to pay double what the Sonorans would likely pay." Joaquin stared at his feet. "This ugly witch has promised me muskets and powder in trade for these mules."

"Let's take a look," I said.

The white man revealed a toothless mouth and two wagons loaded with weapons. I studied his face and then motioned for Benito and Joaquin to follow me.

"Where are his friends?" I asked.

Joaquin waved an arm. "His friends think they are hidden from me, but they are merely down the river a bit."

"All Americaños?"

"Mostly, but he has a few blacks and a few red men and lots of long rifles."

"Where does he hide the whiskey?"

"The whiskey is under the guns in the two wagons."

"We've got to kill this sonuvabitch, take his guns, and hightail it north," Benito said.

Joaquin held up his hand. "We wouldn't last two nights before his men wiped us out." He looked at the ground again. "I made a mistake in talking with this man. Even if he'd offered triple what the Sonorans offered, I should have walked away from him."

"What can we do?" I asked.

"The best we can do is leave this place, tonight, and with no words. We must leave him with both the mules and guns."

"Do you have some deal with this snake?" Benito moved a hand toward his knife. "Are you playing us for fools?"

"The guns were bait, and I swallowed the hook." Joaquin kept his hands still and away from any weapon. "His whiskey is full of poison. He has fifty men who are ready with their rifles."

The sun was a red disk over the western hills. "What of the Paiute of this area? Will they join us against the Americaño?"

Joaquin shook his head. "A few have maintained their sanity, but most are dead or dead drunk."

"The Quachan are two days' ride—what of them?"

Joaquin smiled his beautiful smile. "My cousin Three Finger and my brother Tomàs left me four days ago, and now the Quachan await your orders, José Jesus."

For the first time in my experience with him, Benito smiled and said, "Someday I may grow to like you, Joaquin Murietta, witch's eye and all."

"May that day shine soon upon us both, Benito."

I returned Joaquin's generous smile. "It appears that you were prepared to act with the Americaños or with me, depending upon the variables of danger and profit that you could tally. Am I correct in that assumption?"

"Those were two of the viable options that we three thieves considered."

"Are you now committed to me?"

"Certainly, Tipne Man; it appears the greatest profit will show with you as our partner."

"Where are the Quachan?" I asked.

Joaquin waved his arm. "Down the river a bit. They've got the high ground over the Americaño fools."

"Do the Quachan know about the rifles?"

"Yes, certainly. It is my brother Tomàs who suggests that the Quachan attack just before the next dawn. He has noticed that every evening the white men demonstrate to the Paiute the merits of their whiskey. At dawn they sleep, Paiute and white man together."

"Tell the Quachan that they will receive half of the mules and half of the weapons," I said.

Again Joaquin smiled. "The Quachan have agreed that all the mules and half of the weapons will seal the bargain."

"So be it," I said.

My vaqueros woke in the early light to the quiet blue flames of burning whiskey and the whiskered mule-man tied to stakes hammered into the sand. I spoke to a Paiute tipne who had helped trap the trapper. "His face is unspeakably ugly," I said.

The Paiute kicked the man in the ribs. "Smith, he is called by the White Others."

"He must be one who has learned to bend red-hot metal for horseshoes," I said.

"I've only seen him sell whiskey to my warriors, nothing else."

"Don't these Americaños use metal traps to capture beaver and mink?"

"Yes, some of his men traveled up to the mountain streams for such business." The Paiute tipne paused to pee on the face of Smith. "A few of the invaders made the difficult hike, but most of them stay by the river to drink whiskey all day and lie with the women of our village all night."

"We must kill him," I said.

"Certainly," the Paiute tipne said.

Benito smiled as the Paiute spirit doctor pulled thin strips of skin from the white man named Smith. When Smith was nothing but a bloody slab of meat—silent, barely breathing—Benito leaned close when the Paiute tipne performed a crude surgery on the old man's penis.

"Hey, José Jesus," Benito called. "That's a good Paiute trick we should remember."

"What trick?"

"Snip their penis and then let the white fellows swallow their own cock before they die."

I walked away from the bloody mess.

"Hey!" Benito followed after me. "What's wrong?"

I turned and faced Benito. Foolish, stupid, Benito. "Think of the elders of your village, Benito. What advice would they give about delivering death to an enemy?" I was angry with myself, not Benito. "They would demand that if we must kill our enemies, it must be in the same manner as we dispatch a deer or bear. We must not demean ourselves with this torture."

Benito poked his nose into my face. "Tell me, Tipne Man. Do you forget the padres and their whips? Do you forget the men contained every night in dark, damp rooms?" He shrugged. "A little of their own medicine will scare the White Others away from our land."

"We must remember," I said.

———◆———

Estanislao called his fort La Estacada. Whenever the rains stopped for a short while, he set his men extending the maze of trenches and connecting those tunnels around the perimeter of the fort with tunnels under the walls. He designed a ring of sharpened poles around the fort to form a stockade superior to any built by the Spanish. La Estacada, the fortress of Estanislao, with the large north-flowing river on the east and thick groves of cottonwood and box elder forests on the west.

The People and Miwok and strangers among us all declared the fortress impregnable and called Estanislao a mighty war chief. The storytellers honored him with a lineage that made him brother to the White Eagle of the Miwok people.

———◆———

March 1, 1830

> *My Esteemed and Loving Father Duran,*
> *Sergeant Antonio Soto is dead. Many of his men are dead. My followers attack the ranchos throughout Alta California with impunity. We take*

your horses and cattle as we choose. Every day the red men are stronger, and the whites languish in feeble poverty.

Know this: my fortress is impregnable. Our spirit grows stronger each day. Our ancestors rally us to reclaim the territory wrongfully taken from them. The many women and children you have murdered all scream for revenge.

Return to your own land. Speak to your flock, my good father, and tell them the Indios' spirits are stronger than the feeble god of your book.

Estanislao

—◆—

Corporal Pablo Pacheco marched his forty troops from Yerba Buena. He added a dozen civilians from here and there, and finally, there were also twenty warriors from the village of Chief Solano who joined the expedition. They traveled south from San José to spend their first night at San Juan Bautista. The next few days Pacheco followed cattle trails past Tres Piños and on to Panoche, and finally the corporal bivouacked his army for a satisfying two nights at the hot springs located along the eastern edge of the San Benito Mountains.

On the eighth day of his sojourn, Corporal Pacheco stood on the high cliff at the northeastern corner of our stockade and shouted, "Hey, Estanislao! Send all those Christian Indios back to their missions. Father Duran says you can't keep them here in this damn swamp."

"Come and get them, you woman!" Estanislao shouted back. "You're a coward, Pablo. A coward! You must allow your soldiers to advance into our woods, because they are men. But you must stand back, Pablo. We allow no women among our warriors."

A shower of arrows flew in a rainbow arc from our fortress. One bolt struck a young soldier in the face, and he screamed. Yozocole led a large contingent of his warriors under the fortress wall and into the open meadow, where his troops whooped as they released one arrow after the next. Soon the entire troop of Spaniards was in full retreat. Arrows and insults followed Corporal Pacheco for the next ten days and nights to the very walls of the San Francisco Presidio.

———◆———

Estanislao motioned Yozocole toward his throne. "What were your casualties, Captain?"

"We lost one warrior to a musket ball, and fifteen others suffer from injuries of little concern." Yozocole spoke so those up on the catwalk and those massed in front of Estanislao could hear every word. "Most of those injured have responded favorably to the treatment from our antu doctors."

"What casualties did the enemy receive?"

"Two are dead and buried, and it appears that at least twenty received serious injuries during our daily battles."

"Good, Captain, very good." Estanislao stood and made a grand gesture toward his warriors. "Again we have defeated the Spanish army. Soon the White Others will leave our land. Soon Indios will again rule the land of their ancestors."

The thud of hands on wood and dirt created a violent storm of noise. Dust erupted from Estanislao's fort. "Victory! Victory!" the army of Estanislao chanted.

———◆———

In late April of 1830, I joined Chetic on a raid to gather horses and mules from a rancho east of San Luis Obispo. There was no moon, and dawn was a fuzzy gray band oozing up from the east. Horses were grazing on undulating fields of green oats and white clover. A few stallions challenged us, but the mares and their young continued eating. Quail called to one another. Small patches of fog hugged the damp gullies. Half of Chetic's vaqueros had nearly a hundred head of prime stock milling in a small wooded gulch. I sat my horse and waited impatiently for the other half to return from their raid of the mule corrals.

Chetic spun his horse in a full circle. "Let's go. My people say that Vallejo is in the area."

"What of the other vaqueros?"

"They'll either catch up or fight with Vallejo. Either way, we need to move."

"Wait a bit," I said. "If there's trouble, we need to know which way to jump."

"No! We've got plenty of good horses, and there are no Spanish to the east. Let's go!"

I ignored him. A small breeze stirred the oak leaves, and the sound of hooves moving quickly over soft dirt grew ever louder. A line of riders cleared the hill in brilliant silhouette, and immediately a musket exploded. The vaquero on my left side fell to the ground.

"Run! Separate and run!" I shouted.

I led Chetic and one of his vaqueros toward a gully of poison oak. We slashed our way up the hill and burst through the tangles into an open slope of oak trees. I drew my pistol and fired a single shot into the air. When the huffing horses of the Spanish appeared below me, I yelled, "Women! Can you hear me? Cowards! Go home to your beds." With one additional shot from my pistol, I galloped in a straight line to the east, toward the Great Valley.

At midday I held up my hand, and we stopped at a small rise. I turned and counted thirty-five men maintaining the chase. All were well mounted and unencumbered with equipment. They followed us at the easy lope designed to cover many miles and guarantee the final capture of any quarry. I smiled at their audacity. So few white men, yet they blithely advanced into unfamiliar territory. It was apparent that these white invaders saw only victory for themselves.

"Look," Chetic pointed northeast. "Look again!"

I slowly examined the entire eastern horizon. Signal fires burst from the summits of a half-dozen hills. It was Podnow's system. The intrusion of White Others would soon end. Throughout the Great Valley warriors were ready. Horses and weapons and carefully practiced maneuvers would now merge to form a powerful shield for the People. Tall white columns of smoke boiled to tree level, then began to suddenly dissipate with the strong afternoon wind. The smoke fluttered along oak branches, stumbled into low brush, and spread as a trivial haze in the hot spring air.

"Quickly!" I yelled. "We must serve as winatums to the villages!"

At the next ripple in the land, the vaquero's horse hit a badger hole, flipped head-over-tail, and marked a long dusty path through the scrubby grass. The young rider pushed himself up to stagger a few paces, then collapsed and lay still until a Spanish trooper prodded him with a long steel-tipped lance, once gently, then with great force through the vaquero's chest.

"Faster!" Chetic yelled. "We must warn the villages."

The Spanish edged closer as we approached the first spongy marshland. "Go south!" Chetic yelled to me. He reined his horse to the left. "I'll go north!"

About fifteen of the enemy followed Chetic; the rest followed me. I could hear them yelling and feel their white magic seep into my stomach. The pace of my horse slowed, as if he too understood the futility of our race.

"Go, you traitor!" I struck my heels into the beast's ribs and whipped his neck with the reins. Ahead was a willow thicket, and as we entered the tangle, I jumped from the saddle and rolled under a mass of leaves. My horse continued and the Spanish troops crashed past me, and soon I heard the first musket explode.

Ducks and geese erupted from every moist pocket of the marsh in a thunderous roar. The erratic blasts from Spanish muskets continued as I thrashed my way through the woods until a hill above the Yauelmani village gave me a view of the battle. My eyes watched even as I suffered vile eruptions from my stomach.

The Yauelmani women struggled to fill carry-baskets with rabbit-skin blankets and small children as Vallejo's men charged down the well-ordered streets. The Spanish hacked the elders with swords and poked them with lances. The White Others screamed with joy as they spilled the blood of old men and old women and young children. They whooped at the glory of burning the lodges and storehouses of the People. From my hiding place I watched as greasy smoke spilled toward Tipiknits Pahn.

At dusk the Spanish left the Yauelmani village and rode slowly back toward the western hills. Mariano Vallejo trailed after his troopers. I watched as he turned his horse in larger and larger circles until his men were distant specks on the horizon and he stood alone. "José Jesus!" he yelled.

I stepped into the open, and he rode even closer.

"José Jesus! I want you to whisper a message into the ear of Estanislao. Tell your commandant that he must surrender or die." Vallejo cut the distance between us in half. "Tell Estanislao that he must surrender immediately, or every village of the Great Valley will die." He leaned forward in his saddle. "Hold the dead of this village in your arms, José Jesus. Smell the charred flesh, and then attend to your people. Tell Estanislao that he must surrender to me at once."

Vallejo stared at the smoke and red-blinking embers. He was completely alone. The meadows and distant hills were empty. With the last shadows he turned his horse and jogged into the dusk.

———

I walked into the ruins. The evening breeze fanned flames among the large timbers from the village meetinghouse. Flakes of ash fell like mountain snow.

"José Jesus!" a voice called.

I looked carefully but saw nothing.

"Here! José Jesus. Here, under the elk skin."

The old man was barely alive. I held his gray head in my hands. "Go slowly, old friend," I whispered. "Stay still, and I will fetch some water."

"No! Stay with me, José Jesus. I have no time for water." He moved closer as if seeking warmth from my body. "It was the fault of my bowstring. I could not move my fingers with the necessary speed."

The evening chorus frogs began to scream. The old man struggled to sit upright. "Pokook calls," he said. "In the spirit world I'll be strong again. My fingers will move with the speed of the hummingbird, and I'll kill the white invaders. All of them."

I held the old man close to my chest until he stopped breathing. Then I held him until my tears diminished to the dribble of a drought-year creek.

———

"Who is it this time?" Estanislao asked the winatum.

"Ensign Sanchez," the winatum answered. "They have forty troops and also a cannon." The messenger gave a small cough. "Plus, Sanchez has one hundred Suisun allies."

"Is Chief Solano with his warriors?" I called.

"No, José Jesus," said the winatum.

Estanislao grabbed my arm and pulled me away from the stockade wall. "Stand back, Lieutenant. Do not distract your commandant with intrusive interruptions or tales of village-burning demons." He burned a hard look into my eyes and then turned around to study the western vista.

"Look," Estanislao called to his officers, "Don Sanchez is trying to set fire to the trees upwind from our fort."

We watched as squads of Spanish soldiers ignited piles of gathered wood to send pallid spouts of smoke into the still air.

"Use the hair on your balls, little boys," Estanislao called. "The hair of young virgins will surely start a lively fire."

The laughter of his officers and warriors slowly increased as the smoke diminished into failed wisps. "Hey, snake bellies!" Estanislao called. "Ignite the trees with your beautiful farts. Surely little virgins can start a decent fire with their farts."

Sanchez waved his sword and yelled, "Troopers! Line up in squads! Bring up the cannon, our giant stone-slinger."

A thunderous explosion from the cannon expelled a large round rock a mere twenty paces and pushed the cannon askew from the gun carriage. A short, stout corporal emerged from a black cloud to scream orders at his crew of cannoneers. When a skinny soldier grabbed the still-smoking mouth, he quickly fell backward and shook his hands in obvious distress. Small puffs of laughter burst along the margins of both armies. A second explosion from the repaired cannon provoked equal havoc among the Spanish, and after the third shot dribbled from the black snout onto the grass, Ensign Sanchez shouted, "Leave the cannon! Ready your muskets! Ready to fire! Fire!"

After an erratic siege of harmless musketry, the Spanish army retreated to the first stream west of our fortress and established their camp.

At dawn of the second day, squads of six men, each under command of a corporal, marched back to the edge of our woods, and Ensign Sanchez shouted toward us, "Estanislao! Come to your senses! Surrender, and all your men will live another day. You must surrender, or the villages of the Great Valley will be destroyed."

"Never!" shouted Estanislao. "You are the ones to surrender. Hand over your weapons and leave our land. Surrender, and you will live another day!"

The squads of six made quick little sorties into the woods, fired at the first shadow, and retreated at double quickstep. The tame Indios of the Spanish army lounged about, laughed at nothing, and scratched their balls. Our own powder fizzed harmlessly and rendered our Santa Fe muskets harmless. Estanislao's warriors laughed at their useless muskets. They disregarded the ridiculous efforts of the Spanish soldiers and scattered about the fort to begin their gambling games. The officers of Estanislao dashed about his fort to stir the dust and shout useless orders.

"José Jesus," the winatum whispered in my ear. "I would speak to you."

I pulled him over to a quiet corner. "Speak. I'm listening."

"Four of the white soldiers are walking away from their comrades. They are moving toward the river at a slow pace, and they drag their muskets in the dirt."

Estanislao was moving out of the stockade toward a flurry of activity near the ditches of our southern boundary. Twenty of my vaqueros were squatting nearby, a few gambling, and all waiting for my command. "Hey, you vaqueros," I called. "Take a little walk with me."

In one smooth movement they grabbed their weapons and followed my rapid pace. The winatum led us past the trenches and through the riparian woods until we emerged onto a small brush-covered ledge overlooking the large north-flowing river.

One of my vaqueros pointed. "There! It's two of the Pacheco brothers, plus Manuel Peña and that Mesa fellow." He shook his head. "They're all a useless, lazy bunch."

The four soldiers flopped on the sand to drink water from the river, and then they stood to shake wet hair and laugh the hollow sounds of frightened men.

I pointed to half my men. "You! Move around and cut off any escape route. When we begin shooting our arrows, join to help us."

The men smiled and tapped arrows lightly on bows.

"Look!" the winatum hissed.

A single Spanish soldier emerged from the woods, looked around, then moved toward the river.

"It is Corporal Luis Peña," the winatum said. "He is cousin to Manuel and Antonio Peña."

"Kill him," I shouted, and my vaqueros shot him full of arrows. The corporal faced us, as would an old bear, shook his fist, and then slumped to the ground. The four deserters saw us and began running down the river through shallow water. We shot fat Manuel and chubby Antonio first. My men laughed at the pleasure of putting arrow after arrow into their lard-white bodies. The remaining two friends were skinny and fast, but we caught them and also filled them full of arrows.

<hr />

"Winatum, listen carefully." Estanislao filled his lungs with air. "Go to the villages of the hills and valley. Tell the Yokuts and Miwok of our great victory, and invite them to a celebration here at my fortress." He smiled and waved his arm in a grand gesture. "Go, my winatum. Spread the good news."

In the days that followed our great victory over Don Sanchez, we prepared for the next campaign in our war against the Spanish invaders. Estanislao had us assemble more trenches and pit traps during the day, but during the night he encouraged us to tell about our own moments of glory. The proud warriors of Estanislao also listened to storytellers describe the truth of the old days, and we celebrated those mighty victories at Purisima and Monterey. He had us remain gathered around huge fires until a horn was sounded three times, and then full dark descended with a sudden but ill-defined menace.

The Yokuts and Miwok and strangers among us saw the spirit of Uncle Podnow dance to the beat of the foot drum until sweat from his stomach brought showers of rain down on Estanislao's fort. My dead father rode his winged horse about a lodge crowded with esteemed elders from the many villages. He played with the eagles and sent clouds of eagle feathers among the Yokuts and Miwok and strangers and half-breeds. The spirit of Uncle Shup turned somersaults round and round the huge fire, and even Brother Coyote chased about in my dreams. He crouched and wagged his tail and peed on every stump and weed in sight—the miserable traitor.

"Estanislao!" the warriors and the visitors called through the night. "Estanislao!"

"Death to the white invaders," he called back.

"Estanislao! Estanislao!"

"They come again," the winatum said.

"Who? How many this time?" Estanislao asked.

"There is Ensign Sanchez again, with one hundred troops and two hundred tame Indios. Also, Ensign Vallejo has two cannon and another one hundred troops. They will all meet at Mission San José and then march together until they attack our fortress."

"We are ready," Estanislao said.

———

I sat with my right foot folded atop the saddle to watch the Spanish soldiers and their allies trudge in the dust. The cavalry of Vallejo were mounted and carried their long lances aloft, but most of the leather-armored soldiers and all of the Indios walked. The entire army frequently dissolved into shimmering walls of stultifying heat, and I waited patiently for the ghostly shapes to reappear.

On the third day of observing their march, I watched as the army moved down from the foothills east of Don Tarabél's old ranch. On the way through a rock-rutted gully, a gun carriage lost a wheel, and the cannon tumbled to the bottom of the ditch. Ensign Sanchez called a short halt to inspect the damage and give orders to a sergeant. "Leave two men with this mess. Have them repair the wheel, if possible, then follow the path of our army." The sergeant waved two men to follow him slowly around the gun, two oxen, and carriage, and then he left to catch the distant parade.

A very young soldier found shade under a sentinel oak tree and quickly fell asleep. The mechanic worked through the day and into the early evening in an effort to repair the damaged wheel. He held the metal wheel strip into the heat of his portable forge and beat the malleable iron into shape. His physique and the rhythm of movement were familiar. I crawled through the tall grass.

"Hineh! Cousin!" I whispered. "It's me, José Jesus."

He didn't look up from his work. "Go away or I'll call the soldier."

Hineh continued to pound the hot metal, but we didn't speak again. When I turned to slip away, he immediately stopped working. After a few steps I checked again, and Hineh was staring intently into the blue flames of his fire.

At midmorning of the fifteenth day of June, 1830, the Spanish expedition reached Estanislao's fort. They were greeted with arrows and a volley from our muskets. Vallejo drew his men back and rode his horse around the entire perimeter of our fortress. After the noon meal, he directed his men to pile large mounds of dry wood upwind of our fort. He directed the surviving cannon into a position that overlooked the fortress, and the Spanish troops, with support from their tame Indios, were deployed in large groups downwind from Estanislao's fort. In late afternoon, the quiet time, when even the cicada sleeps, the army of Commandant Vallejo struck.

The waiting piles of wood were torched, and a gusty wind drew the flames quickly into the thick cottonwood trees and greasy brush that bordered Estanislao's fort. Iron cannon balls hammered his stockade wall, and each blow spread splinters and screams among his troops. Ensign Sanchez led his men under clouds of arrows delivered by the tame Indios and past cannon-crushed walls. His troopers fired orderly volleys from their muskets and stabbed incessantly with their lances.

Yozocole and I yelled for our warriors to attack, but they melted away into the smoke. The screams and explosions diminished as the huge oak logs of the fort wall erupted in a blazing inferno. My vaqueros followed a series of ditches to the east side of the fort, where we made a stand against a force of tame Indios. All my men were wounded, but so were those who opposed us. Chetic flopped into the ditch and grabbed my shoulder. "Estanislao has deserted!"

"Damn that coyote!" An arrow grazed my left shoulder, and Chetic yelled into my ear. "You're the only officer left in the fort."

"Vallejo?"

"He's headed in this direction with two squads of Spanish soldiers."

Smoke obscured the enemy, but arrows continued to fly into my men. The glare and boom of musket explosions suddenly slammed toward us.

"Vaqueros!" I yelled. "Leave this place. Scatter where you will. Go! Go!"

I crawled over bodies and away from the fire. Chetic disappeared. My vaqueros disappeared.

At dusk I drank from the river, stumbled toward the eastern hills, and watched the sun disappear into a crimson pool of blood. I could hear Vallejo's army move about in erratic jolts of silence and sound, until eventually there was only a chorus of heron and frog.

When a trickle of fog eased over the riverbank, I returned to the hot ashes of Estanislao's fort. There were many that called for my help, and many more that waited for Pokook's call. I carried water to those who could not move and gave advice to those who could. My own wounds continued to bleed, and just before dawn the drumbeat in my head gave one final blow, and I fell into a black pit.

The sun was near the top of a hazy sky when an explosion jarred my eyes open. Vallejo was there in the meadow with his troops. Four of his Indios beat skin-covered drums, ten others blew wooden whistles, and the Spanish troopers cheered as a single cannon exploded once more. Ensign Vallejo waved his sword and shouted. "Follow me, good Christians. We must punish these Indios for their sins against God." He pointed with arm and sword. "Forward! God's work must be done!" The ranks formed behind his sorrel horse, and they all moved eastward, away from the acrid smoke.

I moved my flock of wounded men south, toward the tule marshes. The ravens and redheaded vultures gorged on the eyes and flesh of the Yokuts and Miwok and strangers among us. Smoke from burning villages drifted about the central portion of the Great Valley.

I asked survivors who brushed against me, "What of Estanislao?"

"He was uninjured when he deserted," they said.

"Chetic?"

"Nothing; we have not seen your brother."

"Yozocole?"

"He was killed with the first cannonball."

"What of the other captains and lieutenants?"

"We can tell you nothing about the others, José Jesus."

CHAPTER 30

1830–1832

SOME SAID SEDIT WAS UP in one of the hill villages above the southern reach of the Great Valley, so I looked up and down one creek after another, but could not find her. Others said she might have escaped from Vallejo's rampaging army with a few Miwok and headed northeast, but again I could not find her. From early winter to the next spring I threw in with some hairy-faced trappers, and they gave me whiskey and beans to go with what tanai I could find. In exchange for the whiskey, I provided some sad-faced widow women for the invaders. One of the toadstool men had different needs, and I gave young orphan boys into his care.

Lugardo, the leader of my southern army, plus one of my vaqueros from the mission days, pulled me away from the trappers just before summer heat settled into the valley. They told me that Chetic had been killed when he fell under a burning timber. "He's dead," Lugardo said. "Flames from the fort cooked him dead," said the other.

I called and called for the spirit of Chetic, but he never answered. Tanai I found or stole. Whiskey I got with a little work here and there. The tanai and whiskey blurred the next few seasons into a gray void until one morning my hands and feet refused to move. My eyes opened and shut for a while, and then they didn't work either. A brilliant sun burned red stars into my eyes. Someone dropped sand onto my fingers. Sticky sand, the kind that stuck one grain to the next, and soon there was no feeling in any appendage, only an increasing weight on my hands and arms and body. "Whiskey," I mumbled. "Give me some whiskey."

I coughed sand from my lips and forced one crusted lid to open. A man sat at my left shoulder. "What?" I croaked. "Who are you?"

He dabbed my eyes and lips with a damp rag and poured a few drops of water into my mouth. I managed to lift my head enough to see that my arms and legs were tied to stakes driven into the sand. "Who are you?" I repeated.

"Quiet, José Jesus. You must suffer the sun, for there is no other way to remove the poison."

His belly was soft and large, his penis the useless appendage of an old man. "Shade my eyes so that I can see your face," I said.

"Remember the white man named Smith, and you will see my face."

I strained to lift my head and shoulders, but the rawhide rope crossed hips and chest and arms and legs. My eyes fluttered in the strong sun. "The Paiute tipne," I said.

"Yes."

"Will you kill me?"

The old man put a damp pebble in my mouth. "You are already dead, José Jesus. It is my task to pull your spirit back to this land of pain."

"Pull the skin from my body," I said. "Stuff my penis into my mouth. Leave my spirit alone."

"The spirits of my dreams say that you must live."

"Put the sand over my face. Let me die."

"Listen to Pokook," said the Paiute tipne.

The spirit owl called with a tiny tremolo that I could barely hear. *Coo coo. Coo coo,* Pokook called.

"There are those who call for your help," the Paiute tipne said. "There are spirits who search for José Jesus. They speak of your son and a brother held in common."

"Carlos my son? Chetic?"

"Those two and many others, tipne man. Many from the spirit land call your name, and also there are many from this land of the living who need your help."

"I have failed the People—let me die."

The Paiute tipne doctor sloshed a wet poultice over my body. "You must live again, José Jesus." I heard a clapper stick start a slow, persistent beat. Two fast clacks followed by one slow. Over and over, *clack-clack-claaak*, as the herbs and my sweat cooked into fragrant soup. "Estanislao wants to speak with you, José Jesus." *Clack-clack-claaak.* "The wandering shades who cannot find their way to Tipiknits Pahn and the spirits with no name—all want to speak to the Tipne Man."

A Miwok winatum led me across a small river, a larger river, then through a wide brown valley. I felt cold ocean fog push against the heat of late fall.

"What is this valley called?" I asked.

"The white invaders call it Amador." He pointed south. "Over those hills you'll find Mission San José. He's waiting for you."

Estanislao led me through a pear orchard west of San José Village. "Let me guess," I said.

He nodded.

"Once again you are Father Duran's alcalde."

"Yes," Estanislao said.

"Do both red and white spirits whisper into your ear, my king? Do they keep you awake at night with their wild arguments?" I ignored his royal mandate and stared directly into his eyes. "Does the white father command your attention or does the red mother?"

"I honor my mother and detest the seed of my father. I am of the Miwok people and no other."

I nodded my head but remained silent. What sense was there in debating with a foolish king?

"It's over," Estanislao said. "The old magic is useless. The time of our ancestors is a distant memory; now there is only the white invader."

We both stood mute, waiting for the other, until finally Estanislao asked, "Tell me what you see. What is next for those who survive the invasion?"

I saw my dead father scatter eagle feathers from high in the sky. In the far distance Uncle Shup smiled, then disappeared in a giant twisting somersault. Uncle Podnow danced around the edge of my mind for three turns, then he also disappeared. "I see nothing," I said.

"Nothing?"

"Well, your highness, maybe Shup will lead me to the correct path for my sojourn. Or maybe he will merely tell a stupid joke and we will laugh at ourselves." I shrugged. "It doesn't matter—the People will survive."

"I think not," Estanislao said.

"We'll see," I said.

End

www.ingramcontent.com/pod-product-compliance
Lightning Source LLC
Chambersburg PA
CBHW030314200626
46816CB00006BA/1776